THE RUBICON

BY

E. F. BENSON

British Library Cataloguing-in-Publication Data
A catalogue record for this book is available from the
British Library

E. F. Benson

Edward Frederic Benson was born at Wellington College (where his father was headmaster) in Berkshire, England in 1867. He was educated at Marlborough College, where he proved himself as an excellent athlete, representing England at figure skating, and published his first novel, *Dodo* (1893), when he was 26. The novel was quite popular, and Benson eventually expanded it into a trilogy (*Dodo the Second*, in 1914, and *Dodo Wonders*, in 1921). Nowadays, Benson is principally known for his 'Mapp and Lucia' series about Emmeline "Lucia" Lucas and Elizabeth Mapp. The series consists of six novels and two short stories, and remains popular to this day, being serialized for Radio 4 as recently as 2008. Benson was also a respected writer of ghost stories – indeed, H. P. Lovecraft spoke very highly of him, especially his story 'The Man Who Went Too Far'. Benson died of throat cancer in 1940, aged 72.

CONTENTS

BOOK III.

BOOK I

CHAPTER I.

The little red-roofed town of Hayes lies in a furrow of the broad-backed Wiltshire Downs; it was once an important posting station, and you may still see there an eighteenth century inn, much too large for the present requirements of the place, and telling of the days when, three times a week, the coach from London used to pull up at its hospitable door, and wait there half-an-hour while its passengers dined. The inn is called the Grampound Arms, and you will find that inside the church many marble Grampounds recline on their tombs, or raise hands of prayer, while outside in the churchyard, weeping cherubs, with reversed torches, record other pious and later memories of the same family.

But almost opposite the Grampound Arms you will notice a much newer inn, where commercial gentlemen make merry, called the Aston Arms, and on reference to monumental evidence, you would also find that cherubs are shedding similar pious tears for a Sir James Aston, Bart., and his wife, and, thirty years later, for James Aston, first Lord Hayes, and his wife. But for the Astons, no marble knights keep watch on Gothic tombs.

The river Kennet, in its green wanderings, has already passed, before it reaches Hayes, two houses, one close down by the river, the other rather higher up and on the opposite bank. The smaller and older of the two is the residence of Mr. Grampound, the larger and newer of Lord Hayes. These trifling facts, which almost all the inhabitants of Hayes could tell you, will sufficiently indicate the mutual position of the two families in the latter half of the nineteenth century.

Grampound House was a pretty, ivy-grown old place, with a lawn stretching southwards almost to the bank of the river, and shaded by a great cedar tree, redolent of ancestors and as monumental in its way as the marble, sleeping figures in the church. It was useful, however, as well as being ancestral, and at this moment Mrs. Grampound and her brother were having tea under it.

It was a still, hot day at the beginning of August, and through the broad, fan-like branches, stray sunbeams danced and twinkled, making little cores of light on the silver. Down one side of the lawn ran a terrace of grey stone, bordered by a broad gravel walk, and over the terrace pale monthly roses climbed and blossomed. Most of the windows in the house were darkened and eclipsed by Venetian blinds, to keep out the sun which still lingered on the face of it; and Mr. Martin, also—Mrs. Grampound's brother—was in a state of eclipse for the time being, for he wore a broad-brimmed Panama hat, which concealed the upper part of his face, while a large harlequin tea-cup prevented any detailed examination of his mouth. Mrs. Grampound sat opposite him in a low, basket chair, and appeared to be thinking. It is a privilege peculiar to owners of very fine, dark grey eyes, to appear to be thinking whenever they are not talking.

Mr. Martin finished his tea, and lit a cigarette.

"They've begun cutting the corn," he said; "it's very early."

Mrs. Grampound did not answer, and her brother, considering that he had made his sacrifice on the altar of conversation, relapsed into silence again.

Perhaps the obvious inference that the summer had been hot reminded her that the day was also hot, for in a minute or two she said,—

"Dear Eva! what a stifling journey she will have. She comes back to-night; she ought to be here by now."

"Where has she been staying?"

"At the Brabizons. Lord Hayes was there. He comes home at the end of the week; his mother arrived yesterday."

"The old witch," murmured Mr. Martin.

"Yes, but very old," said she, whose mind was apparently performing obligato variations on the theme of the conversation. "Haven't you noticed—"

She broke off, and presumably continued the obligato variations.

Mr. Martin showed no indications of having noticed anything at all, and the faint sounds of the summer evening pursued their whisperings unchecked until the distant rumble of carriage wheels began to overscore the dim noises, and came to a long pause, after a big crescendo, before the front door.

"That will be Eva," said her mother, filling up the teapot; "they will tell her we are here."

A few minutes afterwards, the drawing-room window was opened from inside, and a girl began to descend the little flying staircase.

Apparently she was in no hurry, for she stooped to stroke a kitten that was investigating the nature of blind cord with an almost fanatical enthusiasm. The kitten was quite as eager to investigate the nature of the human hand, and flew at Eva's outstretched fingers, all teeth and claws.

"You little brute!" she remarked, shaking it off. "Your claws want cutting. Oh! you are rather nice. Come, Kitty."

But the kitten was indignant, and bounced down the stairs in front of her, sat down on the path at the bottom, and pretended to be unaware of her existence. Eva stopped to pluck a rose from a standard tree, and fastened it in her dress. Her foot was noiseless on the soft grass, and neither her uncle or mother heard her approaching.

"The brute scratched me," she repeated as she neared them; "its claws want cutting."

Mrs. Grampound was a little startled, and got up quickly.

"Oh, Eva, I didn't hear you coming. I was just saying it was time you were here. How are you, and have you had a nice time?"

"Yes, quite nice; but the Brabizons are rather stupid people. Still, I enjoyed myself. I didn't see you, Uncle Tom; anyhow, I can't kiss you with that hat on."

She touched the top of his Panama hat lightly with the tips of her fingers, and sat down in her mother's chair, who was pouring her out a cup of tea.

"We had a tiresome journey," she went on. "Why will people live in Lancashire? Is this your chair, mother?"

Mr. Martin got up.

"I'm going in," he said; "you can have mine. At least, I'm going for a ride. Is the tea good, Eva?—it has been made for some time—or shall I tell them to send you out some more?"

"It seems to me very bad," said Eva, sipping it. "Yes, I should like some more. Are you going for a ride? Perhaps I'll come."

"Yes, it's cooler now," said he. "Do come with me."

"Will you order my horse, then, if you are going in? Perhaps you'd better tell them to have it ready only, and not to bring it round. I won't come just yet, anyhow. If I'm not ready, start without me, and I daresay I'll follow you, if you tell me where you are going."

"I want to ride up to the Whitestones'—to see him."

"Very well, I daresay I shall follow you."

Mr. Martin stood looking rather like a servant receiving orders. Eva always managed to make other people assume subordinate positions.

"How long do you think you will be?" he asked.

"Perhaps half-an-hour. But don't wait for me."

Eva threw off her hat impatiently.

"I have been horribly hot and dusty all day," she said, "and there was nearly an accident; at least, there was a bit of an accident. We were standing in a siding for the express to pass, and we weren't far enough back or far enough forward or something, and it crashed through a bit of the last carriage. That is what made me so late. It is very stupid that people, whose only business is to see about trains, can't avoid that sort of thing."

"My darling Eva," said her mother, "were you in the train?"

"Yes; in the next carriage—I and Lord Hayes. He was dreadfully nervous all the rest of the way. That is so silly. It is inconceivable that two accidents should happen on the same day to the same train."

"I thought he wasn't coming back till the end of the week."

"Yes, but he changed his mind and came with me," said Eva. "The Brabizons were furious. I sha'n't go there again. Really, people are very vulgar. I owe him three-and-sixpence for lunch. He said he would call for it, if he might—he always asks leave—to-morrow morning."

Mrs. Grampound did not reply, but the obligato variations went on jubilantly. Eva was lying back in her chair, looking more bored than ever with this stupid world. Her mother's eyes surveyed the slender figure with much satisfaction. It really was a great thing to have such a daughter. And Lord Hayes had changed the day of his departure obviously in order to travel with Eva, and he was coming to call to-morrow morning in order to ask for three-and six!

Eva, quite unconscious of this commercial scrutiny, was swinging her hat to and fro, looking dreamily out over the green distances.

"On the whole, I sha'n't go for a ride," she said at length. "I think I'll sit here with you, if you've got nothing to do; I rather want to talk to you."

"Certainly, dear," said her mother; "but hadn't you better send word to the stables? Then they needn't get Starlight ready. I must go into the house to get my work, but I sha'n't be a moment. I wonder what you want to talk to me about."

"No," said Eva, "don't get your work. You can't talk when you are working. Besides, I daresay I shall go later. Leave it as it is."

"Dear Eva," said Mrs. Grampound, "I am so anxious to hear what you have to say. Shall I be pleased?"

"I don't know," said Eva, slowly. "Well, the fact is that Lord Hayes—well—will have something to say to me when he comes for the three-and-six. He would have said it at the Brabizons, only I didn't allow him, and he would have said it in the train, only I said I couldn't bear people who talked in the train. I may be wrong, but I don't think I am. I like him, you know, very much; he is not so foolish as most people. But I do not feel sure about it."

"My darling Eva," began her mother with solemn gladness.

"It's all rather sudden," Eva interrupted. "I want to wait a little first. Do you know, I think I shall be out to-morrow when he comes, or I might send him the three-and-six by post. He is not stupid; he would easily understand what I meant."

To say that this was the cherished dream of her mother's heart would almost be understating the fact, and now the cherished dream was perhaps going to be transformed into a most cherishable reality. Mrs. Grampound, if not knowing exactly how to deal with Eva, at least was conscious of her ignorance and was cautious.

"Yes, darling, it's very sudden," she said. "Don't do anything in a hurry—of course I know how heavy the responsibilities will seem to you, as they must to every young girl who goes out from the what's-its-name of home life, and all that sort of thing, to those very much wider spheres, but you will do your best, dear, I know. Eva, darling, I must kiss you."

Mrs. Grampound surged out of her chair, and bent over Eva to kiss her. Eva received the kiss with absolute passivity, but sorry, perhaps, a moment afterwards, for her want of responsiveness, bent forward and kissed her again.

"It wasn't exactly the responsibilities I was thinking of," she said; "it was"—she got up from her chair quickly, and stood quite still, looking down over the lawn to the reddening sunset—"it was that I am not quite sure about myself."

Mrs. Grampound seized hold of anything tangible which Eva's speech conveyed, and sympathised with it.

"Yes, darling, I know," she said. "Just wait a little, and think about it. I think your plan about not seeing him to-morrow is very wise. He will, probably, in any case, write to your father first. It is very faint praise to say that he is not so foolish as most people. A most brilliant and well-informed man! He was telling me, the other day, about a flower he has in his conservatory which ate flies or something of the sort, which seems to me most extraordinary. Such an admirable landlord, too. He has just built some new labourers' cottages in Hayes, and I declare I want to go and live in them myself. I feel sure he will write to your father, and, no doubt, he will talk to you about it."

"You would like it, then, would you?" said Eva. "Tell me exactly what you think?"

Mrs. Grampound had a very decided opinion about it, and she expressed herself fully.

"Darling, that is so sweet of you. Ah, how can I have but one opinion! It is a girl's duty to marry as well as she can. This is a brilliant match. I know so many mothers—good, conscientious mothers—who think only of their children's happiness, who would give anything to have Lord Hayes as their son-in-law. A mother's happiness lies in the happiness of her children. They are bone of her bone, and all that sort of thing. How can they but wish for and pray for their happiness! You see, Eva, you are quite poor; your father will leave you next to nothing. Riches are a great blessing, because they enable you to do so much good. Of course they are not everything, and if you wanted to marry that dreadful Lord Symonds, whom they tell such horrible stories about, I would fall down on my knees and beseech you not to mind about poverty, or anything else. Or if I thought you would not be happy, for it is your duty to be happy. But this is exceptional in every way. You get position, wealth, title and a good husband. No one can deny that the aristocracy is the best class to marry into; indeed, for you it is the only class, and you bring him nothing but the love he bears you, of course, and your beauty."

"Yes; he pays a long price for my beauty," said Eva, meditatively.

"My dear Eva, we are all given certain natural advantages—or, if they are withheld, you may be sure that is only a blessing in disguise—talents, beauty, and so on—and it is our clear duty to make the most of them. Beauty has been given you in a quite unusual degree, and it is your duty to let it find its proper use. Don't you remember the parable of the ten talents? We had it in church only last Sunday, and I remember at the time that I was thinking of you and Lord Hayes, which was quite a remarkable coincidence. And then the good you can do as Lady Hayes is infinitely greater than the good you can do as the wife of a poor man. You have to look at the practical side of things, too. Ah, dear me, if life was only love, how simple and delightful it would all be! This is a work-a-day world, and we are not sent here just to enjoy ourselves."

Eva did not seem to be listening very closely.

"Tell me about your own engagement," she said at length. "I don't know what exactly one is supposed to feel. I have many reasons for wanting to marry Lord Hayes. I like and respect him very much. I believe he is a very good man; he is always agreeable and considerate."

"That is the best and surest basis for love to rest on," broke in her mother, who was charmed to find Eva so sensible. "That is just what I have always said. Love must spring out of these things, darling, just as the leaves and foliage of a tree spring out of the solid wood. So many girls have such foolish sentimental notions, just as if they had just come away from a morning performance at the Adelphi. That is not love; it is just silly, schoolgirl sentimentality, which silly schoolgirls feel for tenor singers, and a silky moustache, and slim, weak-eyed young men. Real love is the flower of respect and admiration, and solid esteem. *Aimer c'est tout comprendre*; and to do that you must have no illusions—you must keep the lights dry—you must regard a man as he is, not as you think he is."

"Yes, I see," said Eva, slowly; "I daresay you are right. I certainly never felt any schoolgirl sentimentality for anyone. I think I shall go for a ride, mother; it is nice to get a breath of fresh air after a long journey."

Mrs. Grampound rose too, and drew her arm through Eva's.

"Yes, darling, it will do you good," she said. "And you can think about all this quietly. Your father is out still; he went down to the river just before you came, to see if he could get a trout or two. And Percy comes this evening. I will ring the bell in the drawing-room for your horse to come round, if you will go and get your habit on. Give me one more kiss, dear; it is so nice to have you home again."

Eva put her horse into a steady canter over the springy turf, and soon caught her uncle up, who was ambling quietly along on a grey pony. He was staying with his brother-in-law for a week or two, before going back to America, being a citizen of the United States. He rode for two reasons—indeed, he never did anything without a reason—both of which were excellent. Riding was a means of progressing from one place to another, and it was a sort of watch-key which wound up the mechanism of the body. He was rather hypochondriacal, and his doctor advised exercise, so he obeyed his doctor and rode. He did much more good than harm in this wicked world, but comparatively little of either.

His sister had married Mr. Grampound early in life. She had a considerable fortune left her by her father, by aid of which, as with a golden spade, she hope to bury her American extraction. This she had succeeded in doing, with very decent success, but her golden spade had, so to speak, been broken in the act of interment, for her husband had speculated rather wildly with her money, and had lost it. Mrs. Grampound cared very little for this; her golden spade had done its work. She had married into the English aristocracy, for the Grampounds, though their accounts at banks did not at all correspond to the magnificence of their origin, and though the family estates had been sold to the last possible acre, held, in the estimation of the world, that position which, though it takes only a generation or two of great wealth to raise, requires an infinite number of generations of poverty to demolish.

Eva found the society of her uncle very soothing on this particular afternoon. He very seldom disagreed with anybody, chiefly because he hated argument as a method of conversation, but his assent was not of that distressing order which is more irritating than a divergent view, for he always took the trouble to let it appear that he had devoted considerable thought to the question at issue, and had arrived at the same conclusions as his interlocutor.

It was nearly eight when they reached home, and the dusk was thickening into night. Mr. Grampound had just got in, when they dismounted at the door, and he greeted Eva in his usual dignified and slightly interested manner. The extreme finish of his face suggested that the number of Grampounds who had been turned out of the same mediæval mould, was very considerable.

Eva's father held the door open for her to pass into the inner hall, and Eva, going to the table to take a bedroom candle, noticed that there was a note lying there for him. She turned it over quickly, and saw a coronet and "Aston House" on the back. She handed it to her father, who took it and said,—

"From Lord Hayes. I thought he had not come home yet."

Eva was standing on the lowest step of the flight of stairs.

"Yes; he came home with me to-day," she said.

"Was he with you at the Brabizons?"

"Yes; we travelled together."

Eva went up to her room, not wishing to see the note opened in her presence. What it would contain she knew, or, at least, guessed. Five minutes later, Mr. Grampound also came upstairs and tapped at the door of his wife's room. She had not begun to dress, and he came in with the note in his hand. His cold, clean-shaven face showed a good deal of gentlemanly and quiet satisfaction.

"Of course there is only one answer," he said when she had finished reading it. "It is a splendid match for her."

"Eva spoke to me about it this afternoon," said his wife.

"Well?"

"She does not want to be hurried. She wants to have time to decide."

"There is no time like the present," observed Mr. Grampound.

"I hope you won't press her, Charles. You will get nothing by that. She wants to marry, I know; and I said a great many very sensible things to her this afternoon. She wants more than a quiet home-life can give her, and she likes Hayes."

"I must send some answer to him; and I certainly shall not tell him to keep away."

"Give her time. Say he may come in a week. There is no harm in waiting a little. Eva will not be forced into anything against her will."

"I shall speak to her to-night."

"Yes, do; but be careful. I must send you away now; it is time to dress. Percy has come."

Eva, meanwhile, was thinking over the talk she had had with her mother. Mrs. Grampound's affectionate consideration for her daughter's feelings, Eva knew quite well, might only be the velvet glove to an iron hand. But she was distinctly conscious that there was a great deal in what her mother had said. She had decided for herself that she was not going to fall in love with anyone; men seemed to her to be very little loveable. At the same time, she knew that, in her heart of hearts, she longed for the possibilities which a great marriage would give her. Perhaps then the world would open out; perhaps it was interesting after all. Her home-life bored her considerably. They were in the country nine months out of the twelve, living in a somewhat sparsely-populated district, and Eva was totally unable to make for herself active or engrossing occupation in the direction of district-visiting or Sunday schools, or those hundred and one ways in which "nice girls" are supposed to employ themselves. Her vitality was of that still, strong sort which can only be reached through the emotions, and is too indolent or too uninitiative to stir the emotions into creating interests for themselves. The vague imperative *need* of doing something never wound its horn to her. She could not throw herself into the first pursuit that offered, simply because she had to be doing something, and her emotional record was a blank. The pencil and paper were there, for she was two-and-twenty, but she had nothing to write. She was quite unable to transform her diversions into aims, a faculty which accounts completely for the busy lives some women lead.

Dinner was not till half-past eight, and, when Eva came down, the drawing-room was untenanted. The shaded lamp left the room in comparative dimness, but through the windows, which were open to let in the cool, evening air, the last glow of the sunset cast a red light on to the opposite wall. She stood at the window a moment and looked at the river, which lay like a string of crimson pools stretching west; and then, turning away impatiently, walked up and down the room, wondering where everyone was. That peaceful, sleeping landscape outside seemed to her an emblem of the quiet, deadly days that were to come. The slow to-morrow and to-morrow seemed suddenly impossible. The door was open to her—the door leading on all that the world had to offer. Perhaps it was all as uninteresting as this, but it would be something, at any rate, to know that—to be quite certain that life was dull to the core. Then she thought she could rest quiet, and, perhaps, would not mind so much. What vexed and irritated her, was to suspect that the world was interesting and not to find it so, and she was disposed to lay the blame of that on her own particular station in life. Yet—yet—she could hardly say she had an ideal, but there was that shrouded image called love, of which she only saw the dim outline. It would be a pity to smash it up before the coverings came off. It might be worth having, after all.

Her eye caught sight of a book on the table with a white vellum cover. Eva took it up. It was called *The Crown of Womanhood*, and something like a frown gathered on her face.

It was almost a relief when her mother entered rustling elaborately across the room, and snapping a bracelet on to her comely wrist.

"Ah! Eva, you are before me. Percy has come. I didn't expect him till to-morrow."

"I'm glad," said Eva listlessly.

"Such a lovely evening," continued Mrs. Grampound with a strong determination to be particularly neutral, and entirely unconscious of her talk with Eva before dinner. "Look at those exquisite tints, dear. The blue so tender as to be green," she quoted with a fine disregard of accuracy.

"Yes, it's beautiful," said Eva, not turning her head. "Ah! Percy, it's good to see you."

Eva got up and walked across to meet the newcomer. Percy was a favourite of hers, from the time he had teased her about her dolls onward.

"How long are you going to stop?" she continued. "Percy, stop here a long time; I want you."

"I can't," he said. "I'm going off to Scotland on the 12th, to the Davenports. I promised Reggie."

"Who's Reggie?"

"Reggie? Reggie Davenport. He's a friend of mine. I'm very fond of him. Haven't you ever seen him. He falls in love about once a fortnight. He's very amusing."

"He must be rather a fool," said Eva.

"Oh, but he's a nice fool. Really, he is very nice. He's so dreadfully young."

"Well, you're not very old, my lord," said Eva.

"But Reggie is much the youngest person I ever saw. He'll never grow old."

"Ah! well," said Eva. "I expect he's very happy."

The gong had sounded some minutes, when Mr. Martin shuffled in. He wore a somewhat irregular white tie and grey socks, and was followed almost immediately by Mr. Grampound.

Eva had already written a little note to Lord Hayes, and told her maid to enclose a three-and-six-penny postal order. She had also expressed a vague hope, so as not to block her avenues, that they would meet again soon. Her chief desire was to obtain a respite; the whole thing had been too sudden and she wished to think it over. Meantime, it was nice to see Percy again.

"What have you been doing with yourself?" she asked. "I notice that whenever young men go away in novels, they always fall in love before they get back, or get married, or make their fortunes or lose them. How many of these things have you done?"

"None of them," said Percy; "though I've been to Monte Carlo, I did not play there. It doesn't seem to me at all amusing."

"I suppose you haven't got the gambling instinct," said Eva; "that's a great defect. You know none of the joy of telling your cabman that you will give him a shilling extra if he catches a train. It's equivalent to saying, 'I bet you a shilling you don't;' only he doesn't pay if he loses, and you do. But that's immaterial. The joy lies in the struggle with time and space."

"Do you mean that you like to keep things in uncertainty as long as possible?" asked her father, looking at her.

Their eyes met, and they understood each other. Eva looked at him a moment, and then dropped her eyes.

"Yes; I'm sure I do."

"Even when you have all the data ready, do you like not deciding?"

"Oh! one never knows if one has all the data; something fresh may always turn up. For instance—"

"Well?"

"I was thinking just before dinner that I didn't know what in the world I should do with myself all the autumn, and now you see Percy's arrived. I shall play about with him."

"I go away in two days," said Percy.

"Oh! well, I daresay something else will turn up. I am like Mr. Micawber."

"No, not all," said Mr. Grampound; "he was always doing his best to make things turn up."

Mrs. Grampound remarked that things were always turning up when you expected them least, and Percy hoped that his gun would turn up, because no one could remember where it was.

The evening was so warm that Eva and her mother
sat outside on the terrace after dinner, waiting for the
others to join them. Mr. Grampound never sat long over
his wine, and in a few minutes the gentlemen followed
them. Eva was rather restless, and strolled a little way
down the gravel path, and, on turning, found that her
father had left the others and was walking toward her.

"Come as far as the bottom of the lawn, Eva," he
said; "I should like a little talk with you."

They went on in silence for some steps, and then her
father said,—

"I heard from Lord Hayes to-day. Your mother told
me that you could guess what it was about."

She picked up a tennis-ball that was lying on the
edge of the grass.

"How wet it is!" she said. "Yes, I suppose I know
what he wrote about."

"Your mother and I, naturally, have your happiness
very much at heart," said he, "and we both agree that
this is a very sure and clear chance of happiness for you.
It is a great match, Eva."

Eva as a child had always rather feared her father and
at this moment she found her childish fear rising again in
her mind. Tall, silent, rather scornful-looking men may

not always command affection, but they usually inspire respect. Her old fear for her father had grown into very strong respect, but she felt now that the converse transformation was very possible.

"You would wish me to marry him?" she asked.

"I wish you to consider it very carefully. I have seen a good deal of the world, so I also wish you to consider what I say to you about it. I have thought about it, and I have arrived at the very definite conclusion I have told you. I shall write to him to-night, and, with your consent, will tell him that he may come and ask you in person in a few days' time. You know my wishes on the subject, and your mother's. Meanwhile, dear Eva, I must congratulate you on the very good fortune which has come in your way."

He bent from his great height and kissed her.

"I don't wish to force you in any way," he said, "and I don't wish you to say anything to me to-night about it. Think it over by yourself. I needn't speak of his position and wealth, because, though, of course, they are advantages, you will rate them at their proper value. But I may tell you that I am a very poor man, and that I know what these things mean."

"I should not marry him for those reasons," said Eva.

"There is no need for you to tell me that," said he. "But it is right to tell you that I can leave you nothing. In the same way I hope that any foolish notions you may have got about love, from the trash you may have read in novels, will not stand in your way either. I will leave the matter in the hands of your own good sense."

His words had an unreasonable mastery over Eva, for her father never spoke idly. He was quite aware of the value of speech, but knew that it is enhanced by its rarity. "No one pays any attention to a jabbering fool," he had said once to his wife, *à propos* of a somewhat voluble woman who had been staying in the house, and of whose abilities he and his wife entertained very contrary opinions. Eva had seldom heard him express his philosophy of life at such length, and she fully appreciated the weight it was intended to convey.

CHAPTER II.

Lord Hayes found Eva's note waiting for him when he came down to breakfast next morning, but its contents did not take away his appetite at all. He was quite as willing that she should think it over as her father or mother, and he had no desire to force her to refuse. He was fairly certain that at his time of life, for he was over forty, he was not going to fall in love in the ordinary sense of the word; that sense, in fact, which Eva had herself confessed she never felt likely to experience. He had had a succession of eligible helpmeets hurled at his head by ambitious mothers for many years, and in sufficient numbers to enable him to draw the conclusion that the majority of eligible helpmeets were very much like one another.

They had ready for him smiles of welcome, slightly diverting small-talk, pretty faces, and any number of disengaged waltzes; and after having basked in their welcoming smiles, submitted to their small-talk, looked at their pretty faces, and hopped decorously round in their disengaged waltzes, he always finished by stifling a yawn and making his exit. It would convey an entirely wrong impression to describe him as either a misanthrope or a cynic; the charms of marriageable maidenhood simply did not appeal to him. But though he was neither misanthrope nor cynic, a little vein of malevolence ran through his system, and he had more than half made up his mind that he would have none of these. He was quite rich enough to afford a wife who would bring him nothing but unpaid bills; and provided that wife brought him something which he had not yet found, he was willing to pay them all.

That he was going to marry some time had long been a commonplace to him, but the sight of his forty-fifth milestone had lent it a loud insistence which was becoming quite distracting. The thought had begun to haunt him; he saw it in the withered flowers of his orchid house, it stuck in the corners of his coat pockets, his garden syringe gurgled it at him with its expiring efforts to emit the last drop of water; even the toad which he kept in his greenhouse had the knowledge of it lurking in its sickly eye.

He was very seldom at Aston; but in one of his visits there, he had met Eva and had been considerably struck by her. She was introduced to him, and bowed without smiling. He had asked her whether she played lawn-tennis, and she said, without simpering, that she did. He asked her whether she enjoyed the season, and she replied, without affectation, that she had got so tired of it by the middle of June that she had gone down into the country. He remarked that London was the loser, and she reminded him that, therefore, by exactly the same amount, the country was the gainer. Her eyes wandered vaguely over the green distance, and once met his, without shrinking from or replying to his gaze. She was astonishingly beautiful, and appeared quite unconscious of her charms. She looked so radically indifferent to all that was going on round her, that he had said, "These country parties are rather a bore!" and she replied candidly that she quite agreed with him. In a word, he felt that he might go farther and fare worse, and that he was forty-five years old.

During the next few months, he had come across her not infrequently, both in the country and in London, and at the end of the season they had both met at the Brabizons, where two Miss Brabizons were alternately launched at his hand and heart—*via* brilliant execution on the piano and district-visiting—by their devoted mother, and Eva's calm neutrality was rendered particularly conspicuous by the contrast. His attentions to her grew more and more marked, and Mrs. Brabizon metaphorically threw up the sponge when he changed the day of his departure without ceremony, in order to travel with Eva, and declared that she couldn't conceive what he found in that girl.

His mother always breakfasted alone, and spent the morning by herself, usually out of doors. Lord Hayes was vaguely grateful for this arrangement. Mr. Martin, as we know, had described her as an old witch, and even to her own son she seemed rather a terrific person. She was tall, very well preserved, and a rigid Puritan. Her hobby—for the most unbending of our race have their hobby—was Jaeger clothing. She wore large grey boots with eight holes in them, a drab-coloured dress, and a head-gear that reminded the observer of a volunteer forage cap. This hobby she varied by a spasmodic interest in homœopathy, and she used to walk about the lanes like a mature Medea, gathering simples from the hedges, which she used to administer with appalling firmness to the village people; but, to do her justice, she always experimented with them first *in propriâ personâ*, and declared she felt a great deal better afterwards. For the practice of medicine-taking generally, she claimed that it fortified the constitution, and it must be confessed that her own constitution, at the age of sixty-five, appeared simply impregnable.

But in the morning her son was conscious of an agreeable relaxation. He was a neat, timid man, with a careful little manner, and he inherited from his mother a certain shrewdness that led him to grasp the practical issues of things with rapidity. For instance, on this present occasion, when he had finished his breakfast, he again read over Eva's letter, put it carefully away, and was quite content to wait.

Outside one of the dining-room windows opened a glass-covered passage leading into an orchid house, and he went down this passage with the heels of his patent leather shoes tapping on the tiles, and a large pair of scissors in his hand. Every morning he attended personally to the requirements of this orchid house; he snipped off dead sprays, he industriously blew tobacco smoke on small parasitic animals, and squirted them with soapy water, and this morning, being in a particularly good humour, he went so far as to tickle, with a wisp of hay, the back of the useful toad. That animal received his attentions with silent affability; it closed its eyes, and opened and shut its mouth like an old gentleman awaking from his after-dinner nap.

It was a warm morning, and when he had finished attending to the orchids he strolled round outside the house, back to the front door. The house stood high above the river, and commanded a good view of the green valley; and, in the distance, two miles away, the red-roofed village slanted upwards from the stream towards the downs. He stood looking out over the broad, pleasant fields for some moments, and his eyes wandered across the river to where the red front of Mr. Grampound's house, half hidden by the large cedar, stood, as if looking up to his. The flower-beds gleamed like jewels in the sunshine, and he could see two figures strolling quietly down the gravel path toward the river. One of them was a girl, tall, almost as tall as the man who walked by her side, and to whom she was apparently talking. Just as Lord Hayes looked, they stopped suddenly, and he saw her spread out her hands, which had been clasped in front of her, with a quick dramatic movement. The action struck him as slightly symbolical.

He was roused by the sound of crunched gravel, and, turning round, saw his mother walking towards him. She was in her hygienic dress, and had a small, tin botanical case slung over her shoulders. In her hand she held a pair of eminently useful scissors, the sort of scissors with which Atropos might sever the thread of life. Lord Hayes wore a slightly exotic look by her side.

"The under housemaid has fallen into a refreshing sleep," she announced, "and the action of the skin has set in. In fact, she will do very well now. And how are you, dear James, this morning?"

"I am very well," said he; "very well indeed, thank you, mother."

His mother looked at him with interest.

"You've got a touch of liver," she remarked truculently.

"No, I think not. I feel very well, thanks."

Lady Hayes snapped her scissors.

"I'm afraid the harvest will be very bad this year," she said. "There's been no rain, and no rain means no straw."

"Yes, the farmers are in a bad way," said Lord Hayes. "I shall have to make a reduction again."

"Well, dear," said his mother, "all I can say is that we shall probably be beggars. But porridge is wonderfully sustaining."

"We've still got a few acres in London," he remarked. "Really, in these depressed times, I don't know how a man could live without an acre or two there."

Old Lady Hayes laughed a hoarse, masculine laugh, and strode off, snapping her scissors again. Half-way across the lawn she stopped.

"The Grampounds are at home, I suppose," she said. "I want to see Mrs. Grampound some time."

"Oh, yes; I travelled with Miss Grampound yesterday. She said they were all at home."

"Ha! She is very handsome. But a modern young woman, I should think."

"She's not very ancient. She was staying with the Brabizons."

His mother frowned and continued her walk.

Lord Hayes always felt rather like a naughty child under his mother's eye. He did not at present feel quite equal to telling her what his relations with Eva were. Modernity was the one failing for which she had no sympathy, for it was a characteristic of which she did not possess the most rudimentary traces. To her it meant loss of dignity, Americanisms, contempt for orthodoxy, and general relaxation of all that is worthy in man. She preferred the vices of her own generation to the virtues of newer developments, and almost regretted the gradual extinction of the old three-bottle school, for they were, in her opinion, replaced by men who smoked while they were talking to women, while the corresponding women had given way to women who smoked themselves. For a man to drink port wine in company with other men was better, as being a more solid and respectable failing, than for him to talk to a woman with a cigarette between his lips.

Eva, as Lord Hayes had guessed from his point of vantage by the front door of his house, had strolled out into the garden after breakfast with Percy. She had not told him of Lord Hayes's offer, but she could not help talking to him with it in her mind. It was like a bracket preceded by a minus sign, which affected all that was within the bracket.

"I wish you weren't going away, Percy," she said. "When I woke up this morning, I thought with horror of all the slow days that were coming. I don't care a bit for doing all those things which 'nice girls' are supposed to do. I have no enthusiasms, and the enthusiasms of the people I see here are unintelligible to me. The sight of a dozen little boys in a Sunday school, with pomatum on their heads, inspires me with slight disgust—so do bedridden old women. I suppose I have no soul. That is quite possible. But, but—"

"Yes, I'm luckier than you," said Percy; "I like little quiet things. I like fishing, and reading the paper, and doing nothing."

"Yes, you're luckier than I am just now," said Eva, "but when I do get interested in things, I shall be in a better position than you. I'm sure there are lots of interests in the world, but I don't realise it."

"Well, I daresay you will discover them sometime," said Percy, consolingly.

"Who can tell? There are lots of women who do not feel any interest in anything—though, perhaps, fewer women than men. But why does London interest you so? It seems to me just as stupid in its way as this place."

"I like the sense of there being loads of people about," said Percy. "A lot of people together are not at all the same as a number of units."

"How do you mean?"

"Well, it's just the same as with gunpowder. One grain of powder only spits if you set light to it, but if you were to throw a pound of gunpowder into the fire the result would be quite different from the effect of a thousand spits."

It was at this point that Lord Hayes was watching the two from his front door. Eva stopped suddenly in her walk, and spread out her hands, stretching her arms out.

"That's what I want," she said. "I want to develop and open. I fully believe the world is very interesting, but I am like a blind man being told about a sunset. It conveys nothing to me. And I don't believe that fifty million Sunday schools and mothers' meetings would do it for me. It must touch me somehow else. Religion and philanthropy are not the keys. I long to find out what the keys are."

"It's a pity you don't want to marry," said Percy.

"How do you know I don't want to marry?"

"You've told me so yourself, plenty of times. You said only a few weeks ago that you thought all men most uninteresting."

"Yes, I know. But I'm not so egotistical as not to suspect that the fault is mine. I don't know any men well, except you, and I don't think that you are at all uninteresting. If only I could be certain—"

Eva broke off suddenly, but Percy asked her what she wished to be certain about.

"If I could be certain that I was right—right for me, that is—certain that for me life and men and women were quite uninteresting, I don't think I should mind so much. I would cease thinking about it altogether. I might even teach in the Sunday school. If all things are uninteresting, I may as well do that, and cease to expect interest in anything."

"But aren't you conscious of any change in yourself?" asked Percy; "and doesn't the very fact that you are getting more and more conscious that everything is very dull go to prove it?"

"I don't quite understand."

Percy looked vaguely about, mentally speaking, for a parallel, and his eyes, sympathetically following his mind, lighted on an autumn-flowering bulb, which was just beginning to push its juicy, green spike above the ground.

"There," he said, "are you not, perhaps, like what that bulb was three days ago? If it were conscious it would have felt, not that it was growing, but that the earth round it was pressing it more closely. Perhaps you are on the point of sprouting. It couldn't have known it was sprouting."

Eva stood thinking for a moment or two.

"What an excitement it must be, after having seen nothing but brown earth and an occasional worm all your life, suddenly to come out into the open air and see other plants and trees and sky. If I am sprouting, I hope the sky will be blue when I see it first."

"I expect grey sky and rain makes the bulb grow quicker."

"Oh! but I don't care what is good for me," said Eva; "I only care for what is interesting. Otherwise, I should

have done all sorts of salutary things, all my life—
certainly a great number of unpleasant things; one is
always told that unpleasant things are salutary."

"I don't believe that," said Percy; "I think it's one's
duty to be happy."

"Oh! but, according to the same idea, the salutary
and unpleasant things produce ineffable joy, if you give
them time," said Eva.

They walked back to the house in silence, but on the
steps Eva stopped.

"Perhaps you're right, Percy," she said; "perhaps I am
sprouting, though I don't know it. Certainly I feel more
and more confined by all these dull days than I used to. I
wonder what the world will look like when I get above
ground. I hope you are right, Percy; I want to sprout."

"It is such a comfort to think that no crisis ever fails
to keep its appointment," said he. "When one's nature is
prepared for the crisis, the crisis comes. Anything will do
for a crisis. It is not the incident itself that makes the
difference, but the change that has been going on in
oneself."

"Yes, that's quite true. It is no use wanting a crisis to
come, or thinking that one is ready for it, if one only had
a chance. If one really is ready for it, anything is a crisis.
People who get converted, as they think, by hearing a

hymn sung, think it is the hymn that has done it, and they don't realise that it is what has been going on in themselves first. Anything else would do as well."

For the next few days all Eva's surroundings combined to strengthen her already existing bias. Percy went away; her father was more stern and exacting than usual; her mother, Eva felt, was watching her, as one watches a barometer the day before a picnic, and tapping her to see whether she was inclining to fine weather or stormy. Moreover, the little talk she had had with Percy strengthened her desire to see and judge the world. Perhaps she would always find it uninteresting. If that was so, the sooner she knew it the better; but the probability was strongly against it, and if it was not uninteresting to the core, she was simply wasting time. These August days were more tedious than ever; she read novels, but they bored her; she tried to paint, but got tired of her picture almost before she had drawn it in; all the neighbours—and there were not many of them— seemed to be away. Lord Hayes's apparently was the only house open, and of him she naturally saw nothing.

It was four days after Percy's departure that Lord Hayes came to call. Eva was sitting on the lawn behind the house when he arrived; she saw him coming out through the open French window in the drawing-room, and down the little iron staircase. She rose to meet him, and told the footman to bring tea out. Her choice, she knew, was imminent, and she had one momentary impulse to stop him, to give herself more time, but the instant afterwards the other picture rose before her—that flat perspective of level days, a country without hill or stream, her own life at home, and, on the other hand, the possibilities of her new sphere—the world and all it contained. Was this man, perhaps, the owner of the key which would unlock it all to her? Among other men she ranked him high, perhaps the highest; he had never pestered her, or stared at her as if she was a picture; he had never bored her; perhaps he understood her need; perhaps he could supply it.

They shook hands, and stood there for a moment silent. Then he said,

"You promised to show me your beautiful garden. I can see it like a jewel among the trees from Aston."

"Yes; the flowers are very bright just now," she said, speaking naturally. "Let us go down the terrace."

At the bottom of the terrace he stopped. The cedar hid them from the house, and they were alone.

"Your father told me I might call here," he said, "and tell you why I have come."

Eva was standing about three feet off him, with her hands clasped behind her. He made a step forward.

"Eva, you know—"

Still she made no sign.

"I have come to ask you whether you care for me at all—whether you will be my wife?"

"I will be your wife," she said, without smiling, but letting her hands drop down by her side.

He took one of her disengaged hands in his, and bent forward to kiss it. She looked at him steadily, as if questioning him—and the long perspective of level days had passed from her life for ever.

CHAPTER III.

The account of Eva's wedding, the description of her dress, the dramatic tears which Mrs. Grampound shed as her daughter was led to the altar, the size of the celebrated family diamonds, are not these things written in the *Morning Post*? And as they are recorded there, by pens better fitted than mine to do honour to the glories of the old embroidery on Eva's train, the Valenciennes lace on her dress, the tulle, the pearls, the white velvet and all the unfading splendours of the matrimonial rite, I will merely say that everything was performed on a scale of the utmost magnificence, that two princes were there, and several dukes, one of whom was heard remark out loud in church, "By gad! she's exquisite," that another exalted personage replied, "Lucky fellow, Hayes," that the wife of the exalted personage fixed her lord with a stony stare and said "Sh-sh-sh-sh," and that he, in spite of his strawberry leaves and his pedigree and his frock coat, trembled in his patent leather shoes, and in his confusion was vividly impressed with the idea that his prayer-book consisted entirely of the service for the visitation of those of riper years, to be used at sea on the occasion of the Queen's accession. As these portentous facts are not recorded in the *Morning Post*, I have thought fit to mention them here, with one other little detail that escaped the vigilance of the newspaper reporters. It was merely that the bride smiled when she was asked whether she would love, honour and obey her husband. But she promised to do so in a firm, clear voice; so, of course, it was all right.

And now two months had passed, and the newly-married pair had emerged from those blissful weeks of solitude, which are designed to make them more used to their happiness, to help them to realise that nothing can come between them but death, that they have awoke from what seemed a dream and found that it was true, that a new life has begun for them, and that the gates of Paradise are henceforward going to stand permanently open.

They had been to the Riviera, where Lord Hayes had bought a large, white umbrella, under which he used to smoke innumerable cigarettes and go little strolls along the beach, sometimes with Eva, but oftener alone. Eva quite fulfilled all the requisites he had wished for in a wife; she was dignified, rather silent, more than presentable. It pleased him that crowds should stand and stare at his wife as she walked up and down the fashionable promenades at Monte Carlo, in her still scornful beauty, with her deep, unregarding eyes wearily unconscious of their scrutiny; that the magnates of the earth should stand by her chair, as she lounged the southern afternoons away, indolently indifferent to the gay chatter round her. She used to play sometimes at the Casino, with the same air of utter *ennui*; though, at times, when the luck went heavily in her favour or against her, her eye would brighten. She played by no system whatever. "If I had a system," she said, "the game would cease to interest me; by the doctrine of probabilities, my losses or gains would be slight if I stuck to the same number; in fact, in the long run, it would diminish the element of chance almost to nothing. But to me the whole point of the game lies in the utter uncertainty of it; just the blind rolling of that ball, the momentum of which no one knows, not even the man who sets it rolling."

On two occasions she laughed out loud at the tables. The first of these occasions was when she had been staking wildly on any number that happened to occur to her, and she had won, by almost miraculous luck, six times in succession. The other occasion was when she had lost ten times that sum, in a few minutes, by always betting on the same number. She liked the sensation of measuring herself with infinite and immeasurable forces, as exhibited in the laws of gravity and momentum.

But Lord Hayes had made, as the reader will have perceived, one grand mistake. He had wanted a presentable, dignified and reserved wife, a wife who was not silly, who did not simper or smirk, and he had got her. But what he had not recognised was that such characteristics do not make up a woman's soul, but are only one expression of it under certain circumstances, and that the soul that expressed itself in such a way was capable of expressing itself differently under other circumstances; that all these may only be the natural and legitimate signs of a want of development, and that they give no hint whatever as to what form that development will take, or what the developed soul will be. In the month of June you may see everywhere, on chestnut trees, certain compact pyramids of folded buds, slightly glutinous to the touch. If you take one of these off a hundred chestnut trees, you will be unable to detect the least difference between them. But two months later, three-quarters of those chestnut trees are covered with spires of white blossoms, and one quarter with spires of red—*Fabula narratur*. But the presumption was that any given one would be white? Certainly; but it is well to remember that a certain number will be red.

Once or twice, then, Eva had shown, as it were, the first hint of a coming blossom, which, somehow, was strangely disconcerting to her lord; it was not quite the fair white blossom he had led himself to expect. Certain of these little episodes will be worth recording.

They had spent ten days at Mentone, among other places, and had met there a certain Mr. Armine, a young man of about thirty-two, of charming appearance and manner, who was amusing himself abroad for a month or two, while an army of contractors, builders and decorators were making his father's country house, to which he had succeeded by that gentleman's death, into a place more fitting for a fashionable young man to spend half the year in. He knew Lord Hayes rather well, and was quite willing to advance to the same degree of intimacy with his wife. Everyone called him Jim, for no better reason apparently than that his name was Plantagenet, but that, after all, was reason enough.

Eva had received this heavily-gilded youth with some cordiality, and he was clever enough to take advantage of it without subjecting the silver cord to too severe a strain. The silence and apathy of a Grecian-browed, velvet-eyed divinity is construed in quite a different manner to the interpretation put on the identical phenomena when exhibited by podgy though admirable members of the same sex. It is quite impossible to imagine that behind the Grecian brow, lurk thoughts that are not distinguished by the same magnificence as their frontlet.

In other words, Eva's silences, her long glances over the weary, blue horizon, her indifference to those round her, challenged conjecture, and roused eager interests, which the vivacity and attractiveness of other women might quite have failed to awaken.

Jim Armine began by finding immense pleasure in watching her beauty, as he might have watched a Greek statue, but in a few days his mere æsthetic pleasure in looking at her had dwindled to insignificance beside the fascination of something apart from her mere beauty. In those few weeks of married life, an essential change had come over her; her soul had awakened with throbs of surprised indignation, and it found its expression in a gathered intensity of indifference in her husband's presence.

She had no need to ask him why he had married her; the sense of his possession of her made itself felt as an insult and an outrage. She felt she had been duped, deceived, hoodwinked. The consciousness that she was his was like an open wound. She had sacrificed all her undeveloped possibilities to a loveless owner; all she had was no longer hers. Truly the red flowers were very different from the white.

To another man who was something of an observer, the signs of this which appeared on the surface, as the surface of dark water heaves and is stirred mysteriously and massively when the depths are moved, were profoundly interesting. The full import of this stirring, of course, he did not, could not guess. All he knew was, that this admirably beautiful woman had moods as profound as they were mysterious; he was pre-occupied with her, interested, fascinated.

They were sitting together on the verandah of the Beau Site one afternoon, in the enjoyment of the bright, winter sun. Lord Hayes had departed with his white umbrella, to see about the purchase of a small villa which was for sale, and which stood high and pleasantly among the olive woods.

They had been for a sail in the morning, and Eva said to herself that she was tired and would stop at home. She did not trouble to make any excuse at all to her husband. He had mentioned to her that he was going to see about the villa which she had admired.

"It will be a pleasant drive up there," he had said, "if you care to come. You said you wanted to see the villa."

Eva had rather wanted to see the villa, but the prospect appeared suddenly distasteful to her.

"I think I shall stop at home," she said, and left him standing on the hotel steps.

Jim Armine, it appeared, was going to stop at home, too, and the natural consequence of this was that, half an hour later, they met on the great verandah facing south.

"This place gets stupid," she said, seating herself in a low, basket chair. "I think we shall have to go away."

"Where are you going to?" he asked.

"I had thought of Algiers; we can't go north yet. They are having blizzards in England. Besides, February in England is always intolerable."

"I have never been to Algiers," said Jim, pregnantly.

Eva looked at him a moment.

"Well, I suppose there's no reason why you shouldn't come with us. We haven't got a monopoly of the line."

"I shouldn't come if you didn't want me," he said, rather sulkily.

"Fancy asking a bride on her honeymoon whether she wanted another man with her!" she said. "There is only one man in the moon, I've always heard."

Poor Jim found it rather hard to keep his temper, more especially as he knew that he had nothing to complain of. He shifted his position in his chair, and fixed his eye on a sail on the horizon, so that he could see Eva without looking at her.

"Algiers is quite a model place for a honeymoon, I should think," he said. "Of course, the object is to get out of the world. There is too large a piece of the world at Mentone. Don't you find it so?"

Eva raised her eyebrows. This last speech seemed to her to savour of impertinence, and needed no reply. Jim was clever enough to see that he had made a mistake, and his tone altered.

"Where are you going to stay in Algiers? I believe it is pleasanter out of the town, on the hills."

"Oh! Hayes has got a villa somewhere in Mustapha Supérieure. He has a passion for villas. He has a strong sense of possession. We have been making a sort of triumphal progress. He has a villa at Biarritz, which we stayed in, and now he has bought one here. Personally, I prefer a hotel, but, of course, villas are more suitable to honeymoons. You are more alone there. But they are rather spidery affairs if they are never lived in."

"Oh! spiders belong to the class of idyllic insects," said Armine. "They swarm in hayfields on Sunday evenings, which is one of the most recognised idyllic settings."

"I don't think I can be idyllic," remarked Eva. "I never want to sit in hayfields. They make one feel creepy, and all sorts of strange things crawl down your back. It may be idyllic, but the consciousness of the creepy things makes one want to go for the idylls with a broom. Besides, spiders are so like a certain class of odious men."

Jim recalled at that moment a little thing that had struck his attention the same morning. Lord Hayes had been breakfasting in the verandah on the usual continental breakfast—a couple of rolls, two pieces of creamy butter, coffee, and a saucer of honey. A fly had found its way into the honey, and Hayes had extracted it with the butt end of his teaspoon. There was a methodical eagerness about this action that had made Jim think at that moment of a spider disentangling a fly from its web, and at Eva's words the scene flashed up before him again.

"I think I know what you mean," he said, feeling his way.

Eva, too, had noticed the scene in the morning, and Jim's remark made her wonder whether he also had it in his mind. When she had compared spiders to an odious class of men, she had not in the least thought of her husband. The possible impertinence of his first remark received some confirmation. She was willing to be like a spider, too, if necessary.

"I daresay you do," she said. "There is nothing very subtle about it. I remember thinking this morning that you looked so like a spider when you were helping that fly out of your honey. Not that you belong to the odious class of men."

Jim flushed. The whip tingled unpleasantly on his shoulders.

"It was your husband who rescued the fly out of his honey," he said.

"Was it?" asked Eva, negligently. "I thought it was you."

She did not feel angry with him. He had made a mistake and had been punished for it. Justice had been done.

"It's getting rather cold," she went on. "Take me for a stroll, and give me your arm if you care for convention as little as you say you do. I am a little tired."

They walked up and down the gay street in front of the hotel for half-an-hour or so. Eva felt a vague stimulus in the homage of this presentable young man, in spite of his slight awkwardnesses. She felt he was not a man whom it was easy to make a fool of, but she was making a somewhat complete fool of him, and it pleased her. For the first time, perhaps, she caught a glimpse of her own power as a beautiful and attractive woman. That glimpse roused no vanity in her, but considerable interest. The sense of personal power is always pleasant; no man or woman who is alive, in any sense of the word, will acquiesce in being a unit among units, or will fail to feel a delicate growing love of power. We brought nothing into the world, and we shall assuredly take nothing out; but while we are in the world, how we cling, with a persistence that no creed will shake, to the passionate desire for more and more and more. Eva was, in fact, on the threshold of the house called "Know Thyself." It is a house of varying size. To her it appeared large and well furnished.

They walked along the sea-wall westwards, and Eva sat down on the low balustrade. The air was still and windless, and forty feet below lay the smooth, grey backs of the rocks still shining with the salt water.

"What a frightful coward one is," she said, "not to throw oneself down and see what happens next. I always flatter myself that I'm brave; but I am not brave enough to risk anything, really. I think a year ago I might have thrown myself down if it had occurred very strongly to me, because I had nothing to risk. But now things are beginning to be interesting. I should risk a certain amount of amusement and pleasure if I just stepped over that wall. I wish you would step over and see, Mr.

Armine; only that would be no good, you couldn't come and tell me about it afterwards."

"Of course, lots of things are a bore," said he, "but I can't imagine any existence where that wouldn't be the case. I couldn't frame a life in my mind where one wouldn't be bored."

"Well, I sympathise with you. I probably am incapable—in fact, I know I am incapable—of many emotions, but I feel bored no longer. I used to feel nothing else."

Armine was sitting near her, looking the other way.

"What emotions can't you feel?" he asked suddenly.

Eva laughed.

"Oh! plenty, and perhaps the most important of all. That is why I fully expect not to feel all the emotions that Algiers should inspire in me."

Armine thought this remark much less inconsequent than it sounded, but he kept his reflections to himself.

Two days afterwards, Eva and her husband left Mentone for Marseilles. Jim walked down with them to the station, accounting for his action by saying that he expected a box from England, and it had not arrived, though it was two days overdue. To Eva this appeared the most shallow and unnecessary of subterfuges. There was some slight delay in starting, and he stood by their carriage window with his arms on the sill until the train moved.

Eva was leaning back in her corner, talking slowly but somewhat continuously.

"I hope your box will have come," she was saying with fine cruelty. "You must have been very eager about it to come down through these dusty streets, when you might be having a sail. I really thought you were coming to see us off till you explained about the box. I think I should have been rude enough to ask you to stop at home if it had been so. I hate being seen off. There is never anything to say; you feel as if you ought to make pretty little farewell speeches, but the farewell speeches always hang fire, I notice. And no one can continue an ordinary, rational, desultory conversation with fifty engines screaming at him. It is much better for everyone to pretend they are not going till the last moment, and then jump up quickly, say good-bye, and bundle into the cab. But at a railway station it is impossible to pretend you are not going. The apparatus of going is too obvious. Everyone is fussy and stupid at a station. Ah! we are really off, are we? Good-bye! I wish you were coming with us."

Eva smiled rather maliciously. The first impertinent remark had been settled with now, and they were quits again.

Jim Armine stood on the platform watching the smoke of the receding train. He made a monosyllabic remark which is not worth setting down, and went back to the hotel. The box which he was expecting might languish alone in the parcel office for all that he cared.

The bridal pair crossed in one of the French Transatlantique steamers, which are built long and narrow for the sake of speed, and the accurate observation of the effect of a cross sea. Eva, with her serene immunity from human weaknesses, was sitting near the bows of the vessel, enjoying the warm, winter sun, and watched the great heaving masses of water, rushing up against the side of the vessel, with a sympathetic gladness in their glorious unrestraint. The position presented itself in a somewhat different light to her husband, who retired, under the influence of the same glorious unrestraint, with anything but sympathetic gladness in his heart. Eva felt a little contemptuous pity for him, but enjoyed being alone. It was drawing near that supreme hour when the sun just touches the horizon of water, and the depth of colour in southern sea and sky grows almost unbearable in its cruel fulness, in its air of knowing something, of being able to tell one, if one could only hear its message, some mystery that would make things plain. Eva was sitting on the windward side of the vessel, looking west, and her eyes were filled with a still, questioning wonder. She had arrived at that most agonising stage of feeling sure that a mystery was there, without grasping what it was to which she wanted any answer. Her mind was full of a vague wonder and expectancy—the wonder and expectancy of a mind just awakened from its dreamless sleep of indifference. One arm was thrown back, and her hand grasped the taffrail to steady herself. She had taken off her hat, and her hair was blown about in the singing breeze. The human interest which had begun to dawn in her, which had stirred and woke from its sleep with a sudden, startled cry, a few weeks ago, would not let the other wonder slumber. The sense of the eternal mystery of things watched side by side with the sense of the eternal mystery of men. But for this half-hour she was alone with it; she was unconscious of the heaving and tossing of the vessel; all she knew was that she questioned, with something like passionate eagerness, the great walls of wine-dark water with their heraldry of foam, the hissing monsters that rose and fell round her, the luminous miracle that was sinking in the west.

In the meantime, Lord Hayes had got, so to speak, his second wind, had emerged from the privacy of his cabin, and was walking along the deck towards her with a battered, dishevelled air. The punctuation of his steps was rigidly but irregularly determined by the laws of gravity as exhibited by a vessel pitching heavily in a fluid medium. Eva had not seen him coming, and he stood by her a few moments in silence.

"I feel a little better," he remarked at length, in precise, well-modulated tones.

Eva started and frowned as if she had been struck. She turned on him with angry impatience.

"Ah, you have spoiled it all," she cried.

She looked at him a moment, and then broke out into a mirthless laugh. He had wrapped a grey shawl round his shoulders, and on his head was a brown, deerstalker cap.

"My dear Hayes," she said, "you are in vivid contrast with the sunset, and you startled me. I was thinking about the sunset. However, it is nearly over now. You look like a sea-sick picture of twilight. That grey shawl is very twilighty. Come into the saloon and get me some tea."

That gentleman was in too enfeebled a condition to feel resentment, even if he had been by nature resentful. It is notorious that certain emotions of the mind cannot exist under certain conditions of the body. No normal man feels a tendency to anger after a good dinner, or a tendency to patience in the ten minutes preceding that function. No one feels spiritually exalted in the middle of the morning, or heroic when suffering from slight neuralgia, and I venture to add that no one has spirit enough to feel resentful after an hour or two of sea-sickness.

The villa at Algiers was a charming, Moorish house, with a predominance of twisted pilasters and shining tiles, and bold, purple-belled creepers flaunting it over the white walls. It stood on the hills of Mustapha Supérieure, above the Eastern-looking town, surrounded by a rich, melodious garden, where the winter nightingales sang in the boughs of orange groves, which were bright with flower and fruit together, and where tall, listless eucalyptus trees shed their rough, odorous fruits thick on the path. But this soft beauty suited Eva's mind not so well as the bold, golden sun dropping into a wine-dark sea; in fact, she cordially detested the place. How much of her hatred was due to the fact that she was alone with her husband she did not care to ask herself. Certainly, the even monotony of one face, one low, well-modulated voice, was displeasing to her.

She found a malicious pleasure in giving him surprises. Her freshly-awakened interest in the human race sometimes took the bit in its teeth and ran riot, and, when it ran riot in his presence, she took no care to check it, but talked in a voluble, rather vicious vein, that startled him. For instance, at dinner one day, she had discussed certain books which he did not know women even read, and announced, somewhat vividly, views on life and being which were scarcely conventional. After dinner, they had sat out in the little passage that ran round the open square in the centre of the house, supported on twisted pillars, and Eva continued her newly-found confession of faith.

"Men seem to expect that women should be sexless replicas of themselves," she said. "All they would allow them is the inestimable privilege of being good. Virtue is its own reward, they say—so they cultivate their own pleasure with a fine disregard of virtue, and a curious pride in performing actions which certainly will lay up for them no store of virtuous and ineffable joy, while to the women they say, 'Be good; here is a blank cheque on the bank of Providence. The bigger the better. *Au revoir.*' A delightfully simple arrangement."

Lord Hayes gave a little cough, and added sugar to his coffee.

"I should always wish," he said, with the air of an after-dinner speaker; "I should always wish women to fulfil to the uttermost their own duties, which none but women can do."

"The duty of being good," said Eva. "Exactly so."

"I fail to see the justice of your remarks about the tendencies of men to regard women as sexless replicas of themselves," he said. "The province of women is quite different from that of men."

"Ah! let me explain," said Eva. "Men are bad and good mixed. Whether the bad or the good predominates is beside the point. Leave out the bad, and introduce no vivid good, and you get the sexlessness, and what remains is a sexless goodness, which is, as I say, the sexless replica of the man. That is a man's woman."

"No doubt it is my own stupidity," said Lord Hayes politely, "but I still fail to agree with you. You do not take into account what I ventured to call the province of women, which, I say again, is quite different from the province of men."

"*Da capo*," murmured Eva. "Let us agree to differ, Hayes. I am rather sleepy; I think I shall go to bed."

Lord Hayes lighted a candle for her, and waited till it had burned up.

"Good-night," said Eva, nodding at him.

He bent forward to kiss her, and, as before, she surrendered her face to be kissed.

The length of these episodes calls for an apology, but there is just this to be said. Life, for most of us, consists of episodes, of interruptions, of parentheses. We can few of us keep up the epic vein and go sublimely on, building up from great harmonious scenes a great harmonious whole. The scene-shifter perspires and tugs at his mighty cardboard trees and impossible castles in the forest; they are stiff, they will not turn round. And he sits down—does this irresponsible and wholly unbusinesslike scene-shifter—and meditates. After all, is life really surrounded by these giants of the theatrical forest? Do we go into remote and virgin woods and chant our love in irreproachable epics? When we have made our great scene, when we stand in the pure, unselfish, heroic, villain-massacreing, devoted climax of our existence, are we quite sure that some one will throw the ethereal oxyhydrogen light on to us at the right moment? Will the audience recognise how great we are: and, even if they do, will not the slightest accident with the oxy-hydrogen light turn our climax into an ante-climax? The irresponsible scene-shifter begins to see a more excellent way. Roll off your forest trees; send the manager of the oxy-hydrogen light home, give him eighteenpence to get drunk on—he will like it better than your heroic vein— let us have no scenery even. Just a few chairs and tables, a plain, grey sky, and no herpics. A few little episodes dealing of men who are not saints or silver kings, a few women who are not abbesses or Portias, who are in no epic mood, but in the mood of the majority of weak, unsatisfactory, careless, human beings, who can be unselfish and pure, but who are at times a little uncertain about the big riddle, unscrupulous, unkind, worldly. Besides, we are only in the first act at present. Perhaps the gigantic forest trees and the white light will come on later, but we do not promise. The irresponsible scene-shifter is right. So much, then, in praise of episode.

To return from the point at which we started before these unconscionable episodes found their way into the text, the honeymoon was over, the month was April, and Lord and Lady Hayes had returned to England. They were to spend a few days at Aston, and, after Easter, to go straight up to London. Old Lady Hayes was staying with her niece, who had married a certain Mr. Davenport, and had one son. Reggie Davenport was a favourite with the dowager, who bullied him incessantly, and who sometimes got furious, because he never lost his temper with her. She was to spend a fortnight in London with the Hayes, as a great concession, in order to make Eva's acquaintance, and would join them as soon as they had settled. It may be stated at once, that she regarded her son's marriage as a most unprincipled and selfish act, and as an insult levelled directly at herself.

Mrs. Grampound came up to see her daughter on the first day after their arrival.

"Your father would have come with me," she explained, "but he and Percy are away. I am quite alone at home. You are looking wonderfully well, dear, and I'm sure I needn't ask you whether you are happy?"

"Of course," said Eva, "those are the things that are taken for granted."

"I've come to have a little cosy talk with you," said Mrs. Grampound, settling herself in a chair and taking off her gloves.

A cosy little soliloquy would perhaps have been a more accurate description. She wandered on in a sort of pious intoxication at the contemplation of her daughter.

"The mistress of a great house like this has very great responsibilities, my darling," she said. "If dear James were not such a thoroughly able and upright man, I confess I should feel a wee bit nervous at seeing my darling whirled away into such a circle. Be very sure exactly how you are going to behave. There seems to me something very beautiful in the life of all those dear last-century, great ladies, whose husbands used to treat them with such charming old-fashioned courtesy, and lock them up whenever they went away, which must have been most tedious. Yes, and send a servant to tell the groom of the chambers to ask my lady if she would receive him. Dear me, yes."

"I don't think Hayes means to lock me up whenever he goes away," said Eva. "We haven't got a groom of the chambers, either."

"No, dear," said Mrs. Grampound; "I was just saying, wasn't I, that all that was changed. Husbands lounge in their wives' boudoirs now, and smoke cigarettes there. So much more human and natural. You don't mind the smell of smoke, do you, dear?"

"On the contrary," said Eva; "I smoke myself."

"Gracious, how shocking! What a wicked child. Of course, there's no harm in it, dear; lots of nice women smoke. I should not let Hayes know that. When a difficult time comes—there will be difficult times, of course, my Eva—there is no rose without its thorns—Let me see, what was I saying—ah! yes, those little indulgences, like letting a husband have a cigarette in the drawing-room every now and then, are very much appreciated. A little womanly tenderness," continued Mrs. Grampound, getting rather breathless, and volubly eloquent, "a little tact, a little wifely sympathy, just a look, the 'I know, I know,' which women can put into one little look, is all that is required to make those difficulties real advantages—concealed facilities, one might really call them; real renewals of the marriage vow; the rough places shall be plain, in fact, if we may use those words."

"We get on admirably together," said Eva; "he is most considerate for me, and most kind."

"I declare I positively love him," cried her mother. "Of course, in any case, I should teach myself—should compel myself—to love the man of your choice, but the first time I saw him, I said to myself, that is the husband for my Eva. It was one June evening," continued Mrs. Grampound with an impressional vagueness, "and we were dining somewhere, I can't remember where, and he was there too; dear me, I recollect it all as clearly as if it was yesterday. I remember old Lady Hayes telling us all that brown sherry was rank poison, and that she would as soon think of drinking a glass of laudanum. We all laughed a great deal, because our host had very famous brown sherry."

"It must have been very pleasant," said Eva.

"Dear old Lady Hayes," said Mrs. Grampound; "such a wonderful woman, such strong, shrewd common sense; I wonder if she will go on living with you, Eva? I don't think it's a very good plan myself—there is sure to be some little unpleasantness now and then."

"In spite of her strong, shrewd common sense?" asked Eva.

"Dear child, how you catch one's words up! Of course, her presence would be invaluable to you, if she stopped, and with such a guest constantly by you, of course you would learn a great deal. But I should make it quite plain what your relative positions must be. You are the mistress of the house, Eva; she is your husband's pensioner. Be very kind, very courteous, but very firm. Your rights are your rights. I daresay she will go to live at Brighton or Bournemouth or Bath, all those watering-places begin with a B; no doubt she has money of her own. You didn't think of asking Lord Hayes what would be done about that, did you, Eva? You might suggest it very gently and feelingly some time soon. Of course, you needn't express any opinion till you see what she is likely to do. Then, if it appears that she is proposing to live with you, just say very quietly that you will be very glad to have her. That will show, I think, that you know and are ready to insist on her occupying her proper position in the house. And you went to Algiers, did you not?" continued her mother; "that dear, white town set like a pearl and all that on the sapphire sea. I forget who said that about it, but it seems to me a very poetical description. I could almost find it in my heart to envy you, dearest."

"Yes, it's a very pretty place," assented Eva.

"Darling, why do you tell me so little," said Mrs. Grampound, more soberly. "I have been thinking so continuously about you all the time you have been away; you have lived in all my thoughts. I have said to myself, 'Eva will be at home in four weeks, three weeks, two days, one day; to-day I shall see my dearest again.'"

"What is there to tell you?" said Eva, slowly. "You assume I am happy, and I don't deny it. I am also amused and interested. I find things very entertaining. If you like I will show you some photographs of Mentone and Algiers. I lost two thousand francs at Monte Carlo. Hayes is very generous about money matters, and he has the further requirement of being very rich. He is bent on my being magnificent, and so, for that matter, am I. You shall see some fine things. I have, as you told me before my marriage, great natural advantages in the way of beauty. Diamonds suit me very well, and I have quantities of diamonds."

Poor Mrs. Grampound's mental intoxication was passing away rapidly, leaving behind a feeling of depression. At no time did her thoughts present themselves to her with distinctness; they were like seaweeds waving about close to the surface of the water. Sometimes, after a big wave had passed, sundry little ends of them appeared above the sea for a second or two, and Mrs. Grampound made anxious little grabs at these before they disappeared again. Consequently, her descriptions of them, as reflected in her conversation, were somewhat scrappy and inorganic.

She appeared, in the short silence that followed Eva's remarks, to have got hold of a new sort of sea-weed—a bitter, prickly fragment. At any rate she said, somewhat piteously,—

"Eva, Eva, tell me you are satisfied. You don't blame me, do you, for urging it on you?"

Eva could be very cruel. The foam-born Aphrodite, when she came "from barren deeps to conquer all with love," had, we may be sure, many undesirable suitors, and to these, I expect, she did not show any particular kindness or sympathy. She was, to judge by her face, too divine to be cruel in petty, irritating ways, but she was too divine not to be very human.

Eva raised her eyebrows.

"Why should I blame you? I am amused and interested. After all, that is more important than anything else. Surely I ought to be grateful to you. But to speak quite frankly, I did not marry to please you; I married to please myself, and Hayes, of course," she added.

Mrs. Grampound was very nearly shedding a few vague tears, but the appearance of Lord Hayes made her decide to postpone them.

"My charming mother-in-law," he said, "I am delighted to see you. Very much delighted, in fact. And am I not to see my father-in-law? How do you think Eva is looking?"

"Eva is looking wonderfully well," said she briskening herself up a little. "She has been giving me the most delightful accounts of your honeymoon. Mentone, Algiers, all those charming, romantic places. But Monte Carlo! Really, I was shocked. And Eva tells me she lost two hundred thousand francs—or was it two thousand, Eva? In any case, it is quite shocking, and I feel I ought to scold you for leading my child into bad ways."

"He didn't lead me," said Eva. "I went by myself. I think you remonstrated, didn't you, Hayes? You didn't play yourself, I know. However, I got a good deal of fun out of it. It was really exciting sometimes. After all, that is the chief thing. Two thousand francs was cheap. Tell mother about the new villa. I must go—I've got a hundred things to do."

Old Lady Hayes also made inquiries of her son as to what was to happen to her. She was a direct old lady, and she said,—

"And what is to become of me?"

Lord Hayes quailed under these unmasked batteries and felt most thankful that he would not have to meet them alone any longer. He had great confidence in Eva's courage, and felt that she would be quite up to the mark on such occasions. But he had, for the present, to trust to his own forces, and, with the idea of making the scene as little unpleasant as possible, he replied,—

"Of course, dear mother, you will do whatever suits you best. Your position in the house will necessarily be somewhat changed."

"Necessarily," said Lady Hayes.

Her son found no pertinent reply ready.

CHAPTER IV.

There is something peculiarly substantial and English about those houses which our aristocracy brighten with their presence, in the more fashionable parts of London, during several months of the year. Those lords of the earth, who cannot manage to breathe unless they have a thousand or more acres round their houses in the country, being sensible folk, are content to live, shoulder by shoulder, in rows of magnificent barracks, when they are in London. A porch supported by Ionic pillars, with a line of Renaissance balustrade along the top, a sprinkling of Japanese awnings, a couple of dozen large, square windows looking out on to what is technically known as "the square garden," partly because it is round, and partly because it is sparsely planted with sooty, stunted bushes, scattered about on what courtesy interprets to be grass, and surrounded by large, forbidding railings, are the characteristics of the best London houses. They may not be distinguished by any striking, artistic beauty, but they are eminently habitable.

Along one of these rows, one June afternoon, a smart victoria was being driven rapidly. It was hung on the best possible springs, and the wheels were circumscribed with the best possible india-rubber tires. A water-cart had just passed up the street, and the air was full of that indescribable freshness which we associate in the country with summer rain, and which, in London, makes us feel that art is really doing a great deal to rival Nature. The progress of the well-appointed victoria was therefore as free from noise, jolts, and dust as locomotion is permitted to be in this imperfect world. There was only one occupant of this piece of perfection—for, of course, the coachman and footman are part of the carriage—and she was as perfect as her equipment. In other words, Lady Hayes was going home to tea.

The carriage drew up with noiseless precision at the curb-stone, and Lady Hayes remained apparently unconscious of the stoppage till the powdered footman had rung the bell, and turned back the light crimson rug that covered her knees. Then she rose languidly and trailed her skirts across the pavement to the house. Above the porch was a square, canvas tent, with one side, away from the sun, open to admit the breeze, and Eva, as she passed upstairs, said to the man standing in the hall, "Tea upstairs, above the porch." This tent opened out of a low window in the drawing-room, through which Eva passed, and in which was sitting, as gaunt and forbidding as ever, her respected mother-in-law. That lady had grudgingly complied with the popular but misguided prejudices of London with regard to the skins wherewith the human animal clothes itself, but her stiff, black silk gown was as awe-inspiring as her grey, Jaeger dress and the boots with eight holes a-piece in them.

They had all been in London nearly a month, and the excellent old lady was living in a permanent equipment of heavy armour, with which to repel, assault, and batter her daughter-in-law. Eva, on the contrary, despised the old methods of warfare, and met these attacks, or led them, with no further implements than her own unruffled scorn, and a somewhat choice selection of small daggers and arrows, in the shape of a studied delicacy of sarcasm and polite impertinences. She resembled, in fact, an active and accomplished pea-shooter, who successfully pelted the joints of a mature and slowly-moving Goliath. The dowager glanced up as she entered. One of her laborious mottoes was "Punctuality is the root of virtue," and Eva, in consequence, held the view that punctuality is the last infirmity of possibly noble minds. She was quite willing to believe that her mother-in-law had an incomparably noble mind; she did not underrate her antagonist's strong points; in fact, her whole system was to emphasize them.

"Ah, you've come at last," said old Lady Hayes. "And pray, when are we to have tea?"

"I am late," said Eva. "I always am late, you know. Why didn't you have tea without me? Is Hayes in?"

"The servants have quite enough to do with the dance to-night without bringing up tea twice."

"Ah, that is so thoughtful and charming of you," said Eva, drawing off her long gloves. "The merciful man considers his beast. That is so good of you."

"And he considers his servants as well," said the dowager.

"Oh! I think servants are meant to be classed as a sort of beast. The good ones are machines, with volition; and if they are bad servants, of course they are beasts."

The dowager turned over the leaves of the current number of the *Lancet* with elaborate unconsciousness.

Eva finished taking off her gloves, and whistled a few bars of a popular tune.

"I don't know if it's customary for women to whistle now-a-days," said the old lady, for whistling, as Eva knew, was a safe draw, "but in my time it was thought most improper."

"Isn't there a French proverb—I daren't pronounce French before you—about 'we have changed all that?' That is a very silly proverb. It is the older generation who changed it themselves. They made their own system of life impossible. They reduced it to an absurdity."

The dowager, who spoke French with a fine Scotch accent, and knew it, finished buckling on, as it were, her greaves and cuirass, and presented arms.

"I confess I don't understand you. No doubt I am very stupid—I should like very much to know how we have reduced our life to an absurdity."

"I don't say the modern generation are not quite as absurd," said Eva, "but the difference is that they have not yet learned their absurdity. You see, the whole race of men, since b. c. 4004—that is the correct date, is it not?—have been devoting themselves to the construction of any theory of life which would hold water, and one by one they have been abandoned. The new theory, that nothing matters at all, has not yet been disproved, and considering that no theory hitherto has ever been permanent, it would be absurd to abandon this one till it is disproved in as convincing a manner as all its predecessors."

"I imagine that no previous age has ever sunk so deep in mere sensuous gratifications," said the dowager, lunging heavily.

"Ah, do you think so?" said Eva. "Of course, it is impertinent in me to try to argue the matter with you, as experience is the only safe guide in such matters, and you have experience of at least one more generation than I. But that seems to me altogether untrue. As we know from the Bible, desire shall fail, because it has been gratified to the utmost that human desire can conceive, I imagine. Well, I think desire has failed to a great extent. The men of your generation, for instance, and the generation before, drank so much port wine that this generation drink none. The daily three bottles that our grandfathers and great-grandfathers indulged in, has fulfilled the desire of port to the uttermost. No one gets drunk now. I don't think I ever saw a man drunk. They used to fall under the table, did they not? What a charming state of things! But it has at least produced a fastidiousness in us, which considers heavy drinking coarse and low.

"My father was a teetotaler, and so was my husband," said the old lady, rather wildly.

"I think that the habit of drinking in men," continued Eva, "is really the fault of the women; you, of course, are an instance in point. Your husband was a teetotaler—surely, through your influence. If the men of the last generation were vile, the women, I think, were viler still. What is the word? Oh! yes, vicarious. The men sinned vicariously for the women."

"It is easy to speak lightly of the virtues of your forefathers," remarked the dowager; "much easier than to practice them yourself."

"Ah! you misunderstand me," said Eva. "Heaven forbid that I should speak lightly of them! Their virtues were as gigantic and as loathsome to them, as their vices are to me. They used to go to church with the most appalling regularity, and eat salt fish in Lent, and have their clergyman to dinner on Sunday, which meant no port wine to speak of. Of course, they made up for it by having a little quiet cock-fighting on Sunday afternoon, but you cannot expect perfection."

"Cock-fighting seems to me no more brutal than butchering hand-reared pheasants," said the dowager.

"Ah! that is the war-cry of people who don't know anything about shooting," said Eva. "The hand-reared pheasant comes over the guns at the height of about sixty feet, at forty miles an hour. I watched them shooting last year at home. There was a big wind, and Hayes missed seventeen birds in succession. Take a gun and try for yourself. Of course, you say the same thing about partridge-driving. You say the manly thing is to walk your partridges up instead of having them driven to you. The truth is that one of the reasons why men go partridge-driving now is because it is so much more difficult than walking them up. Certainly Hayes's butchery of hand-reared pheasants was a most humane proceeding. Did you ever see a cock-fight?"

"Cock-fighting improved the breed," said the other, "though I disapprove of it entirely."

"Well," said Eva, "it killed off the weak ones. The survival of the fittest, of course. And we reap the benefits by having particularly large eggs to eat; at least, I suppose a stalwart chicken begins life in a stalwart egg."

Old Lady Hayes rose with dignity.

"I think tea must be ready," she said. "In fact, it is probably cold by this time."

"Time does pass so in conversation," said Eva, languidly. "Ah! they have sent some orchids. How nice and cool they look." She snapped off a spray of the delicate, cultured blossoms, and fastened them, in her dress. "I think tea is put in the room above the porch. I rather expect Jim Armine," she said, as she settled herself in a low, basket chair. "I wonder when the absurd custom of women pouring out tea will go out; why a woman should have that abominable trouble I cannot think. Of course, when tea was rather a rarity, a sort of up-to-date luxury, it was natural. The hostess gave her guests a smart little present."

Old Lady Hayes accepted the challenge. She said:

"It used to be held to be the province of women to be matronly and womanly and domestic. They were in their places at the fireside, at the tea-table, not in the smoking-room and in grand stands."

"I am referring to the manual labour of pouring out tea," said Eva; "but whatever the province of women may be, they seem to me to fill it very inadequately when their husbands go to bed drunk every night. It is such a comfort to know that your father and husband were teetotalers, for I can say these things without being personal. Your father was a Presbyterian minister, was he not? How do you call it in the dear Scotch language— meenister, isn't it?"

"He was a learned, upright man."

"How nice!" said? Eva. "I can add a meenister to my ancestry. Do you know who my great-grandfather was? He was a crossing-sweeper, originally, in New York. Then he went West, you know, and, being 'cute, made a pile."

"You have very distinct traces of your American origin," said the old lady with asperity.

"And you of the dear Scotch talk," said Eva. "I always like the Scotch so much. They are so honest and sterling and serious. Hoots, mon!" she added meditatively.

The dowager took a second cup of tea. She had been accustomed to consider tea as a destructive agent in the days of seven o'clock dinner, but as Eva refused personally to dine till half-past eight, she found that, though perhaps destructive, it was less unpleasant than pure inanition. She had enunciated some startling warnings as to what would happen to people who dined at half-past eight earlier in her sojourn in London, and Eva had told her, with great courtesy, that she was quite at liberty to dine at seven or half-past six, or six if she liked, but she was afraid that her daughter-in-law would be unable to share the meal with her. Whether her mother-in-law's constitution had become so strongly fortified by the use of drugs that she could now afford to play tricks with it, we are not called upon to say; at any rate, the half-past eight dinner had, at present, made no perceptible inroads on her digestive or vital powers.

Eva had finished tea, and proceeded to light a cigarette.

"After our dreadfully keen encounter," she explained, "I want soothing. Argument is very trying to the nerves. Tobacco, on the other hand, is eminently soothing. Permit me to soothe myself."

Old Lady Hayes watched these proceedings through eyelids drooped over vigilant, irritated eyes.

Eva's whole personality was radically abhorrent to her. Her complete modernity seemed to her an epitome of all that is unsuitable to woman. Even her best points—her extreme tolerance, her cold purity—were repugnant, because they were the outcome of what she considered a wrong principle. Tolerance, according to the old lady's code, was the fruit of charity—Eva's tolerance was the fruit of indifferences. In the same way, the purity, the utter stainlessness of Eva's mind was the result of fastidiousness, which, according to the other, was the sinful opposite of charity. Purity *via* fastidiousness, not morality, was to her the fig on the thistle, the grape on the thorn, which, however excellent in itself, could not be good because it must partake of the nature of its parent stem.

"Of course, I know how utterly you must disapprove of me," continued Eva with sincerity; "my whole system, or rather want of system, of life, must seem to you to be utterly inexcusable. Life is a complicated business and rather tiresome at the best. It is continually fractious and annoying and irritating. Its whole object seems to be to make one angry. But my plan is to bear with it; to treat it as a tiresome child, not to let it irritate and annoy me, to avoid all possible collisions with it—and, to do all this, you mustn't be serious or too particular."

"I was brought up to believe in moral responsibilities," said the old lady, "in some idea of duty, in a notion that it was not our mission simply to amuse ourselves and disregard others."

"Just so," said Eva; "that illustrates very well what I mean by reducing things to an absurdity. Duty dominated everything, and the port wine affairs were merely regarded as interludes. Of course, if men are brought up to believe in these ponderous responsibilities, they must have interludes. We have done away, or rather you made it inevitable that we should do away, with responsibilities and interludes alike."

"And not unnaturally you have nothing left."

"Quite so. We are human beings who find themselves in a state of consciousness, and a state of consciousness demands that you should do something or think something. We fulfil those demands to a certain extent, but we do not make a mumbo-jumbo of them. You see there have always been a certain number of people with a desire to do certain things—to be kind, to be respectable and reasonable; and a certain number of these have a tendency—we all have tendencies—to construct a theory about what they do. They have, to begin with, a genius for doing their duty, and doing your duty is an unremunerative occupation in this wicked world. Then there comes in their inexorable need of making a theory. Duty is unremunerative here, but amusing oneself is remunerative. Therefore there must be a place and a time when the balance is struck, when to have done your duty is remunerative, and not to have done your duty is unremunerative; and the Paradiso and the Inferno are already made."

The blood of all the clans was up.

"Do you mean to say," gasped the dowager, "that you deny the existence of—'

"Ah, my dear lady," said Eva, "do not let us say things we shall be sorry for afterwards. I deny nothing, and I affirm nothing. I am only pointing out that many people do deny and affirm a great many things. The fault lies with them. If they had affirmed nothing, and denied nothing, would the fact that I did the same seem so horrible to you? Would you have evolved all your system of denials and affirmations out of your own inner consciousness?"

This was a little too much. Old Lady Hayes surged up out of her chair and confronted her.

"You believe nothing—you fear nothing—you love nothing. All you care for, are your wretched little hair-splittings about tendencies, and the modern view of life. When you call my beliefs superstitions and inventions, you think you have annihilated them."

"Excuse me," said Eva, "I have no wish to annihilate them, nor do I pretend to do so. I wish I shared them. It must make everything so very easy if it is labelled right or wrong; if every choice is like a cross road with a sign-post, 'Heaven and Hell.' It must be so like those little allegories about children with bare feet walking along a dusty road, with flowers by the side, and lions and tigers hiding among the flowers. Having read the allegories, of course, you know that if you only keep to the road, it will soon become flowery, and beautiful boots will mysteriously grow on to your feet. And you have the inestimable satisfaction of seeing the lions and tigers gnawing at the bones of the people who go to pick flowers, and of reflecting that not only do they have no beautiful boots, but that the lions and tigers have eaten them up, so that the beautiful boots would be no use to them even if they had them. No doubt you expect me to be seized upon soon, and eaten. It must be very unpleasant. I notice that you never go to help them; you are too much occupied in walking along your tight-rope road."

"This is mere burlesque."

"And who is the author of this burlesque?" asked Eva.

"Perhaps it is another characteristic of your generation to ridicule the most sacred beliefs of others," she replied. "I should have thought any code of good manners would have forbade that. Jews take off their hats when they come into a Christian church."

Eva rose without any show of haste or impatience.

"*Au revoir*," she said. "You will excuse me, I know. I have half-a-hundred things to do."

She went through the open window into the drawing-room. As she passed the head of the stairs, she saw a well-known figure coming up, preceded by a footman.

"Ah, Jim," she cried, "how late you are. Come to my room. I have been discussing religious questions with my mother-in-law, and, well—and so we parted in more senses than one. Have you had tea? No? Bring Mr. Armine some tea to my room."

"She's rather a powerful old lady, isn't she?" asked Jim, who, since the Hayes' return from abroad, had managed to establish himself on a fairly intimate footing.

"She has been abusing me with immense power and vigour," said Eva. "I am the incarnation of all that is horrible in her eyes. The one incomprehensible thing to that generation is this generation."

"The converse holds, too," said he.

"No; I understand them perfectly. Their nature is the basis of ours; we are the heirs of all previous ages, just as they were. The later development has incorporated the earlier, but it is contrary to the nature of the earlier to understand the later. Just in the same way, I understand what I was a year ago, though, if I saw now what I should be in another year, it would probably be incomprehensible to me."

"I shouldn't have thought you would change much."

Eva took a book from a small table near her, and opened it with a quick, dramatic movement.

"It is like that," she said. "Whether I have changed, or only discovered, I don't know. But a year ago the book was shut, and now I have read the first chapter."

"At any rate, you have some ideas about the last chapter, then; I suppose all the characters have come on the stage?"

"Ah! but who can tell what will happen to them? No character can be uninfluenced by circumstances. If it is a book worth reading, they will have altered by the end. Circumstances have led me to open the book, they will determine my subsequent career; and circumstances, in the shape of gout or cancer or something, will make me close it."

"Is it interesting reading?"

Eva looked at him, with a smile gathering on her mouth.

"Particularly interesting," she said. "I am sure you are interested too."

In the silence that followed, a tap came at the door, which was repeated, and Lord Hayes entered. He was irreproachably dressed in a black frock coat, with a fine gardenia in his button-hole. He was rather short-sighted, and blinked in the manner of a small, tame owl.

"I am sure I beg your pardon," he said; "but I tapped, and there was no answer, and so I came in."

Eva turned to him.

"It is of no consequence. Have you had tea?"

"I found some tea in the drawing-room, thank you. I am bound to say it was rather cold?"

"Have you seen your mother?"

"Yes; she was not cordial. Her manner implied that she had been a little upset about something. She is going to stay with the Davenports for a week, in Hyde Park Gardens, she said, before she goes down into the country. She has, in fact, determined to leave us on the day after to-morrow, instead of stopping till next week."

Eva pointed to a box of cigarettes.

"You may smoke," she said; "Jim, the matches are by you."

"A cigarette would be very refreshing," said Lord Hayes. "The heat and the noise have made me a little fatigued. And, I suppose, we shall be up very late to-night. My mother informed me she would not be present at our little dance."

"Not even at the cotillion?" asked Eva.

"The cotillion ought to be very pretty," said he. "I am satisfied with the appearance of the room. I sent word to Aston not to spare the choicest orchids. Have you seen the staircase since they put the flowers in?"

"Yes," said Eva; "it looks charming. I am much obliged to you for taking all that trouble."

Lord Hayes bowed.

"I am delighted," he said. "I am very glad you are satisfied. Princess Frederick is coming, is she not?"

"Yes," said Eva; "I met her this afternoon. I did not know she was in London. Of course I asked her."

"It will be very brilliant," said her husband, solemnly.

Jim Armine rose to go.

"You will be here to-night?" asked Eva. "We don't begin till eleven."

"The heat is getting very oppressive," said Lord Hayes, politely, as he opened the door for him. "The thermometer was standing at eighty-two degrees in the Window of White's."

Eva was sitting back in her chair, in an attitude that was common with her, with her two hands clasped over one knee. She had developed a great power of doing nothing; whether it was a survival of the days of the blank white page, or an effect of the change that had given her so much to think about, is doubtful; probably the habit of the first was adapted to the needs of the second. Life was interesting and amusing—a new book in a new language. She had found herself suddenly transplanted from a silent, pleasant garden to a crowded reception-hall. Her tastes did not lie in the direction of gardens; they seemed to her very monotonous. The beautiful but silent and weary-looking girl, who had been looked at and passed by, found London a different place when she learned that the rows of eyes in the reception-room looked to her as a sort of center. There is nothing so inexplicable as the phenomenon called "the rage." The opera screamed and starved unheard for years in London, when suddenly the whole of London became aware that it was the most delicious thing in the world. It had been there all the time; it was advertised in the morning papers, but nobody cared. In the same way with Eva—she was living before, and she was living after; she had been advertised at balls and concerts, but the advertisement had been entirely unremunerative. Then a middle-aged peer had remarked that Miss Grampound seemed to him worthy of the highest compliment that a man can pay a woman, with the consequence that all London was of one mind that she was exactly what they had been looking for so long. Eva's head was not turned, nor was her heart touched, but the effect was that she became conscious of herself, and conscious of other people. Pygmalion had touched Galatea and Galatea sprang to life.

Pygmalion inevitably has the worst of it. When a whole race of men bursts almost simultaneously on one woman, it is not to be expected that she will single out one. They are all queer and interesting, some are attractive. Poor little Pygmalion may beat his breast in the corner and say, "It is mine, it is all mine," but no one will listen to him; least of all Galatea. His best course is to keep on good terms with his handiwork, and be very polite and obliging. He is compelled to act as bear-leader to this incarnated stone, but he had better not allude to the time when he called her off her pedestal; and unless he is a fool, he will not try to put any finishing stroke to his handiwork. He let her have a soul, let him remember that he did not let her have it. The material is his, her flesh and blood, for he paid for it when it came from the quarries, but his possession ends there. The rest is hers and all the world's.

Lord Hayes sat down again on the chair he had just left, and repeated his remark about the thermometer at White's. Eva stifled a yawn.

"I suppose that was in the shade, was it not?"

"Oh, yes," he said; "in the sun the temperature would have been much higher."

"Your mother and I had a somewhat plain-spoken conversation this afternoon," she said; "I came in for a good deal of abuse."

"I imagined her sudden departure was owing to something of the kind," he said. "I am sorry it has occurred; personally, I always avoid quarrelling with anyone."

"It is a mistake," said she; "but if two people disagree, they must quarrel some time. Besides, I didn't quarrel with her. I was even amused, I am sorry to say."

"That is—if you will pardon my saying so—the surest method of quarrelling."

Eva looked at him gravely.

"You have admirable good sense," she said; "I always thought you had. But, after all, it is a good thing to be amused."

BOOK II.

CHAPTER I.

There are certain hours of the day which seem to exist only in England, and one of these is the hour before dinner in winter. We are quite certain that there is a certain time in all countries which is identical, according to the statements made by clocks and other clumsy contrivances, with this sacred time, but it is not the same thing. Where else in the world may we look for that sense of domestic comfort, that hour thought away before the fire, after a long day's tramp in the snow, or an afternoon on black, patient ice, that lends itself to be drawn and scribbled on by the ringing, clear-cutting skates? The hour is there, the pitiful, unmeaning sixty minutes, from half-past six to half-past seven, but it is a mockery, a delusion, with no more soul about it than a photograph or a bust. Let us look at the real thing.

Firelight—no candles, but bright firelight—enough to think by. A chair drawn up on to the hearth-rug, and two large feet resting on the fender. If you look about, you will see two evening shoes lying near, and, if you are human, you will sympathize with the impulse that led to their temporary want of employment.

The proprietor of these large feet is proportionately large. He has half-dressed for dinner; that is to say, a rough, Norfolk jacket takes the place of a dress coat and he has no shoes on. He has been out shooting all day, and got a very fair bag, with twelve woodcock among it, which is truth, not grammar. When he came in, after a bitterly cold and entirely satisfactory day, he drank no less than three cups of tea and ate an alarming quantity of muffins. Then, being still very cold and extremely dirty, he wallowed for a quarter-of-an-hour in a bath about as large as a small pond, and became warm and clean. Then he dressed for dinner, barring the dress-coat, came into the smoking-room, where he kicked off his shoes, lit a briar-wood pipe, and proceeded to spend the next half-hour in looking at the fire, enjoying the particular peace of mind which is inseparable from a sane mind and a sane body.

While he looks into the fire and finds entertainment there, we may as well take a look at the room and then at him. It is always a good plan to look well at anyone's room, for everyone leaves on a room they frequent a personal impress which is almost always infallible. An aquiline nose or a deep, dreamy eye are often the legitimate outcome of an ancestry with certain tendencies, which may have dropped out of existence in any particular case, though their corporeal stamp remains, but no Crusader or king of Vikings will be able to touch with their ghostly fingers the particular sanctum of any man or woman in the nineteenth century. Their portraits may frown down from the walls of the dining-hall, but the clank of their swords, the rhythm of their oars, is not heard in the smoking-room.

A table-cloth, betwixt and between the table and the floor, and half-a-dozen cartridges, which act as a drag on its slipping further, may be of too ephemeral a nature to lay much stress on, but they are indications which will be useful if borne out by confirmatory evidence. A book-case—that is better. Badminton on shooting, Badminton on hunting, Badminton on coursing, Badminton on racing, Badminton on fishing; let us not forget the six cartridges. A book upside down on the top shelf, with not more than forty pages cut—*Robert Elsmere*. Remember that. Four volumes of Dickens, bearing the mark of a well-spent and battered existence. *Tess of the D'Urbevilles*—not more than half cut, but the last six pages also cut. That also, in conjunction with the state of *Robert Elsmere*, is distinctly important. *Ravenshoe*—signs of wear—in much the same state as Pickwick. *Demosthenes' de Corona*—dog-eared and filthy, with the meanings of many unpardonably irregular Greek words, I am sorry to say, written down in the margin in a minute hand. The utterly abandoned, dishevelled appearance of the rest of the book suggested that the extreme care with which these were written was not wholly owing to any reverential adoration of that immortal author. A small Greek Lexicon, from γ to ψ inclusive, also filthy, with several crude but vivid illustrations in red ink. A volume of Browning. Certain lyrical poems, with pencil marks by the side—a difficult factor, but not inexplicable.

Such were the habits, so to speak, of this room, to which we confidently hope to find a key in the habits of the six feet something of flesh and bone warming itself in front of the fire. Making all possible allowance for the deceptive character of appearances, we may at once hazard two epithets on him—well-bred and English. In spite of the thorough tanning his skin had undergone, you would be right in concluding that he was a pure Englishman, who had been subjected lately to a tropical sun; in fact, he had only been a fortnight in England. His name, to descend to less metaphysical matters, was Reginald Davenport, the son of a Mr. Davenport, who has been mentioned incidentally in this history as being the nephew, by marriage, of old Lady Hayes, and whose house the dowager had selected to be her ark of refuge, after she had been driven out, with loss, by Eva's criticisms on religion and the last generation. Eva had never seen her handsome young connection, for he had been travelling for the last year, and only came back to England, as I have said, two weeks before we discovered him in the smoking-room—some five months after Eva had left London. He was a friend of Percy, Eva's brother; in fact, that gentleman was expected here this evening, to do murder and sudden death among the woodcock. And some one else was coming, who, to tell the truth, interested Reggie far more than any number of his other friends. Percy had intimated that he was in the habit of falling in love once a fortnight, and he had just done so to such good purpose that he was definitely and irrevocably engaged. These periodic fallings in love were slightly embarrassing, because the charming girls with whom he fell in love—he never fell in love with anyone who was not charming—sometimes fell in love with him; and the emotional atmosphere of his neighbourhood became extremely electrical and exciting.

On the whole, I feel inclined to risk another epithet in this preliminary skirmishing round Reggie. Yes—indubitably boyish. By boyish, I mean the power of enjoying life without thinking about it. Such a gift—the gift of serene receptiveness, of complete irresponsibility—is rare, fascinating and, at times, intensely irritating. The majority of ordinary work-a-day folk have, as Eva said, a certain capacity for doing their duty, and forming theories about it. Reggie knew no obscure idol called Duty, to which he owed obedience, but he was ruled by a quantity of cleanly, wholesome instincts, that made him honest, good-natured, lovable and affectionate. The worst of drawing your morality from the springs of your nature is that, if a mischievous hand gets to meddling with those springs, to diverting the course of the water, or, perhaps, putting a little piece of something not entirely wholesome in that clear fountain, your moral digestion is considerably disorganised. At the same time, an innate morality is productive of a more lively faith than a collection of dried plants from the gardens of other men's experience. They may be the same plants, but they are alive, not pressed and sapless.

Reggie never hazarded any guesses as to the answer of that Gordian riddle called life. The how, why and wherefore of existence cannot even be said to have been uninteresting to him—such questions did not exist for him at all. But, by virtue of an innate sweetness of disposition, he had an undoubted capacity for being content to live, and be nice to those in the same predicament of living as himself. Such natures are not often saddled with great mental gifts; but very often hold a great capacity for loving and being loved, with the restful love one feels for shady places on dusty roads, for the "times of refreshing" that are so divinely human. This gift is one which many children possess, and which few retain beyond childhood. It is dangerous, fascinating, dazzling, seductive and very unsettling, but it is very sweet.

This fathom of well-bred, boyish, English life was nearly asleep, but not quite. In fact, a very slight sound made him particularly wakeful, for it was a sound for which he had been listening—the sound of carriage wheels outside. He went quickly out of the room, and was in the hall before the front door was opened. Ah! well, the meeting of two young lovers is very pretty, but it has happened before.

Percy arrived in time for dinner, and when Mr. Davenport retired from the smoking-room soon after eleven, he left there the two young men, who did not seem inclined to go to bed. Reggie, in fact, had an alarming number of things to say, and he proceeded to say them with guileless straightforwardness.

"I am awfully glad you were able to come," he began; "I wanted you to see Gertrude very much. You must be my best man, you know. We're not going to be married yet; not for a year. You see, I was half-engaged when I went to India, and we settled to wait then for two years. Well, one year's gone, that's something."

"You're a detestably lucky fellow," said Percy, on whom a charmingly pretty and thoroughly nice girl had made her legitimate impression.

"Oh! I know I am; detestably lucky, as you say. Doesn't she sing beautifully, too? Hang it all, I won't talk about it, or else I shall go on for ever, and it's rather dull for you."

Percy laughed.

"Oh, don't mind me. I'm very happy. Pour out your joyful soul, but pass me a cigar first."

"Cigars!" said Reggie. "I really had quite forgotten about smoking. That's what comes of being in love. Really, old fellow, you had better fall in love as soon as you possibly can. Depend upon it, there's nothing like it. Here, catch!"

Reggie chucked a cigar case across to him.

"Have you seen your new cousin yet?" asked Percy.

"Who? Oh, Lady Hayes. No, I haven't. She's perfectly lovely, isn't she?"

"Eva has always been considered good-looking," remarked the other solemnly.

"I don't particularly care for Hayes himself," said Reggie. "He's so awfully polite and dried up. But I expect your sister's made him wake up a bit. I want to know her. Where is she?"

"They're abroad again, at present. Jim Armine's with them."

"Jim Armine?" said Reggie, doubtfully. "That pale chap with a big place in Somersetshire?"

"Probably the same. I don't know why Eva likes him so. I can't bear him."

"He's an oily sort of fellow," remarked Reggie, frankly. "But lots of women like him. He's too clever for me. I'm awfully stupid, you know."

"They met him abroad on their honeymoon," said Percy, "and he hung about a good deal, I fancy."

"I'm blowed if I'll have another man hanging about on my honeymoon," said Reggie.

"No; I don't suppose you will. It does seem one too many to the unbiassed mind. Rather like the serpent in paradise, who was certainly *de trop*."

"What serpent?" said Reggie, who was obviously thinking of something else. "Oh, I see, the devil, you mean."

"No, I didn't mean the devil exactly; I meant any third person."

"We're going shooting to-morrow over the High Croft," said Reggie, after a pause, in which he had determined, by a rapid mental process, that he was unable to initiate any more statements on the subject of the serpent, "and Gertrude and mother are going to bring us lunch. You and father will have to shoot alone after lunch; I'm going to drive on with Gertrude, just round about and home again."

Gertrude Carston certainly seemed a most desirable partner for Reggie; they were really both of them detestably lucky people. She had considerable beauty, of a large, breezy order; she was quite as adorably child-like as he, and showed quite as few signs of any tendency to grow up. She was fond of hunting, lawn-tennis, animals, loud hymns, anything, in fact, of a pronounced and intelligible stamp; she was quite ridiculously fond of Reggie, and they both behaved in the foolish, delightful manner in which people in such a predicament do behave. They had both settled to get up early the next morning and have a short walk before breakfast, which was not till a quarter to ten, but in the morning they both felt it quite impossible to do so, and came down feebly a few minutes after the gong had sounded, and pretended that they had been up an immense time waiting for the other, till that particularly flimsy falsehood broke down, and they both laughed prodigiously. It was obviously a good, honest love-match; for each of them only the other existed, in no ethereal, mysterious form, but simply as a capital, honest human being, lovable in every part. There were no regrets, no unsatisfied longings, no sentimental, half-morbid affection that was exacting or jealous. Love, like Janus of old, is a two-headed god. On some he smiles, to others his eyes are full of strange, bewildering doubts; on his lips there is a smile that is half a sigh, that wakes at times a tumultuous happiness, a bitter aching at others, and never brings content. That love may be more complex, more worthy of the agonised questionings with which men and women have worshipped him, more deserving of the reproach, the longing, the dread, the reviling, that has found its expression in bitter verses and heart-broken epigrams, but the simple, smiling face is there for some to see, and those are blest who see it. Their love may be on a lower level, but it is very sweet, and lies among pleasant gardens and by melodious streams; for such there is no mountain top, compassed about by heaven; earth lies about them, not beneath them, and for them there is no painful climbing, no bleeding hands or panting breasts, and perhaps, at the top, nothing but clouds and cold, palpable mist.

Such, at any rate, was their love at present, yet nothing is safe in this uncertain world. An earthquake may rend the pleasant garden, an east wind may wither its flowers, drought may drink up its melodious stream. But now it was the June of love, and the garden was very fair.

It was nearly luncheon time, and Reggie, in spite of the woodcock, looked on to the cottage, where a thin, blue smoke rose, on a hill above the trees, wondering whether Gertrude had come yet. The beat lay over uneven ground, with some thick cover, interspersed with heathery, open places, on the edges of which many woodcock rose in silent and ghostly flight for the last time. Reggie was an excellent shot, and was having a match with Percy—a shilling a woodcock—which promised to be an investment with good security, and quick returns. He was just arguing a disputed point, in which Percy stoutly upheld that a certain bird, at which they had fired simultaneously, was his own, not Reggie's, and that Reggie ought never to have shot at it, as it did not rise to him, when Gertrude appeared on the scene.

She had seen the party approaching from the cottage, and, as it was cold, she had walked on to meet them.

Percy felt much evil satisfaction at her appearance. The ways of women at shooting parties were known to him. Reggie was looking about in a bush, with the keepers, for a bird he had killed, and Gertrude stopped with him. She fully justified Percy's expectations.

"Oh! Reggie, what a pretty bird. It's an awful shame to shoot them. Poor dear! Oh! I am sure I saw it flap its wings. It can't be dead. Oh! do kill it quick. I think you're perfectly brutal. Now, you've killed it," she added with reproach, as if the object of shooting woodcock was to render them immortal.

They soon caught up the others, and Percy's wicked wish was fulfilled. No man in the world can shoot when his affianced is walking by him, making remarks on the weather, and on his homespun stockings, and telling him that she was sure he didn't hold his gun straight that time. But Reggie did not feel as if he had lost very much, when he handed Percy one-and-ninepence at lunch, which was the nearest equivalent he had for two shillings.

Mrs. Davenport was sitting by the fire when they came in, preferring to get warm passively, rather than actively.

"Well, boys," she said, "have you had good sport? Fifteen woodcock? How jolly!"

"And we should have got four more if Gertrude hadn't joined us," said Reggie. "Why did you let her come, mother?"

Gertrude looked at him in genuine, wide-eyed astonishment.

"What *have* I done, you stupid boy?" she exclaimed. "I only told you to hold your gun straighter; you were aiming at least five feet from the bird. Besides, it's horrid to kill woodcock; they're such jolly little beasts—birds, I mean."

"Then why did you tell me to aim straighter?" asked Reggie, with reason.

"Oh, I thought it would please you to kill them, my lord," she said. "At least, that's why you went out, wasn't it?"

Reggie was emptying his pockets of cartridges in the porch, and Gertrude was standing in the doorway, so that they were in comparative privacy.

"Would you rather please me than save the woodcock?" he asked softly.

"Reggie, I know those cartridges will go off if you drop them about so. Yes, oh the whole, I would. How dirty your hands are. Oh! is that blood on them?"

"No, dear, it's red paint, like what the Indians put on when they go out hunting."

"You extremely silly boy. Go and wash them, and then come to lunch. I'll come with you to the little pump round the corner. You can't be trusted alone."

"You'll catch cold standing about," said Reggie, not without a purpose.

"No more than you will. Besides, I want to talk to you."

"Talk away, I'm listening."

"Oh, well, it's nothing, really. I only meant to chat."

"Let's chat, then."

"Well, stoop down, while I pump on your hands. Do you know, I'm rather happy."

"What a funny coincidence; so am I."

And they went back to the house, feeling that they had had quite a successful conversation. But that was all they said.

Mr. Davenport was to join them after lunch, and go on shooting with Percy, and they had nearly finished when he entered. He was a stout, hearty-looking man of fifty, and inexpressible satisfaction was his normal expression.

"Well, you people look pretty comfortable," he said. "What sport, Reggie?"

"Oh! rabbits, lots of them, a few hares, ditto pheasants, and fifteen woodcock," said Reggie, with his mouth full of bread and cheese, whose naturally healthy appetite had not been spoiled by love.

"Reggie's going to take Gertrude a drive after lunch," said Mrs. Davenport; "and I shall walk home; I want a walk."

Gertrude and Reggie looked at each other, but acquiesced.

"Reggie, dear, give Gertrude my furs. She will be cold driving, and I sha'n't want them walking," said Mrs. Davenport, as the two started to go.

Reggie took them, and with those little attentions that a woman loves so much when they are offered by somebody, wrapped them closely round her.

"Well, I'm sure I ought to be warm enough," she said, as they left the door.

"Reggie will take off his coat if you're not, I daresay," murmured Mrs. Davenport, as she watched them start. "Dear boy, how happy he is."

"He hasn't got much to complain of," said his father. "How old it makes one feel."

He stretched out his hand to his wife, and she took it silently. Parents feel old and young when they see the young birds mate.

"Reggie was recommending me to fall in love as quickly as possible, last night," remarked Percy. "He said there was nothing like it."

Mr. Davenport laughed.

"Cheeky young brute," he said. "He gives himself the airs of an old married man. He quite patronised his uncle the other day, because he was a bachelor. He and Gertrude together don't make up more than forty-five years between them."

"Reggie's only just twenty-four," said Mrs. Davenport, "and she's barely twenty. How dreadfully funny their first attempt at housekeeping will be. Reggie never knows what he's eating, as long as there's plenty of it, and I don't think she does either."

"Ah! well, shoulder of mutton and love is a very good diet," said his father. "Are you ready, Percy? If so, we'll be off."

Mrs. Davenport sat a little longer over the fire before she set out on her homeward walk, and observed, with some annoyance, that it had begun to snow heavily, and half wished she had driven home with Reggie. The keeper's wife wanted to send a boy with her, as the short cut across country, which she meant to take, was hardly more than a sheep-track, running across a flat stretch of bleak moorland.

There is, perhaps, nothing so bewildering as a snow-storm. The thick net-work of falling flakes conceals all but the nearest objects; and the small, familiar landmarks of the path are soon lost under the white trouble. The consequence was that, half-an-hour after Mrs. Davenport had started, she was entirely at sea as to her position, and, after trying in vain to retrace her steps, she found herself, at the end of an hour's tedious tramp, at a little cottage some six miles from home. She was known to the labourer who lived there, but, as she was too tired to continue walking through the snow that was already beginning to lie somewhat thickly on the path, he sent out a lad to the neighbouring village to procure any sort of conveyance. All this took time, and Mrs. Davenport was impatient, for the sake of those at home, to get off as soon as possible. Her husband, she knew, would be very anxious; and there were people coming to dinner.

Meanwhile, Reggie and Gertrude had got safely home after a most satisfactory drive. In fact, they rather liked the snow, which compelled them to go slower, for the sake of that sense of extreme privacy—a sort of cutting off from the rest of the world—which it lent them. He had said once, "I am afraid mother will have a horrid walk," and Gertrude was filled with an evanescent compunction for having taken her furs, but no more allusion was made to it.

They reached home about half-past four, and, half-an-hour later, were joined by the shooters, who had given up when the snow began in earnest. They were sitting at tea in the dark, oak-panelled hall, by a splendid fire of logs when Mr. Davenport suddenly said—

"I suppose your mother is changing her things upstairs, Reggie?"

Reggie was sitting on the floor, with his long legs drawn up, and a tea-cup balanced somewhat precariously on his knees. His back was supported against the head of the sofa, on which Gertrude was sitting. She had put on an amazing tea-gown, of some dark, mazarine stuff, trimmed with large bunches of lace, and was feeling intensely happy and rather languid after the day in the cold air. She had just asked Reggie some question, and he did not hear, or, at any rate, did not fully take in his father's remark.

Ten minutes passed, and Mr. Davenport rose to go.

"You'd better ring the bell, Reggie," he said, "and get your mother's maid to take her some tea upstairs, or it will be getting cold. I am afraid she must have got very wet."

"I don't think mother's come in yet," said Reggie, placidly.

"Not in yet," he said quickly. "Why didn't you tell me? She must have lost her way over the High Croft."

The irrepressible satisfaction had died out of his face. He rang the bell sharply.

"Tell two men to go at once, with lanterns, over the High Croft. Mrs. Davenport must have lost her way."

Gertrude got up.

"You're not anxious about her, are you?"

"No, no, dear," said he, "but it's a horrid night. The snow may be lying very thick, and perhaps she has lost her path. There's no anxiety."

Gertrude looked down with a little impatience at her long-limbed lover.

"Reggie, you goose, why didn't you remember she hadn't come in?"

Reggie looked up.

"I thought nothing about it. There are lots of cottages about. It was stupid of me to forget. Can I do anything, father? Shall I go out with the men?"

He was perfectly willing to do quite cheerfully all that was required of him, and he would have got back into his damp shooting clothes, and left this comfortable hall and Gertrude without a murmur.

"No, never mind," said he. "I think I shall go with them, because I couldn't keep quiet at home. But I wish you'd remembered sooner."

Reggie had risen and was standing by the fireplace.

"I wish you'd let me go, instead of you," he said.

"No; there's no need whatever. I only go for my own sake."

Reggie was quite content. If he was not wanted to go, he was quite happy to stop. He was extremely fond of his mother, and the thought of her possible discomfort was most unpleasant to him, but what was the good of worrying? There was absolutely no danger. Mrs. Davenport was an eminently sensible person, and he could not lessen her discomfort by thinking about it. Let us be sensible by all means; let us take things as they come, without thinking about them when there is nothing to be done. Truly these boyish natures are a little irritating at times!

Mr. Davenport left the hall, and Reggie resumed his place on the floor, and had another cup of tea.

"Poor mother!" he said with sincerity; "how dreadfully wet and cold she will be."

Percy had retired to the smoking-room, and the two were alone.

"Your father was rather vexed," she said.

"I'm afraid he was," said Reggie. "I wish he'd let me go instead of him."

"Why don't you go with him?"

"That would do no good," said Reggie. "He's only going because he is anxious. I'm not the least anxious. Mother is sure to have turned in at some cottage to wait till the snow was over, or until she could get a carriage. If I could save her anything by going out, of course I'd go."

Gertrude was frowning at the fire.

"I think I'll ask him whether I may come with him," she said.

Reggie raised his eyebrows.

"Oh, nonsense," he said. "He wouldn't let you, anyhow. Sit down, Gerty, and talk."

"Oh, well," she said, "I suppose it's all right."

There was no need, however, for Mr. Davenport to go out, for before he came down again with thick boots, and rough clothes on, his wife had arrived.

Reggie sprang up and welcomed her with great eagerness and affection.

"Dear mother," he cried, "I am so glad you have come. Oh! how wet you are."

He led her to the fire, and poured out a cup of tea with almost feminine tenderness.

"I hope you and Gerty weren't anxious," she said.

"Oh, no," said Reggie, frankly, "not a bit. I knew it would be all right. But I'll run to tell father. He was going out with two men to look for you."

"Reggie wanted to go instead of him," said Gertrude, feeling that her lover's conduct was capable of some slight justification.

"Dear Reggie is never anxious," said Mrs. Davenport, warming her hands. "It is a great comfort for him."

Gertrude was rather relieved. There was no need for her, apparently, to turn advocate.

CHAPTER II.

Theology, in theory, at any rate, teaches us that human beings are living things with souls; experience, on the other hand, which deals with facts capable of proof, insists that, whatever theological truth this statement may embody, for practical purposes, human beings are born without souls. The soul awakes, or, as experience says, is born at varying times. Some men and women reach maturity of body and mind without it, some, we cannot help thinking, reach death without it; some, on the other hand, are but children when that perplexing gift is handed over to their bewildered keeping. But the soulless human animal often has at its disposal and use a quantity of instincts which partake of the soul-like nature; the soul, at any rate, when it is born, takes them over entire. There is no need to adapt them, or to purify them, for they are already clean and pure; it hardly ever vitalises them, for they are already very living; it merely shows them their kinship to itself, and they are forthwith embodied in it.

This birth of the soul, like all births, is the consummation of bitter pangs; it is brought forth in sorrow, through some rending asunder of the inmost fibre, not by any elegant musing on devotional books, nor in a flash of blinding ecstasy, but in silence, save, perhaps, for the bitter cry, in darkness, in solitary desolation, for the sufferer does not know what is happening until the end of his pain has come; the blind pangs get fiercer and fiercer, and are still unexplained till the light breaks.

It would, perhaps, be an insult to the reader to state baldly the bearing of these remarks, for it will be already, we hope, obvious to him that, in this sense, Reggie, in spite of his frank charm, his susceptibility, his pretty face, his capacity for receiving and inspiring affection, was, at heart, soulless. His strong, hearty liking for his betrothed was of that genial, animal kind, which, however wholesome and satisfactory, has no more to do with the soul than his power of aiming straight at woodcock. Happily, or unhappily, for him, the abstruse side of life was scarcely less remote from Gertrude than it was from himself. She had at present no wish and no power to give anything but the same genial, hearty liking that she received, a thorough, wholesome affection in which the nature of both, as far as they were aware of their nature, shared to the full. Neither Reggie nor Gertrude had ever fallen in love with an idea, which is, perhaps, the most exacting lover that man or woman ever has, but which, being wholly abstract, is of an entirely different nature from the love of two young people who admire and like each other enormously, mind and body. This abstruser side of life was a complete puzzle to Reggie. To take a very small but wholly appropriate illustration; he could sympathise with his mother, who might, perhaps, be wandering on the High Croft in a snow-storm, with a good deal of feeling, but the instinct that made his father put on his damp shooting clothes, and prepare to go out, not for any assistance he could give, but for the eminently unpractical reason that his wife was in the snow and he was having tea, seemed inexplicable to his son. If he could have done a jot or a tittle of good by standing in the water butt for five minutes, there is not the shadow of doubt that he would have done so, shiveringly but contentedly and without question; but it would have seemed absurd to him to put his nose outside the hall door, if nothing was to come of it.

With a less sweet disposition, he would have been a profound egoist; but in his manliness was salt enough, as the phrase is, to keep him sweet. The egoist rates himself higher than he rates the rest of the world; he thinks more of himself, consciously or unconsciously, as he thinks less of others, whereas Reggie, though he was incapable of those intricacies of feeling, which, for all practical purposes, are different, not merely in complexity but in kind, from the simpler forms, and which make the spectacle of the human race so vastly interesting, and produce, it may be, love of the complex order, never contemplated himself at all, and, however little he knew of others, at any rate he knew nothing of himself. His mind resembled, it is true, a being of two dimensions, which is unable to contemplate the existence of a third, but in its two dimensions it moved very smoothly, and had a very charming smile for its own plane horizon.

Gertrude stopped with the Davenports nearly a fortnight—a fortnight of pleasant, quiet days, which are paradise to a mind content, and she was supremely content. Reggie was all that a lover, whom she would choose, should be; he was uniformly cheerful, affectionate, charming, full of the thought of her; and, ah! how much that means! Reggie was one of those who show their best side when they are in love; whereas many men, who are otherwise reasonable beings, behave like spoiled children when they are in that predicament; they become observant, jealous, exacting, when they should be serene, indulgent, large-hearted.

But once, just at the end of that fortnight, there arose out of the sea a little cloud like a man's hand, which broke the blue horizon, though Reggie was unconscious of it. A little hint of it had occurred once before, on that evening when Mrs. Davenport lost her way over the High Croft, but on that occasion it had soon passed away.

Percy, it must be owned, was not so jovially contented with the spectacle, as the days went on, as the actors themselves. He was a deductive young gentleman, and, to his mind, this affair resembled too strongly Reggie's previous flutterings in the feminine dovecotes to strike him as something altogether different from a flirtation on a large scale. A flirtation, after all, is only a superficial exhibition of love, an attraction on one side, a liability to be attracted on the other; and the question occurred to him, whether it is possible to keep a flirtation up permanently, and what was left if it broke down? A strong, deep love, like the Nile in flood, leaves, like a sediment behind, which in so many cases renders marriages, from which the tumultuous stream has passed, happy and stable, an alluvial deposit, which makes the earth rich and fruitful in the sober green of friendship; but when the slender, light-hearted streamlet is dried up, the effect of its passage is only too often seen in the uncovering of ugly roots and stones, and a removal, not a deposit of sediment. Of course he knew more about those previous affairs, which, to do Reggie justice, were superficial and innocent enough, than did that gentleman's mother. A young man, whatever his relations with his mother may be, will choose some other confidant in such cases. They argued, in fact, nothing more than a very great susceptibility on Reggie's part to the influence of charming young women, and the sage Percy asked himself whether the constant propinquity of one specimen of this attractive product would necessarily secure him from the influence of the others. That unlucky resemblance between his previous skirmishes and this engagement seemed to him too close to be altogether satisfactory. A flirtation on a large scale, he argued, is not very different from a flirtation on a small scale.

Mrs. Davenport had immense confidence in Percy. He was three years older than Reggie, and was possessed of a certain soundness, of which that young gentleman stood in need. He had been of great use to him in the thousand and one unconscious ways in which one young man can help another slightly younger than himself. He had a practical mastery of details that led him to reliable conclusions on their sum, which is a gift as useful as intuitive judgment, though less striking in its process, as it partakes of the nature of industry rather than brilliance. But Reggie's mother did him justice, and found herself consulting him as she would have consulted an older man, with considerable respect for his opinion.

"We are all so delighted about Reggie's engagement," she said to him one evening after dinner. "His father thought, and so did I, that a long engagement was better. You see they are both very young, and they ought to know each other well. No one should marry on an enthusiastic first impression, least of all Reggie, because he has so many of them."

"Certainly there are no signs of wavering yet," said he. "They are as fond of each other as—as two children."

"Why do you say that?" she asked.

"They are so healthfully fond of each other," he said. "They were trying to read two of Browning's lyrics this morning, about one way of love and another way of love, and they gave it up in about three minutes and read Pickwick instead."

"Poor Reggie, I'm afraid he'll find that his way of love is neither one nor the other, but I think it's a good way for all that."

"There's no nonsense about it, anyhow," said Percy, without meaning to make reflections on the lyrics in question.

"It isn't tumultuous exactly," said Reggie's mother, "but it's very thorough. Still waters do run deep, you know, in spite of the proverb."

"But the stillness is not a proof of their depth."

"No; but when a stream is in the rapids, so to speak, it is. The rapids, I mean, which come just after the waterfall, the plunge into love."

"Oh, but Reggie's always falling in love."

"So I gathered; though, of course, the boy wouldn't tell me about that. But I don't think that's against his present engagement."

Percy was silent, and Mrs. Davenport adjusted her bracelet before she added,—

"I believe it's a healthy thing for a young man to be in a chronic state of devotion. The vague adoration is all sucked into the particular adoration when that comes."

"But is falling in love with a series of particular girls to be called a vague adoration?"

"Yes, certainly, just as a circle is an infinite number of straight lines. He falls in love with womanliness in many forms."

"I see. No doubt you are right. Certainly he is standing his long engagement very well."

"Poor boy! he wants to shorten it very much, which is just the very reason why I want it to be long."

"Miss Carston is satisfied, I gather?"

"It looks like it," said Mrs. Davenport, smiling, and indicating with her eye a shady corner of the room where the two lovers were sitting.

"Old Lady Hayes was staying with us for a week in London last summer," she continued, after a pause. "She was defeated in a great battle, apparently, with your sister, and came here to bind up her wounds by bullying us all. I have an immense admiration for anyone who can rout her."

Percy laughed.

"I heard something about it. Eva behaved abominably, I expect."

"I met her several times in London," said Mrs. Davenport. "She has a wonderful way of appearing to notice no one, and obliging every one to notice her."

"I never saw anyone so changed in a short time as Eva," said Percy. "She has suddenly found men and women extraordinarily interesting. A year ago, she was exactly the reverse. She disliked most women, and never remembered any man."

"That was the impression she gave me in the summer."

"Ah! but that manner is only a survival. She is often silent; at other times she talks a great deal. In the old days she seldom talked at all."

"Poor Hayes is terribly afraid of her."

"I think most people are afraid of her. She can be very cruel."

"A woman with such beauty as that has an unfair advantage. Her shots must always tell."

"She is one of those people who always make an impression," said Percy; "because she doesn't care at all what impression she makes."

"That is the sort of impression that produces the deadliest results," said Mrs. Davenport. "If a man sees that he is being made a fool of, he can be on his guard, but the effect of the other is that he is dazzled, piqued, maddened. The women who don't care are always those for whom men care most passionately."

"I wonder if Eva will ever fall in love," said Percy half to himself.

"It will be a fine sight if she does; she will teach all these bloodless people how to do it. I think she has more force than anyone I know. Does she ever talk to you about her marriage?"

"Oh! there's nothing in the world she doesn't talk about. She has begun to take an immense interest in herself, as well as in other people, and she watches her own development with much entertainment. She never forces anything; she quietly waits till the change is made, and then finds out exactly what has happened."

"Her scene with old Lady Hayes must have been wicked," said Mrs. Davenport. "I can imagine her so well, lolling back in her chair with infinite languor, smoking cigarettes probably, and uttering slow, polished blasphemies about all her mother-in-law's most cherished beliefs."

"They are out in Algiers now," said Percy. "Eva suddenly expressed a wish to go there again. She likes the languid heat of the place. Jim Armine is with them."

"Ah!" said Mrs. Davenport, softly. "She is very cruel."

"She had the greatest distaste for her ordinary home life. Last year my father lost a lot of money, and we had to live very quietly at home in the country and retrench. Eva couldn't endure it. She had quite made up her mind that she would never fall in love at all. She will do something sublime if she does. She is quite capable of sacrificing herself or anybody else."

"A clear stage and a crowd to see," thought Mrs. Davenport, "and may I be in the stalls."

Meanwhile, the two lovers were talking at the very farthest corner of the drawing-room, but before the evening was over, the little cloud, which had just appeared over the horizon on the occasion when Reggie's mother had lost her way in the snow, gathered again, and this time it seemed to Gertrude to leave a little film of mist behind. Like the other two, they had been talking about Percy's sister, and Reggie had said suddenly,—

"She is perfectly lovely, I believe; they call her the most beautiful woman in London. Percy showed me her photograph. I want to see her very much."

This speech, made in absolute thoughtlessness, jarred somehow on Gertrude's sensibilities.

"I daresay there are many actresses as beautiful," she said, rather unnecessarily. "I don't think I should like her a bit. There was a man staying with us the other day who said she was perfectly reckless about what she did."

"Oh! a woman as beautiful as that can afford to be reckless," said Reggie. "She sets the fashion."

"I don't think recklessness is a good fashion to set, then," said Gertrude, with some asperity.

"Oh! nor do I," said Reggie. "I only meant that one excuses it more, somehow."

"I don't see why you should excuse it because a woman is beautiful," said she, seeing the cloud rising out of the sea.

"I don't know," said Reggie. "You must take a person all round; beauty is an advantage, and you set it off against a corresponding disadvantage."

"Do you mean that an incomparably beautiful woman is excusable if she does unpardonably nasty things?"

"I suppose it comes to that in extremities," said he, doubtfully. "You see, it is impossible to believe that such a woman could do anything quite unpardonable."

"Reggie, you're absurd," she cried; "don't talk such utter nonsense, and be thankful I don't believe you mean what you say."

Reggie turned round in surprise.

"Why, Gerty, what's the matter?" he asked.

"You hurt me when you talk like that," she said.

"Oh! what have I been saying?" said he, with an air of perplexity. "You know the worst of me is, I never know what I'm talking about. When I begin talking I get dreadfully puzzled."

"Most people explain what they mean by talking, not obscure it."

"Well, it's just the opposite way with me," said he, serenely. "I know what I think all right before I begin to say it, but as soon as I begin to say it, I begin not to know what I think."

This confident assertion failed to satisfy Gertrude.

"You said you didn't mind a woman being immoral, if she was only beautiful," she said.

"Oh! I never said a word about immorality," exclaimed Reggie. "I don't think it's right to talk about such things. Gerty, what *do* you mean. As if I should say such things to you, especially since I never think them at all."

The open candour of her lover's face had its due effect.

"Well, you're quite sure you meant nothing of the sort, are you?" she asked, ready to be mollified.

"Of course I am," said he with sincerity. "I don't understand what you mean."

"What did you say, then?"

The cloud had begun to drift, but the horizon was not clear yet.

"Oh! don't ask me," he said tragically. "I tell you I never know what I say, and I get so dreadfully confused. I said—Oh, Lord! what did I say. I said that an ugly woman—oh, dear!—that an ugly woman can't do the things which, if a beautiful woman did, she wouldn't be thought a beast," he explained, with a fine disregard of coherency.

"Oh! but, Reggie, that's exactly what you said you didn't say."

"No, it isn't," said Reggie, who, though not exactly bored, wanted to talk about something else. "I said something about a beautiful woman being the fashion, which an ugly woman can't be."

"What do you mean by the fashion?"

"Why, I mean the fashion," said Reggie; "the rage, the *comme il* something, the thing everybody else does—balloon sleeves and dachshunds, you know."

"Are you sure you only meant that sort of fashion?" asked she.

"Oh! yes, of course I am. Oh! do let's talk about something else."

But Gertrude was vaguely dissatisfied. The cloud had left a little drift of mist behind.

And Reggie? Well Reggie's cleanly, honest instincts gave him no directions on this subject; they drew in their feelers like sea anemones when a foreign substance touches them. A soul would have had a word or two to say to him about it, but Reggie unfortunately knew nothing about that.

They sat silent for a minute or two, Reggie trying to think of something to say which should be sufficiently remote from this puzzling topic, Gertrude still rather troubled in her mind. In after years, she remembered that night as the first occasion on which a certain, vague pain had begun, the first of a series of blind pangs that stirred a new sort of feeling in her, that tore asunder some fibre in her inmost being. An elegant musing over devotional books is, as I have mentioned before, the accredited source of such an awakening.

The unerring instinct of a lover in Reggie, divined, though very dimly, that some little change had taken place. He felt that Gertrude had felt something that he had not felt. In spite of his recent sense of irresponsibility, of utter contentedness on his own part, he could see that the edge had been taken, ever so slightly, off hers. You may observe something like this in the case of the more human animals. A dog sometimes will know that it does not understand, if the bond between itself and its human friend is very strong. Its inability to understand is something quite different; it is the knowledge of this inability that is rare, and Reggie felt this now.

As is natural, he recovered himself first. After a twinge of pain, one is prone to sit quiet a minute or two, and regain one's normal level. But the pain had been all on one side, and Gertrude required a little space to steady herself in.

"Gerty, let's play a game of some sort. Come and see what the others are going to do."

He got up and stood in front of her.

"Pull me up," she said.

Her white hands lay in his great brown paws, like little patches of snow in some sheltered nook of the hills. But they were warm with life and love, and she was very fair. He bent down and kissed them gently, first one and then the other.

"You sha'n't kiss my hands," she said. "Come, let's go to the others."

The troubled look had gone from her face, but Mrs. Davenport, with a woman's swift, infallible intuition, saw that something, ever so small, had happened. There was still in her eyes the shadow of a vague wonder.

Ladies, I believe, have a bad habit of going to each other's bedrooms when they are thought to have gone to bed, and sitting by the fire, talking things over. It is a bad plan to talk things over at night, because, while you are talking, there forms in the air, without your seeing it, a little grey ghost, to which your words give birth. There are no such things as barren words; all words uttered by you go to make up a little series of figures, who come and talk to you when nobody else is there. And the sort of conversation that Gertrude and Mrs. Davenport had that night gave rise to a little, pale, anxious, grey ghost, that sat by Gertrude's bedside, and, as soon as her body had had enough sleep—the ghost always allows his victims the necessary minimum—it tapped fretfully on her shoulder, and said, "Come, wake up, let us go on talking!" And Gertrude stirred in her dreamless sleep, and knew that the little ghost had come to talk to her.

It is a time-honoured custom for an author to describe the personal appearance of any character when he decides to lay his reflections before a discriminating public, and the neglect of this custom is a red rag to the stupid, furious bull called criticism. So, since this little ghost's personal appearance is only to be described by retailing the conversation which took place between Gertrude and Mrs. Davenport the night before, this obedient and peace-loving author complies with the eminently English demand.

Gertrude was sitting before her fire in her dressing-gown, when Mrs. Davenport came in. Her eyes still wore a troubled look, and the pictures in the fire were not so pleasant as she had known them.

Mrs. Davenport noticed it at once. It was the same look as she had seen before that evening, a little intensified.

"Are you tired, dear?" she asked. "Would you rather I left you to go to bed instead of talking?"

Gertrude looked up.

"No, I want to talk very much."

"Gerty, dear, is anything the matter?"

"I don't know."

There was a short silence. Mrs. Davenport was far too wise to press her. Then Gertrude said,—

"Do you know Lady Hayes?"

Mrs. Davenport was puzzled. The carrier-pigeon always takes a few wide circles before he sets out on his unerring flight home.

"Oh! yes, quite well," she replied. "Percy and I were talking about her this evening. It's funny that neither you nor Reggie have even seen her."

She was feeling her way with tactful discretion. But it was a very narrow path down which Gertrude meant to go, and Mrs. Davenport not unnaturally had missed it.

"What is she like?" asked Gertrude.

"Ah! what isn't she like? She is the most beautiful woman in England, I think, also one of the most reckless, and, I believe, very generous. I should call her dangerous as well. But she is so interesting, so unlike others, that you forget everything else, which is harder than forgiving it."

Gertrude turned round and faced her.

"Ah, you too," she said.

"I don't quite understand, dear," said Mrs. Davenport, gently; "have you and Reggie been talking about her? Tell me, Gerty. I saw something was a wee bit wrong. I'm sure you haven't been quarrelling, though. What has been the matter?"

"I couldn't love Reggie more than I do," said Gertrude, irrelevantly, "and I don't think he could love me more than he does. It's odd that I should be troubled."

"Yes, dear, I am sure of your love for each other," said Mrs. Davenport. "But tell me what is wrong. It does one good to tell things; they become so much smaller in the telling. Those vague thoughts are like those great spongy puff balls that we noticed to-day; as soon as you really examine them, you find there is nothing in them. What is it?"

"I don't know," said Gertrude again.

Ah, that infinite patience of womankind! Mrs. Davenport waited a moment, and then, by an unerring instinct, laid her hand softly on Gertrude's, and pressed it gently. The touch had power in it, and the dumb soul spake.

"I've got no right to be troubled," said Gertrude, "and I feel it's horribly ungrateful of me, when I think of what Reggie is to me, and how good you are all to me. But—"

Her voice got tremulous, and she stopped abruptly.

"Yes?" said Mrs. Davenport, softly, wanting to hear more for Gertrude's sake.

"It's just this," she said at last, speaking rapidly, and with a splendid self-control. "Reggie said something this evening which hurt me. He said that recklessness mattered less in a beautiful woman than in another."

"Is that all?" said Mrs. Davenport, with considerable relief.

"No, that's not all," said Gertrude. "That was all nonsense; of course I know he doesn't mean that. But he didn't see it hurt me. Oh! it's so hard not to give you a wrong impression. I don't mean that he was inconsiderate at all—he never is anything but considerate—but he simply didn't know. It wasn't tangible to his mind. If I cut my finger he'd be miserable about it, but somehow he was unable to understand how this hurt me, and so he could not see that it did hurt me. It hurt me somewhere deep down, ever so little, but the feeling was new and strange. This sounds horribly selfish, I'm afraid, but I can't help it."

"Ah, I think I see," said Mrs. Davenport.

"It's like this," said Gertrude. "Hitherto I've always felt so entirely at one with Reggie. If I feel a thing, he's always seemed to feel it too, like an echo, and the same with me. But just this once I listened for the echo and it didn't come."

Mrs. Davenport paused a moment.

"Did you ever hear of the man who was out riding with his wife when her horse threw her, and in dismounting to help her he dropped his whip, and while he was picking it up, the horse kicked her and killed her?" she asked. "It seems to me that you are just a little like that man, Gerty. Love is a very big thing; one's own small sensibilities are very little things. Take care of the big thing, never mind the others."

"But they're so mixed up," said the girl. "You see the little thing is a part of the big thing."

"You are right—that is quite true. But there are many very lovely things which it is right to look at as a whole. Love is one of those. All philosophers, from the beginning of the world, have addled their brains over that impossible analysis. You and Reggie are not philosophers, Gerty; you are young lovers, and it is not your business to analyse or dissect, but to enjoy."

Mrs. Davenport was at the sore disadvantage of having to temporise. She could not but suspect what was at the bottom of this. But all she said was quite sincere. She fully believed that the strength of Gerty's love would fill the interval, if there was to be an interval between her and Reggie. It is best that the woman be better, finer, bigger than the man, for the beautiful indulgence of a woman's love has more passive endurance in these early stages than a man's. In the perfect marriage, the two eventually are mixed "in spite of the mortal screen," but such mixings are rare at first. They rushed together, they will inevitably recoil a little, and a woman has more power of waiting than most men. Gertrude seemed somewhat relieved, but it was not quite over yet. The grey ghost was waiting for his frillings.

"I was just a little disappointed, you understand?" she said. "I waited for the echo, but it never came. Ah! well, I am very happy. Yon are very good to me."

"God forbid that I or mine should ever give you pain," said Mrs. Davenport, warmly.

"And what am I to do?" said Gertrude, to whom the practical side of things always presented itself.

"Be natural, dear," said the other, "as you always are. You are both very young; well, that is a gift almost more worth having than anything else. It lies in your power a great deal to keep it. And, if you guard it well, it will build up in you the only other gift which is worth having, which will last you to your grave. They will melt into each other."

Gertrude looked at her inquiringly.

"It is called by many names," she said. "It is trustfulness, it is serenity, it is sympathy; it is all these, and many more. Some people call it the grace of God, and I think they are right." She kissed the girl on her forehead very tenderly. "It will tide you over the difficult places, over which youth carries you now, for youth has the gift of a splendid stainlessness—of going through deep waters and not being drowned, of avoiding evil instinctively, without thought; but the time comes to us all when we avoid it with our reason as well, and with our soul."

"It was ridiculous of me," said the girl suddenly. "Reggie didn't know what I felt, and I didn't tell him; and yet I was disappointed. I've probably done just the same to him lots of times, and he never told me. It was abominably selfish of me. I hope he'll forgive me."

"I should think it extremely unlikely," said Mrs. Davenport, with enormous gravity. "I should advise you to cry yourself to sleep. I am going to bed, and so are you. Good-night! Ah! my dear, I pray you may be very happy."

Gertrude clung to her in a long kiss, feeling a new bond had sprung up between them.

But the odious, little, grey ghost, who had been grinning sardonically at her easy enthusiasm, was sitting by her bed, waiting till the renewal of strength, brought by sleep, had quickened her capabilities for listening to his cold accuracies—until that generous, sudden glow had begun to burn somewhat less warmly in her breast.

CHAPTER III.

Lord Hayes had been rather troubled about his health during the winter in which the foregoing events had occurred, though it had not stood in the way of their giving several large house-parties. But at one of these he had suddenly fainted dead off in the middle of dinner, and, when the house was empty again, he had gone up to London to see a doctor.

Eva was sitting in her room when he returned, feeling rather bored.

"Well, Hayes," she said, as he came in, "what did they say to you?"

Lord Hayes adjusted his trousers about the knee before he answered.

"I have all the symptoms of dangerous heart disease," he said. "I may live for many years, and die of something else. Again, I may die almost at any moment."

Eva's book drooped off her knee.

"How horrible!" she said at length. "Can nothing be done? Are they sure they are right?"

"Unfortunately, they are quite sure," he said; "and nothing can be done. They consider the chance of my dying quite suddenly at any time as possible, but not at all likely."

Eva, in her serene health, felt a sudden, great pity for him, but not unmixed with horror. She had no sympathy with disease; it seemed to her hardly decent.

"Poor Hayes," she said. "I cannot tell you how shocked I am."

"I thought it was best to tell you," said he, "but let us avoid the subject altogether. I shall live to bore you for many years yet."

Eva looked at him admiringly.

"You are a brave man. But you are right. Don't let us talk about it."

This took place late in November, but the fact that the symptoms, which had been the result of over-fatigue, did not re-occur, made Eva soon get used to the thought, and, in a measure, her husband too. He took the doctor's advice, did not over-exert himself at all, and found that the discovery they had made did not affect his health. The days soon began to pass on as usual.

Eva had suddenly determined to go abroad for a few weeks, for she had an intense dislike to an English winter. Hence it came about that one morning at breakfast, when she and her husband were alone, she had said to him,—

"What do you propose to do during these next two months, Hayes?"

Lord Hayes looked up from his breakfast, not quite understanding the purport of her question.

"I suppose we shall remain here till Easter," he said. "We are paying some visits in January, I believe."

"I should rather like to go abroad for a few weeks now this horrible weather has begun." She looked out of the window, where snow was beginning to fall heavily, and shivered sympathetically. "I hate this English weather," she said; "it is like being in a cold bath. Dry cold is not so bad, there is something exhilarating about it. But this doesn't suit me in the least. Why shouldn't we go to Algiers again?"

"I thought you didn't like Algiers," he said. "Do you propose that we should go alone?"

"Oh no, we won't make any intolerable demands of that sort on each other. I think it suits us best to have people with us. I daresay Percy would like to come for a bit, perhaps your mother would join us, and then there's Jim Armine, who always wants to go abroad whenever he can."

Eva spoke with the utmost indifference, but her husband found himself wondering whether that indifference was not a very subtle piece of acting. That he had some inkling of the young man's feelings towards his wife was very possible, but he had not the least objection to that. In fact, it rather pleased him than otherwise, as it afforded a sort of testimonial to his own admirable taste in wishing her to become his wife, and to his enviable success in securing her for that purpose. He knew quite well that the *rôle* of jealous husband would not suit him in the least, and he had no intention of being a complaisant one, but he had sense enough to guess that complaisance was not necessary. He had no reason to believe that Eva had a heart at all; and he had no desire to make a mistake. If he suggested to Eva that he would rather not have Jim Armine with them, his remark would be liable to be interpreted in a way which she might with justice resent; in fact, that was the only interpretation open to her, for he liked the young man well enough in himself. He did not even admit the smallest suspicion into his mind; he only realised that there was the possibility of an avenue, down which suspicion might some day choose to walk; and when suspicion was seen by him walking down that avenue, he would go and take its hand, and they would knock at Eva's door, and show themselves.

Eva rose from the table.

"Then you don't mind coming to Algiers?"

It was clearly impossible to say "No; but I do mind Jim Armine coming," and so he proposed a date some ten days off for their departure.

"Why shouldn't we go sooner?" asked Eva.

"There's been some unpleasantness down at the ironworks," he said, "and I think that, as owner, I ought to just wait till it's settled in some form or another."

"Do you mean down at Trelso?"

"Yes; the men are striking, or wanting to strike, for higher wages—more pay, in fact."

"Couldn't you go down there to-day, and see the agents or managers or whoever they are?"

"There is nothing definite yet; we only know that there is a good deal of discontent."

"Surely, then, you can leave it with your manager to deal with, when it occurs. It is absurd waiting in England for a handful of miners to tell you what they want."

"It would be better, I think, if I waited," he said.

"I wish you would explain to me exactly why."

"Simply because, as owner," he said, "they would wish to consult me if anything went really wrong."

"Surely there is a telegraph to Algiers. I should infinitely prefer starting in less than a week. I really cannot stand this sort of weather."

"I feel sure I am right to stop," he said. "It is certainly best."

Eva hesitated a moment.

"Would you mind my going on without you, then? Perhaps that would be the best plan. I daresay Jim will come with me."

Her husband looked at her narrowly. He felt he was playing a losing game.

"I will go down to Trelso to-day, and see exactly what the state of affairs is—how they stand, in fact."

"Very good. I shall start on Thursday, then. I will write to Jim to-day. I hope you won't lose any more money over this."

He smiled rather grimly.

"I hope not. This last year has been very expensive. I don't grudge it in the least; in fact, it is very interesting to me to see how much a woman can spend."

He was conscious of an impotent desire to make it not quite pleasant for Eva, even if she did get her own way in the main, and he was pleased to see her flinch, just perceptibly. She was annoyed with herself for doing it.

"Yes, I suppose you find you spend much more now than you used."

"About ten thousand a year more."

"Dear me, that is a great deal. You can hardly have counted the cost."

"I did not quite realise it at the time. That's what I mean by saying it was more than I anticipated."

"Ah! of course you wouldn't anticipate it," said Eva. "Love is blind, you know."

Lord Hayes was rather sorry he had begun. He was somewhat in the position of a dog which runs out from its shelter to bite a passer-by, and when it gets into the open, discovers that its intended victim carries a stick.

Eva waited long enough to give him time to reply if he wanted, but finding he said nothing, turned and left the room.

Two days after this, as they were sitting at dinner, Eva asked him what had happened about the ironworks.

"I am glad you reminded me," he said. "I told them that I wished particularly to leave England at once, and asked them to telegraph to me in case I was wanted. It appears that they do not expect any immediate disturbance, so I shall be able to come with you on Thursday—in fact, there will be nothing to detain me."

"You had better stop if you think you are wanted," said Eva. "I can manage perfectly by myself, and Jim Armine will be with me; he wrote to-day. But if they don't want you, of course you'll go with me."

"Armine is coming, then, is he?" asked her husband.

"Yes; you don't object to him, I hope?"

"Not in the least."

"If you do, it would have been better if you had said so at once," said Eva, carelessly. "I've asked him now."

"Why should you suppose I object to him?" he asked suddenly.

"You didn't seem very cordial about it. Have you asked anybody else?"

"I mentioned it to my mother when I saw her in Trelso, but she said she wouldn't come."

"Ah!" said Eva, with the ghost of a smile, "did she say why?"

"Apparently it was for your sake—because of you, in fact."

"I expect she meant for her own sake. I should be charmed to have her. There is a straightforwardness, a refusal to compromise, in her behaviour to me, that is very refreshing."

"She speaks of you with bitterness—I might almost say rancour," remarked Lord Hayes.

"I am more sinned against than sinning, then," said Eva. "I always feel perfectly charitable towards her. She loathes me; but, after all, that is not her fault. Really, it is wonderful what a fine order of hatred is compatible with the most orthodox Christianity. But of course I am one of the works of the devil, which she has been led to renounce from a child."

Thus it came about that, before the middle of December, Lord Hayes and his wife, and Jim Armine, were installed in the charming little villa at Algiers. The Gulf of Lyons was kinder on this occasion to the susceptibilities of Lord Hayes, and he produced his white umbrella, and sat on a deck chair in untroubled contemplation. He always wore a yachtsman's cap and brown shoes on calm trips, which were, somehow, particularly aggravating to Eva.

She was sitting on deck when he came upstairs on the morning after their departure from Marseilles, and Eva had a long, malignant look at him as he approached her.

"You look completely nautical this morning," she said slowly. "I hope it won't get rough, for your sake, or you will have to retire. The commodore will be found groaning in his cabin. But, perhaps you are only a fighting sailor, like Lord Nelson, who was always ill, wasn't he? In that case, I hope we sha'n't meet any Moorish privateers. If we are attacked during a storm, you will be completely exposed."

Eva had rarely said anything to him in such simple bad taste, and her husband was surprised. The childishness of her strictures, however, rather amused him than otherwise, for he thought he had the key to them, in a rather awkward little scene which had taken place the evening before. Eva had been arguing some point with Jim Armine, and he had got a little excited. She had just made an assertion which seemed to him to contradict what she had said a moment before, and by an unlucky slip he exclaimed,—

"Why, Eva, you said just the opposite a minute ago."

The mistake was pardonable enough: when a man is in love with a woman, he naturally thinks of her by her Christian name, and it is excusable if, in some momentary excitement, he uses it. Eva was startled. He had never called her that before, and, losing her self-control for one half second, she uttered a sudden exclamation of anger, and glanced at her husband. He was sitting with one leg crossed over the other, looking at the sunset. He turned to Jim Armine, and said politely,—

"I think you must have misunderstood Lady Hayes."

The poor young man flushed deeply, and Eva bit her lips, divided between her annoyance and a desire to laugh. But the annoyance conquered in the end, as the delicate, veiled insult of her husband's speech dawned upon her. His words certainly bore another interpretation, though whether he had meant it or not she was not quite sure, and she could not ask him. But Jim Armine evidently took them in the obscurer sense and was horribly disconcerted, and Eva not unnaturally felt extremely annoyed. He was, possibly, trying to make a fool of her, and she had not the least intention of being treated in such a manner. After a few moments she found something to say, but the conversation was evidently over. Jim Armine soon strolled away to the other end of the deck, and Eva was left alone with her husband.

As soon as the other was out of hearing, she said to him,—

"I do not wish you to speak of me in that way. Please remember that."

"I regret having offended you," replied he, "but I do not choose that Armine should call you by your Christian name, Eva, in fact."

"Your speech implied more than that," she said.

Lord Hayes determined to make a stand.

"You are very quick at finding meanings."

"What you said was insulting."

"It is insulting to you that he should call you Eva?"

"Do you admit, then, that your speech bore another meaning?"

Lord Hayes lit another cigarette.

"I admit nothing of the sort. Not at all."

"You will be so good as to apologise to him."

"I have no reason for supposing that he imagined it to bear any meaning but the obvious one—the one, in fact, which I meant to convey. Of course you are at liberty to explain to him that, if you choose."

For the first time Eva was conscious of a slight disadvantage, and Lord Hayes distinctly saw it. As she sat still silent, he looked at his watch and remarked,—

"I am afraid they propose to give us dinner at seven. It is a barbarous custom. Perhaps you would like to know that it is now five minutes to seven."

He carefully furled his white umbrella, and walked down the deck to the saloon. He made in his mind a careful little note of the occurrence, against that possible contingency of suspicion coming down the avenue. It was characteristic of him that he was as evenly polite as ever to Jim Armine, and advised him to drink white wine and not red, and remarked to him at tea afterwards that the Albert biscuits were stale, but that it was interesting to observe that the English manufactories of biscuits held their own abroad; in fact, that the makers of the stale Albert biscuits were Huntly & Palmer.

This suggestive little scene accounted, in his mind, for Eva's unusual want of politeness on the subject of his yachtsman's cap and brown canvas shoes. But he did not consider that a reason for abandoning them; in fact, they became to him a sort of commemorative medal on the occasion of his victory. A force which has an unbroken record of defeat is apt to dwell on a single and unexpected victory. In the main he was right in attributing Eva's irritation that morning to her slight discomfiture on the evening before, for though she had dismissed, or rather forgotten, the occurrence, there was still in her a latent resentment that unconsciously vented itself in this manner.

They had been at the villa four or five days, and Lord Hayes had got into the habit of observing his wife and Jim Armine somewhat closely. Eva was rather silent; to her husband she hardly spoke at all, though now and then at meals she would begin talking, more to herself than the others. Jim Armine was not a very wise young man, and he said things sometimes, that, with another woman, would have betrayed him, but Eva did not seem to notice them.

They were seated at lunch one day, when Eva took up her parable. She had said nothing at all, as her way was, for some minutes, and Lord Hayes had been describing to Jim how the eucalyptus oil was extracted from the tree.

"You must excuse my silence, Mr. Armine," she said, "but, you know, I have all sorts of recollections about this villa. We were here, you know, on our wedding tour, after we had been on the Riviera—just Hayes and myself—and we used to sit out in the garden and listen to the nightingales singing of love. It was very romantic; no doubt Hayes has spoken to you of it, when you pour out your hearts in the smoking-room, after I have gone to bed. It is always odd to me that men choose that time for being confidential. I should have thought it would have disturbed your night's rest."

"How do you know that we are confidential, then?" asked Jim.

"Why, of course you are; there isn't time to be confidential during the day. Besides, that is the only time when you are sure not to be invaded by women. I shall hide in the smoking-room some night and listen to what you say."

"There is nothing you might not hear," said her husband.

"You mean that, I suppose, in order to deter me from listening, assuming that, being a woman, I only care to hear what is not meant for my ears. But you said it very politely."

"Not at all; it was a formal invitation," said he, "an assurance of how entirely welcome you would be."

"Thanks. Of course you and I are under a sort of mutual compact to delight in each other's society at any time or place."

Lord Hayes laughed.

"One eternal honeymoon. Surely the golden age will return."

Jim Armine, not unnaturally, felt that this was distinctly a comedy *à deux*, and that the presence of a third person was unnecessary. But no man can leave his red mullet half eaten for such reasons. Everything goes to the wall before our material needs.

Lord Hayes's punctilious little manner always vanished in anything like a scene. He began to be self-possessed at exactly that point when most self-possessed people begin to be nervous and flurried, for his punctiliousness was the result not of nervousness, but a desire not to be nervous, and when the occasion was interesting enough to allow him to forget this, his tinge of finished cynicism and indifference to his fellow men assumed its natural predominance. He rather enjoyed a little polite sparring match with his wife, until he began to get the worst of it; as long as the buttons were on the foils he could fence very decently, but the sight of the bare point distinctly discomposed him.

Eva flushed.

"Let us reserve our raptures for when we are alone," she said. "They are slightly embarrassing to a third person."

Lord Hayes smiled. For the second time the banner of victory seemed to wave over his head. He saw his wife flush, and knew that she was very angry. That desire to avenge herself which she had felt so strongly on her return from her honeymoon, the sense that she had been trapped, and was being exhibited as a rare bird in a cage, was very strong in her; the added insolence of the trapper pretending to be on intimate and loving terms with her made her furious, and the consciousness that she had brought it upon herself, did not tend to diminish her rage. For the second time he was trying to make a fool of her before a third person.

How far a scene that took place a day or two after this was brought on by Eva's dislike of her husband and her thirst for vengeance, is not part of this narrative to determine. The chronicler's mission is not to form conclusions, but to present data, and my immediate mission is to present some rather important data.

Even in December, in Algiers, it is often pleasant to sit out of doors at nine in the evening, for the air is cool but dry, and Eva often spent an hour in the little open passage which ran round the central courtyard of the house, and in which, a year before, she had talked to her husband on the position of women. This time it was Jim Armine who was her companion; Lord Hayes had gone upstairs to write to his mother, and he proposed to give her some accurate descriptions, based on observation, about the date palm.

His room looked out on to the aforementioned courtyard, and before beginning his letter, he went across to the window to close it, for he had heard that the night air of Algiers is unwholesome. Just as he was in the act of taking this little precaution, there lighted on his ear the grumbling noise of a basket chair being dragged in passive, grating resistance over a stone floor, followed by the sound of Eva's voice. As he could not see her, he came to the very logical conclusion that she was sitting directly below his window, and where she could not see him, and as she was talking, and Jim Armine was the only person in the house, he pictured her talking to him. After all, the evening air was not unpleasant, and instead of closing the window he stood by it and listened. The emphatic deliberation of this manœuvre was, he felt vaguely, in its favour from a conventional point of view.

The voices, at first, were inaudible to him, for the sense of hearing requires focussing as much as the sense of sight, and he only caught a word here and there. But, for the sake of the reader, it will be necessary to give the inaudible part of the conversation.

The two seated themselves in their basket chairs, and Jim Armine lit a cigarette. There was a small lamp by him, the flame of which burned steadily in the still air. It cast a square of brilliant light into the courtyard beyond, across which, as across a magic-lantern sheet, white moths wandered from time to time, losing themselves again in the surrounding dark. There were several moments' silence, and then he looked at Eva, half of whose face was in brilliant illumination, and said,—

"You look tired to-night."

"No, I am not tired," she said, "but I am feeling blank. Just now everything appears to me extremely uninteresting. I know from experience that things are not uninteresting really, and that is the worst of it. They are there, but I cannot touch them. I live in a grey fog; there is sunshine somewhere, quite close, but I cannot get to it. What else could I expect?"

Jim was attending eagerly.

"Of course I mayn't say how sorry I am for you," he said in a low voice.

Eva did not turn her head, but the least sparkle returned to her eyes. Perhaps things were going to be amusing, after all, for a few minutes.

"I am grateful, of course," she said. "One is to be pitied when the fog is so palpably dense. Of course, it will lift again; fogs don't last for ever. I am glad you are with us, though I don't think you ought to be. After all, nothing matters much."

Lord Hayes had by this time successfully focussed his ear to the indistinct sounds, and Eva's last remark was perfectly audible.

"Ah! but things *do* matter," said the young man earnestly. "And all men are not like some men."

"By which I suppose you mean me to understand that you are not like some men. How can I know that? You have no halo round your head, no dawning of ineffable joy in your face. Why should I suppose you are more than others? You have spoken to me before now of your great aims, your enthusiasms for great causes, by which, as far as I know, you only mean Home Rule, or the Unionist policy—I forgot what your politics are—and even that seems to have been in abeyance lately. You have been with us a week or more, and what have you done, what have you thought about? You seem to prefer, after all, talking to me—"

"You are very cruel, Eva," said he.

Lord Hayes shut his window. Perhaps the night air was unwholesome after all. In any case, he had heard enough. Suspicion was running down the avenue, and growing clearer at every step. He hesitated a moment, and then left his room and walked downstairs. As he came out into the courtyard he heard the echo of Eva's light, cruel laughter.

Jim Armine was standing in front of her, with his arms hanging listlessly by his side. He did not look exactly happy, and the sight of Lord Hayes only added a very slightly deeper shade to his face.

Eva's husband never felt more methodically cool in his life. He had quite determined what to do. She had not seen him approach, and a smile still lingered on her lips. She was lying back in her chair, in indolent languor; only in her eyes was amusement and excitement.

"You looked very fine just then," she was saying to Jim, and turning, she saw her husband.

The smile died off her lips, the amusement from her eyes. Only that air of utter languor was left. But she saw her vengeance coming near, as Lord Hayes had seen suspicion, and she met it joyfully.

Lord Hayes laid his hand on the young man's shoulder.

"The steamers only go twice a week to Marseilles," he said, "and there will be no steamer to-morrow. In the meantime, I am sure you will see the advisability of your spending the next two nights at the Hotel St. George. They say it is a very good hotel. Of course we shall not receive callers."

Eva shifted her position slightly, and looked at her husband.

"Kindly explain why he should go off so suddenly," she said.

"I would not insult you by doing so."

"The insult lies in your silence. I suppose you overheard something."

"Yes," said her husband. "I was listening."

"Ah! that is so like you. What were you listening for?"

"I was listening more or less for what I heard."

"In fact, you suspected something of the sort?"

"Yes."

"And yet you did not warn me. Go away, Mr. Armine, and don't listen, please. Sit down, Hayes; I wish to talk to you. What a lovely night it is. Quite idyllic. By the way, I wish to know whether your suspicions are entirely confined to him."

"Absolutely and entirely."

"You are quite sure?"

"Quite."

"That is good," said Eva. "But naturally I wanted to know. To return—why did you not warn me?"

Lord Hayes found that things were not going exactly as he had foreseen.

"I did not think it would be of any use to warn you," he said at length.

"Then, as you have no suspicions whatever of me, what purpose is served by his going away?"

"His presence here, under this roof, is an insult to you and me."

"Yet you did not warn me," said Eva. "It seems to me that you have cancelled the insult to yourself. Shall I tell you exactly what has happened, or do you know it all?"

"I know enough," he said.

"Possibly, from your point of view. But I am afraid you must have left your box before the end. The end was important. How much did you hear exactly? However, it doesn't matter. He said something—well, extremely ill-judged, and I told him he had mistaken me altogether. I laughed as well. Did you hear me laugh? I said I had not the slightest doubt of his devotion, but that I did not feel the least inclined to accept it. I don't appreciate devotion, except my husband's, of course."

Eva waited a moment. A refined cruelty waits a little every now and then for the full effect of the pain to be felt.

"It is impossible that he should remain here," said he.

"Please listen to me a moment. I have not finished yet. You have insulted me grossly, twice; in the first place, by not warning me, in the second, by listening. I do not like insults in the least, and I have no intention of receiving them. Jim committed an extreme indiscretion, for which you are mainly responsible. If you had spoken to him or me before, this would not have happened. Again, if you had not listened, you would have known nothing of it, and you will be good enough to take my word for it, that no one would have been the worse. He would have learnt a lesson, and I should have had the pleasure of teaching it him. I did not expect this in the least, for I did not think he would have been so foolish as to speak of it."

The degradation which her husband would have imposed on her grew more and more bitter. She stood up with intense anger intensely repressed.

"I choose that he should stop," she said. "I despise you for listening. If you like, you may insist on his going, and, if you do, I shall go too. I tell you I am perfectly reckless, and perfectly determined. Your point is that I have been insulted. It was you who insulted me by not giving me warning, and if you play the spy on me in this way, I owe you absolutely nothing. That is all. You may choose; and choose quickly."

She waited a moment, giving him time to reply.

"Apparently you have nothing to say. In fact, there is nothing for you to say. That is all, then. If you are going to sit out here with us, you had better tell them to bring you a chair. Understand me quite clearly; it is over. I shall never allude to this again, and I must ask you not to, either."

Lord Hayes walked away without saying a word. Eva stood still one moment, steadying herself, and then she called out to Jim, who was leaning against a pillar at the opposite corner of the court.

"You can come back," she said. "We are not going to send you away. Let us go on talking from the last remark but two."

She settled herself again in her chair and laughed. The evening had been unexpectedly amusing.

"He will not listen again, and you will not talk nonsense again, I hope. Really, this is an unique position, and I am the only one of the three who comes out of it with credit. *A* suspects that *B*, his friend, is making love to his wife. Does not warn her, but listens, and hears something that confirms his suspicions. Tries to drive *B* out of the house. They all meet amicably at breakfast next morning."

Certainly, if Eva had felt she had any small score to wipe off against her husband, she had wiped it off very cleanly. He was, for those few moments when she had stood up with her intense anger thoroughly in hand, mortally afraid of her, and she knew it. She had used her anger as a weapon against him, and had not let it act wildly, or unpremeditatedly. She well knew that, as a weapon, anger is most useful when it is skilfully handled, controlled, compressed. A horse without a rider, lashed into the enemies' lines, may, it is true, do some service by promiscuous kicking, but it is a blind, ungoverned force; a skilful rider, however, who adapts its savage strength to his own intelligence, can guide it and direct it, and its destructive potentialities are increased tenfold.

It was as a serviceable though savage brute that Eva employed her anger against her husband; she spurred it and lashed it into fury, but never gave it its head. That cruel, governed anger of women is a very terrible thing; the hot, blustering anger of a man is like a squib that bursts and jumps here and there, sometimes singeing its immediate surroundings and, perhaps, breaking something, but it wastes its force in childish, cracker-like explosions that hurt nothing but sensitive nerves, which regard such exhibitions as a lamentable want of taste. But Eva's anger could not have offended the most fastidious; it gave no annoying little bangs, no unexpected leaps, no fizzing, no unmomentous crackling; it was still, deep, intense, not pleasant to fight with.

Eva and Jim sat in the little courtyard for some half-hour more, which was rather a hard burden for the young man. To Eva it appeared to be no effort to talk as usual. She had required just one moment in which to steady herself, to dismount her quivering, indignant steed, and then for her, as she had told her husband, it was over. She had been angry, furious, insulted, and she had used the whip with a vengeance. The offence and the punishment were past, and she threw the whip into a corner. But Jim was silent, which was not altogether unnatural. He had no taste for scenes, and his great *coup*, his ace of trumps, which, to his shame, had been forced from him, seemed to have fallen very flat. He had played it, and Eva had seen it, but that was all—it had simply been wasted. Naturally enough he felt he had spoiled his hand. Eva had laughed at him, but she had not been offended. Surely such an attitude was almost unprecedented.

When she went upstairs half-an-hour later, she turned into her husband's room to get a book she wanted, and found him sitting by the window, as if expecting her. He rose as she entered, and stood like a servant waiting for orders. But Eva gave no orders, and, having found her book, only remarked that it was growing a little chilly. He did not reply, and she turned to look at him. There was something miserably shrunken about his appearance which was rather pitiful.

"You look tired," she said. "I should go to bed if I were you."

He did not meet her eyes, but continued to look out of the window.

"It has been a terrible night," he said.

Eva frowned.

"It has been nothing of the sort," she said. "Don't be absurd, Hayes. You made a very bad mistake; you did not treat me in the way I wish to be treated, and I was intensely angry with you. But I assure you I am angry no longer. It is quite over, as far as I am concerned. Don't let us quarrel more than is necessary. Just now, it is quite unnecessary to quarrel."

Lord Hayes had a certain potentiality for being malignant.

"It is not the quarrelling," he said; "it is the mutual position that I find we occupy to each other."

She grew a little impatient.

"Let that be enough," she said. "We only waste words."

She came a step nearer to him, and laid her hand on his shoulder, as if he had been a woman, or she a man.

"Come," she said, "be sensible. There is nothing more to say about it. You had better go to bed. Good-night!"

CHAPTER IV.

The little grey ghost which visited Gertrude Carston in the early morning, soon became a *habitué* of her waking hours. He was a very importunate little ghost, and having once been given the *entrée*, he concluded that he was always welcome. But, though he was unpleasant enough at the time, he was slightly medicinal in character, or rather, not so much medicinal as health-giving. He did not exactly correct existing defects, but opened fresh springs within her. So far, however, he was medicinal, in that he was operative after the dose, which always continued bitter to the taste. But the bitterness was a good bitterness, and occasioned not discontent with Reggie, but discontent with herself, and it is always worth a good deal of bitterness to become wholesomely, not morbidly, discontented with oneself. She began to see in her nature unsuspected limitations, a thing quite as salutary, though not perhaps so pleasant, as the sight of unsuspected distances. A consciousness of unsuspected distance is liable to breed content, which is more injurious to the average mind—and she was quite average—than the discouraging discovery of a near horizon of unsuspected limitations, for the latter cause a revolt of something within us—which some call pride, and others spiritual aspiration—which refuses to acquiesce, and insists on those limitations becoming merely landmarks and milestones.

And, indeed, to see such a limitation is a long step towards correcting it. The young mind, to which growth is as natural as it is to the young body, if it has any of that irrepressible, unconscious elasticity, which is the main characteristic of its divine remoteness from age, will never acquiesce in a limitation it sees. It will, somehow or other, clamber over that horizon's rim, and though it may get many a fall, though it may be benighted and foot-sore and weary, that same divine youthfulness, which heals its physical fibres when they are bruised or cut, will repair its mental fibres. Its potentialities for recuperation are as strong as its refusal to be bounded. Youth may be crude, exaggerated, headstrong, but when the advocates of a temperate and bloodless senility have said all they can against it, they must confess that it is young.

What made this inward struggle so trying to Gertrude was, that she was unable, from the essential nature of it, to guess what was happening. All she knew was the sense of tangible limitations and dim tracts beyond, and an imperative necessity to flounder, as best she could, towards them. But she found much comfort in her love for Reggie, and in the knowledge of his love for her; she felt as if she was following some thin golden thread through a maze of bewildering twilight, but while that was secure in her hand, the maze and the twilight and the bewilderment were comparatively unimportant.

The Davenports had moved up to London in April, and Gertrude was with them again for a week before she went abroad to Aix with her mother in May. Mrs. Carston was a weak, fretful invalid, who always insisted on her daughter's cheerful and robust support while she went through a course of somewhat unnecessary baths and massages. The great city was just beginning to settle down to its great effort of amusing itself for three months, and the *Morning Post* recorded, morning by morning, some fresh additions to the big fair. The Davenports, in virtue of Mr. Davenport's modest contribution to the task of governing the nation, had been duly entered on the books for the year, and their blinds in Grosvenor Square testified to the accuracy of the announcement.

Reggie and Gertrude were sitting in the dining-room about half-past ten one morning. Reggie was apt to treat breakfast as a movable feast, and this morning he had been out riding till after ten, and had only just come back. It was a hot, bright day, and he had taken the liberty, which had broadened down from precedent to custom, to ride in a straw hat. This particular straw hat was new, and had a very smart I. Z. ribbon round it, and Gertrude was seeing how it would look on her. She was suffering from a slight cold, and had not gone out with him, but she found it pleasant enough to wait, after she had finished breakfast, and skim the daily papers till he returned.

She was deeply absorbed in the total disappearance of a French poodle when Reggie entered after dressing, and she laid down the paper to pour out tea for him.

"The Row was fuller this morning," said he, "and the Parliamentary train was in great force."

"What's the Parliamentary train?"

"Oh! the string of people who walk up and down very slowly, with a row of grooms behind; you know the sort."

"Any one there you knew?"

"Yes; several people. Gerty, give me another bit of sugar. Percy was there, looking for his sister. Apparently they've come back. Jim Armine was there too, also looking for Percy's sister."

"Lady Hayes?"

"Yes," said Reggie, eating steadily on. "I went and looked too. But we couldn't find her. By the way, Percy wants us to go there to lunch."

Gertrude had a sudden sense that all this had happened before, that she was going to act again in a rather distasteful scene. She had a sudden, instinctive desire not to go there, a quite irrational dislike to the idea.

"Oh! I can't," she said. "I've got a cold."

Reggie looked up innocently.

"Oh! I'm so sorry for not asking. Is it worse? Poor dear!"

Gertrude had a quite unusual dislike of white, excusable lies.

"No, it's not worse; it's rather better," she said.

"Let's go, then."

"Oh! I don't want to, Reggie," she said. "I want to go to the concert at St. James'. They're going to do the Tannhäuser overture."

"That's Wagner, isn't it?" said Reggie, doubtfully. "I think Wagner is ugly."

"Oh, you exceedingly foolish boy," said Gertrude. "You might as well call a storm at sea ugly."

"I don't care," said Reggie, "I think it is hideous. Besides, I want to go to the Hayes."

"Oh, well, then you just sha'n't," said Gertrude. "Really, I want to go awfully to this."

"But it'll be much worse for your cold than going out to lunch."

"Oh, I give up my cold," said she. "I haven't got one, really."

Reggie ate marmalade attentively.

"Do take me to the concert," said Gertrude. "I'm going away in two days. You can go and lunch with the Hayes then. It's a waste of time going out to lunch."

"You see, I promised to go to the Hayes," he said.

"Oh, nonsense! Send a note to say you have got to go to the concert. It's quite true; you have got to go."

"Of course, if I have got to—" said he slowly.

"That's right. It begins at three, doesn't it? No; don't say we can do both, because it is quite impossible. You're very good to me, Reggie."

Gertrude felt intensely relieved, but she could not have told why. There had been something in the conversation she had held with Reggie, six months before, on the subject of Eva, which remained in her mind, and gave her a sense, not of danger, but of distrust. A sensitive mind need not, usually is not, the most analytical, and for this reason, to apply analysis to her unwillingness to see Eva, would yield either no results, or false ones. There is an instinct in animals which enables them to discriminate between their friends and their foes, and the keener that instinct is, the more instantaneous it is in its working. The anatomist can tell us the action of the heart with almost absolute accuracy; he can say how the blood gets oxydised in the lungs, how it feeds the muscles and works the nerves—but the one thing he cannot tell us is, why it does so. And these instincts, like the action of the heart, can be noted and expressed, but the reason of their working we shall not know just yet. An action may be pulled to pieces like a flower, and divided into its component parts, and labelled with fifty crack-jaw names, but the life of the flower ceases not to be a delicate, insoluble mystery to us.

Reggie was very fond of music, but it was compatible, or rather essential, that his particular liking for it prompted him to say that Wagner seemed to him to be "awfully ugly." Nor was it such a far cry that he should assert, that same evening to Gertrude, that he had thought the "Overture to Tannhäuser" "awfully pretty."

Gertrude had been rather silent as they drove back. But something had prompted her to say to Reggie that evening, as they sat in the drawing-room before dinner:

"Ah! Reggie, I am so glad you are good."

Reggie's powers of analysis were easily baffled, and it is no wonder that he felt puzzled.

"I don't like bad people," he said.

"Nor do I, a bit," said Gertrude. "I am glad you don't either. I thought of that this afternoon at the concert."

"Oh! I listened to the music," said Reggie. "I liked it awfully."

"Yes, I know, but it suggested that to me. Half of the overture—all that rippling part seemed so wicked. I think Wagner must have been a bad man. He evidently meant it to be much more attractive than the other."

"I don't see how you can say some parts are wicked and some good. It's all done on the fiddles, you know."

Gertrude laughed.

"I hope you'll never understand, then," she said. "I prefer you as you are. After all, that matters a great deal."

The gong had sounded, and Mrs. Davenport, as she entered the room, heard the last words.

"What doesn't Reggie understand?" she asked.

"Gertrude said she thought some of the overture was wicked," said he, "and I said I didn't know what she meant. Is it very stupid of me?"

Mrs. Davenport looked up quickly at Gertrude.

"No, dear; I think it's very wise of you," she said.

Reggie jumped up.

"I didn't know I was ever wise," he said. "It's really a delightful discovery. Thank you, mummy. Gerty, you'll have to respect me for ever, now you know I'm wise. I shall invest in a sense of dignity."

"I never said you were wise," remarked Gertrude, "and I refuse to be responsible for any opinions but my own."

"Oh, I'll be responsible," murmured Mrs. Davenport.

Reggie looked from one to the other with the air of an intelligent dog.

"I daresay it's all right," he said, "but I don't know what it's all about."

"Oh! Reggie, you do understand," said Gertrude; "don't be ridiculous."

Reggie looked at her with the most genuine frankness.

"I don't understand a word, but I should like you to explain it very much."

Gertrude frowned and turned away to greet Jim Armine, who was dining with them. The vague pain which she had felt before was with her now. Somehow, she and Reggie seemed to have got on to different levels.

It was his moral, not his intellectual, understanding which appeared to her every now and then as almost entirely wanting. What puzzled her was that she had been entirely unconscious of any such defect till a few months ago, and her present knowledge of it struck her somehow as not being the natural outcome of increased intimacy, but rather as if her own moral understanding, by which she judged Reggie, had been developed and showed the want of it in him. But here again the vague instinctiveness of the feeling in her mind precluded analysis. All she knew was that she viewed things rather differently from him, and that this difference had not always been there. But pity is akin to love, and love, when joined with pity, is not less love, but love joined to the most human protective instinct, which, if anything, adds tenderness to passion.

Jim Armine had been lunching with the Hayes, and brought a minatory message for Reggie. Why had he said he would come to lunch and bring Miss Carston, and then never turned up.

Reggie behaved in the most unchivalrous manner.

"It was all Gerty's fault," he said. "She made me go to hear music."

"But you wrote to say so, didn't you, Reggie?"

Reggie began to wish he had taken the blame on himself.

"Yes, I *wrote*," he said.

"And forgot to send it," interpolated Mrs. Davenport. "Reggie, you are simply abominable. You must go to call, and explain."

"Oh, you can write a note to say how sorry you are," said Gertrude, suddenly.

The remark was insignificant enough, but to Gertrude it was the outcome of a feeling not at all insignificant. She felt as if she had inadvertently said something she did not mean to say, without reflecting that, to the others, the words were capable of a much less momentous interpretation. She looked up quickly at Mrs. Davenport, fearing for a moment that her self-betrayal was patent. Mrs. Davenport also remembered at the moment a certain conversation which she and Gertrude had had one night some months ago, and their eyes met. That look puzzled the elder woman; she had not fathomed Gertrude's feeling on the subject of Lady Hayes, when she spoke to her about her, and the mystery remained still unsolved. The idea that Gertrude was in any way the prey of a jealous fear was too ridiculous to be entertained.

The Dowager Lady Hayes, who was staying with them, entered somewhat opportunely at this moment, followed by Mr. Davenport, and they all went in to dinner. That veteran lady appeared to be in a state of mind which, when it occurs in children, is called fractiousness.

She always took a homœopathic dose in globular form before dinner, which was placed in a little wooden box by her place, but to-night the dose had not been set out, and she disconcerted everybody horribly by saying, during the first moment of silence, inevitable, when English people meet to dine together, and in a voice of stentorian power,—

"My dinner pills."

A hurried consultation took place among the flunkies, and, after a few moments' search, the box was found, and handed to her on a salver. Old Lady Hayes held them up a moment and rattled them.

"Pepsine," she announced; "obtained from the gastric juices of pigs. An ostrich couldn't eat the food we eat, and at these hours, without suffering from indigestion. I would sooner eat a box of tin tacks than an ordinary English dinner at half-past eight, without my pepsine."

Mrs. Davenport cast a responsible eye over the *menu*, which, to the ordinary mind, appeared sufficiently innocent. She was always divided between the inclination to laugh and to be polite when dealing with Lady Hayes, which produced an inability to say anything.

Eva, as we have seen, adopted a different method; she neither laughed nor was she polite, but she was respectfully insolent, which is a very different matter. The utter indifference of her manner produced a sort of chemical affinity in those widely-sundered qualities, just as electricity produces a chemical affinity between oxygen and hydrogen, which turns them into pure water, though both gases seem sufficiently remote, to the unchemical mind, from their product.

"*Soufflé*," continued the dowager, glancing down the *menu*, "when composed of meat—that is, of nitrogenous substance—is utterly unsuitable to human food. It produces a distention—"

But Mrs. Davenport broke in,—

"Dear Lady Hayes, let me send for the wing of a chicken. I know you like chicken wing."

A sigh resembling relief went round the table. Mrs. Davenport had broken the charmed circle, who were waiting, like the cities of Sodom and Gomorrah, for the unaccountable brimstone to descend on them. Reggie began to talk very rapidly about the Ascot cup; Jim Armine engaged Mrs. Davenport on the Irish question; and Mr. Davenport, by way of transition, asked Lady Hayes whether gas was not very unhealthy.

But the subject of gas did not appear to interest the old lady. She wished to talk about something else, and when she wished to do anything, she did it.

"My daughter-in-law—" she began.

Reggie was still discussing, or rather enunciating, truths or untruths on the chances of Orme, and Lady Hayes's words did not reach him. But Lady Hayes was accustomed to demand a universal deference and attention for her remarks. So she glared at Reggie, who soon caught her eye—it was impossible not to catch her eye very soon when it meant business—and subsided.

"My daughter-in-law," repeated the dowager— "whom I saw this afternoon, driving a dogcart in the Park—it was quite unheard of for a young woman to drive a dogcart alone when I was young—asked me to tell you all to keep Monday week open. She is sending out cards for a dance on that day—or rather she has sent them out, and she forgot to send them to you. Therefore I am a penny postman. She would be glad to see you all. Personally, I think the dances that are given now are simply disgusting. They are very unhealthy, because everyone sits up at the time when the ordinary evening fever sets in; that is, from twelve to two. But I promised to give her message. I am responsible no further. And the cotillion is indecent."

Mr. Davenport made a bad matter worse.

"I am sure there will be none of that romping which you so rightly—ah!—dislike," he said. "I always think—
"

But what Mr. Davenport always thought will never be known, for her ladyship interrupted him.

"It is based on immorality," she announced; "it is an exhibition that would disgrace any Christian country, and more especially England."

"Why especially England?" asked Jim, who was conscious of a challenge in her words.

"Because English people seem to pretend to a high morality more than any other nation."

"And are you cruel enough to include your daughter-in-law in that category?" asked Jim.

"Eva Hayes is very English," said the old lady.

"I am sure she never made any pretence of an exceptional morality," remarked Jim, eating his nitrogenous food, and getting angry.

"No one would accuse her of being exceptionally moral."

"I said she didn't make a pretence of it," said Jim.

Mrs. Davenport threw herself into the breach, and asked the dowager how digitalis was made.

Gertrude was sitting next Jim Armine, and wished to know more. Old Lady Hayes was well embarked on the structure of foxglove seeds, and she turned to Jim.

"You know Lady Hayes very well, don't you?" she asked.

"I was with them in Algiers last year."

"Do you like her very much?"

"That's a wrong word to use, somehow," he said. "I think she is the cleverest woman I ever saw, and, perhaps, the most interesting," he added, in a burst of veiled confidence.

"Ah!"—it was somewhat discouraging to hear that so many people took this as their main characteristic—"I don't know her at all. But I don't feel as if I should like her."

"I believe women dislike her very much, as a rule," remarked Jim, drily.

Something in his speech made Gertrude angry. It is always annoying, however modest an opinion we may have of ourselves, to be classed as a probable example to an universal rule. She waited a moment before she answered him.

"Why do you say that?"

"Well, there are very few people whom both women and men like much. Of course, I am not referring to the ordinary, stupid, good-natured people who are universal favourites—that is to say, whom no one dislikes—but to the people whom many men or women get excited about. She is one of those."

Mrs. Davenport was beginning to collect eyes—that is to say, she was looking at Gertrude, for no one could collect the dowager's eyes—and Gertrude rose in obedience.

"I think I know what you mean," she said.

Jim was left in excusable uncertainty as to what she meant, and the ladies left the room.

Mr. Davenport sat down again with an air of relief.

"I have always been considered a strong man," he said, "but, by the side of that old lady, I am a cripple and a baby. Get the cigarettes, Reggie."

"She told me that cigarettes were slow but certain death, yesterday," remarked Reggie, "but she cannot make me rude to her. It would be such a pity."

"Oh! she regards you as a possible convert," said Jim. "She hopes that you will go about with eight holes in your boots before long."

"How does she get on with Percy's sister?" asked Reggie, innocently.

Jim Armine laughed.

"Didn't you know you were her ark? She got routed in several pitched battles, and retired precipitately."

"That was when you were abroad last year, Reggie," said Mr. Davenport. "She came here one day with her boxes and medicines, and asked us to take her in. She gave no reason; but Lady Hayes told your mother."

"Was Lady Hayes so rude to her?"

Jim Armine laughed.

"She was so polite, on the contrary. Don't you know her?"

Gertrude went off next morning to meet Mrs. Carston at Tunbridge, and go with her to Aix. Reggie went with her to Victoria, and had parting words on the platform.

"I wish you were coming with me, Reggie," said Gertrude. "We're going to Lucerne in a month from now, when mother has had her course. That will be towards the end of June. Do come. It is an awfully nice place, and you can go up mountains—or row if you like. Will you?"

Reggie thought it a brilliant and feasible idea.

"I don't care a bit about London," he said, "and I do happen to care about you. It will be lovely. Write to me just before you go there, and tell me the hotel, and so on. Of course, I'll come. Ah! good-bye, Gerty."

The train moved slowly out of the station, and Reggie was left standing on the platform, waiting for it to curl away into the dark arch which soon swallowed it up. He had lost a great deal, and he went home somewhat silently.

That evening there was a great reception at one of the Foreign Embassies. Mrs. Davenport was the sister of the Ambassador's wife, and, after dinner, she asked whether anybody was going with her. Her husband eschewed such festivities; like a sensible man, he preferred, he said, to sit quietly at home, than to stand wedged in among a crowd of people who didn't care whether they saw him or not, and fight his way into a stuffy drawing-room. Reggie was sitting in the window, which he had thrown wide open, and was reading *The Field*. He had written a short note to Gertrude because he missed her, and as her bodily presence was not there, he felt it was something to communicate with her, but letter-writing was a difficulty to him, and the note had been very short.

An idea seemed to strike Mrs. Davenport when she saw him.

"Reggie, why don't you come?"

"I'll come if you like. Will it be amusing? Yes; I should like to come. Let me smoke in the carriage, mummy."

The two went downstairs together, and got into the carriage.

"Poor old boy," said Mrs. Davenport, laying her hand on his, "you will feel rather lonely to-night. I thought you'd like to come."

"It's an awful bore, Gerty having to go away," said Reggie, without any obvious discontent, "but it's only for a month, you know. I'm going to join her at Lucerne, if you don't want me. I hope there's something to do there. She said there were some mountains about. I shall climb."

Mrs. Davenport was conscious of a slight chill.

"Well, there'll be Gerty there," she said.

"Oh, yes; of course," said Reggie. "I shouldn't think of going if she wasn't there. You said I might smoke, didn't you?"

"I'm very happy about you and Gerty," said Mrs. Davenport, after a pause. "I should have chosen her of all others for a daughter-in-law."

"Oh! but I chose her first," said Reggie. "That's more important, isn't it? I wrote her a line this evening. I wish I didn't hate writing letters so. I can never think of anything to say. What do you say in letters, mother, you always write such good ones?"

"But you don't find it difficult to talk, Reggie. Why should you find it difficult to write?"

"Oh! but I do find it difficult to talk," said he. "It's dreadfully puzzling. I never talk to Gerty."

"Are you always quite silent, then?"

"No; but I don't talk. At least, I suppose I do talk, in a way. I babble, you know. She does most of the talking."

Mrs. Davenport laughed.

"Babble on paper, then," she said; "Gerty will like it just as well."

"Oh! but I can't. It's so silly if you put it down. Is this the Embassy? I hope I shall meet a lot of people I know."

Reggie's common sense was enormous. Gertrude had gone away, and she wouldn't come back for the wishing. He wished she had not gone very much, but here he was in England without her. Surely England without her was the same as England with her, except that she was not there. Her absence, from a practical point of view, did not take the taste out of everything else. How should it? She was a very charming person, the most charming person Reggie had ever met. But there were other charming people, on a distinctly lower level, no doubt, but they did not cease to be charming because Gertrude had gone to Aix. After all, Reggie agreed with the great materialistic philosophers of all time, though he had never read their works. Mrs. Davenport felt somewhat annoyed with this school of thought as she dismounted from the carriage.

The Embassy stood at the corner of a large square, and a broad, red carpet ran from the door across to the road, for royalty was expected. Inside the house the arrangements all corresponded with the magnificent promise of the red carpet. A row of gorgeous flunkies, a band in the hall beneath the stairs, several hundred pounds' worth of hot-house flowers banked up against the wall, a crowd of perfectly-dressed, bustling aristocrats, crowding up and staring, in the worst possible breeding, at a small space between two pillars, where three princesses were looking rather bored, and a similar number of princes were talking to the few who had managed, by dint of loyal shoves, to edge themselves into the august presences; the smiling host and hostess, the pleasant music of women's voices, crossing the somewhat sombre strains of the band below, all these things are the invariable concomitants of such festivities, and on the whole one crush is rather like another crush.

Mrs. Davenport and Reggie had moved slowly up the staircase, and Reggie certainly was finding it amusing. There were lots of people he knew, and he stood chatting on the stairs while Mrs. Davenport talked for a few moments to her sister.

Later on he was standing in a doorway between two of the big reception rooms, talking and laughing, and commanding, by reason of his height, a good deal of the room beyond, when he saw the crowd by the door opposite to him sway and move, as if a wind had passed over it; and through the room, plainly visible, for the crowd made way for her as she was walking with a prince, came a woman he had never seen before. She was tall, dressed in some pale, soft material; round her neck went a single row of diamonds, and above it rose a face for the like of which men have lived and died. Eva had a habit of looking over people's heads and noticing no one, but Reggie happened to be six foot three, and in his long, eager gaze was something that arrested Eva's attention. She looked at him fixedly and gravely, until the thing became absurd, and then she turned away with a laugh, and asked who that pretty boy was.

Reggie, when the spell of her look was broken, turned away too, and asked who the most beautiful woman in the world was.

"There, there," he cried, pointing at her, regardless of men or manners.

So the great loom clashed and crossed, and two more threads were woven, side by side, into the garment of God.

CHAPTER V.

There is a distinct tendency, if we may trust books on travels and early stages of religious belief among the uncivilised, dusky masses of the world to assign every event to a direct supernatural influence. Certain savages, if they hit their foot against a stone, will say that there is a demon in that stone, and they hasten to appease him by sacrificial sops. We see the exact opposite of this among those nations, which, like those in our own favoured isle, assign every event to pure chance. There is no harm in calling it chance, and there is no harm in assigning the most insignificant event to a local god, and the lesson we may learn from these elementary reflections is, that there are, at least, two points of view from which we may regard anything.

To adopt, however, the nomenclature of the day, this chance that led Lady Hayes to walk down that room at the French Embassy, when Reggie was standing at the door, was a very big chance. One of the least important results of it was that it occasioned this book to be written.

Reggie was, as I have mentioned before, a very susceptible young man. He fully realised, *in propriâ personâ*, Mrs. Davenport's "healthy condition" of being in a chronic state of devotion, and this, coupled to his extreme susceptibility, will fully account for the fact that he moved slowly after Lady Hayes, till, by another chance meeting, she fell in with his mother, who had followed him from the top of the stairs, and got introduced. Mrs. Davenport pronounced the mystic words, "Lady Hayes, may I introduce my son Reggie," and the thing was done.

Lady Hayes was amused to find herself so quickly introduced to the "pretty boy" who had stared at her, and as her prince had gone away, she was ready to talk to him, and it appeared that he was ready to talk to her.

"I was so sorry I couldn't come to lunch yesterday," he began, "and I forgot to send a note to say I couldn't."

"We have lunch every day," remarked Lady Hayes, gravely. "Come to-morrow. I shall think it very rude if you cut me again. So will Percy. I shall send him to call you out."

"I know Percy very well," said Reggie. "I'm awfully fond of him. I don't believe he'd call me out."

Eva looked at him again with some amusement. This particular type was somewhat new to her. He was so extraordinarily young.

"I'm very fond of Percy too," she said.

"Oh, but he's your brother," said Reggie.

"So he is."

She laughed again.

"How extremely handsome he is," she thought to herself, in a parenthesis. "Why was I never so young as that."

Then aloud,—

"I'm going to ask you to give me your arm, and take me to get something cold to drink. Do you like ices?" she asked with some experimental malice.

"Lemon water," said Reggie after consideration, "but not cream ices, they're stuffy, somehow. I'd better tell my mother where we're going, and then I can meet her again afterwards."

"Ah! Lady Hayes," exclaimed the voice of their host's brother, "I've been looking for you. Prince Waldenech wishes to be introduced to you. Adeline sent me to find you."

Lady Hayes raised her eyebrows.

"I'll come by and by," she said. "I can't now. I'm going to eat an ice—lemon water. Tell her I will be back soon—ten minutes."

"Prince Waldenech's just going."

"Then I am afraid it will be a pleasure deferred for me. Come, Mr. Davenport. You shall have a lemon water ice, and so will I."

"That was very kind of you to keep your engagement to me," said Reggie.

"You deserved I should cut you, as you cut me yesterday. But I felt inclined to keep this engagement, which makes all the difference. Of course, if you'd felt inclined to come yesterday you wouldn't have forgotten. One never forgets things one likes."

"Oh, but I did feel inclined to come," said Reggie, and stopped short.

"It was self denial, was it?"

"No, I was wanted to do something else."

"What did you do else, if it isn't rude to ask?"

"Oh! I went to the concert at St. James'. They did the Tannhäuser overture."

"Did you like it?"

"Oh yes, it was awfully pretty."

Eva laughed again.

"I expected you would think it stupid or ugly."

"How did you know?" asked he.

"You told me yourself. I knew almost as soon as you began to speak. Never mind. Don't look so puzzled. You shall come to the opera some night with me, and hear it again. I'm dreadfully rude, am I not?"

"You rude! No!" said Reggie, stoutly. "But you mustn't mind my being stupid."

"I like stupid people."

"I should have thought you would have hated them. But I'm glad you like them," said he, blushing furiously.

"What pretty speeches! But you are quite wrong about my hating stupid people—I don't say you're stupid, you know—but in the abstract. You see I know much more about you already than you know about me. I was right about your thinking Wagner ugly, and you were wrong about my disliking stupid people. There's the buffet. I shall sit down here, and you shall bring two ices—one for yourself and one for me."

It was characteristic of Reggie that he wrote an effusive though short note to Gertrude next day, saying that he had met Lady Hayes at the French Embassy, that she was perfectly beautiful and awfully nice, and that he couldn't write any more because he was just going out to lunch with her, and that three days after this another short note followed this one, saying that Lady Hayes was awfully anxious to meet her—Gertrude—that Gertrude must come home as quick as ever she could, and that Mrs. Arbuthnot was going to Lucerne in July, so that, if Mrs. Carston could join her there, Gertrude could come straight home. He had heard that Lucerne was very slow.

Lady Hayes had been "awfully nice" to Reggie. She had hardly ever seen anything so fresh as he was. About two days after their first meeting, Reggie had told her, with unblushing candour, all about Gertrude, and Lady Hayes was charmed to hear it. Reggie's confession of his young love seemed simply delightful. He was so refreshingly unversed in the ways of the world. He had spoken of Gertrude with immense ardour, and had shown Lady Hayes her photograph. He had been there to call one afternoon, and had found her alone. They had tea in the little tent over the porch, which Eva kept there "*en permanence,*" and in which she had routed her mother-in-law a year ago.

She was sitting in a low, basket chair, looking at the photograph, which Reggie had just put into her hand, and had turned from it to his eager, down-looking face, which appeared very attractive.

"Charming," she said, "simply charming! You will let me have this, won't you? and one of yourself, too, and they shall go on the chimney-piece in my room. Really, you have no business to be as happy as this; it isn't at all fair."

Reggie stood up, and drew in a long breath.

"Yes; I'm awfully happy. I never knew anyone as happy as I am. But may I send you another photograph of her? I can get one from the photographer. You see, she gave me this herself."

"No; certainly not," said Eva. "I want this one. I want it now. Surely you have no need of photographs. You have got the original, you see. And this is signed by her."

"Oh! but I'm sure she'd sign another one for you, if I ask her to."

"If it please my lord the king," said Eva. "No; I want this one. Mayn't I have it?"

"Yes, it doesn't make any difference, does it?" said Reggie, guilelessly. "I've got the original, as you say."

"Thanks so much. That is very good of you."

"Of course it's an exchange," said Reggie.

"Ah, you're mercenary after all. I knew I should find a weak point in you. Very good, it's an exchange. But I don't suppose Miss Carston would care for my photograph. She doesn't know me, you see."

"Well, anyhow, mine must be an exchange."

"You're very bold," said Eva. "Of course you could make me give it you; you're much stronger than I am. If you held me down in this chair, and throttled me until I promised, I should have to promise. I'm very cowardly. I should never have made an early Christian martyr. I should have sworn to believe in every heathen goddess, and the Thirty-Nine Articles long before they put the thumbscrew really on."

"Yes, I expect the thumbscrew hurt," said Reggie, meditatively.

"Don't you miss her tremendously?" said Eva, looking at the photograph again. "I should think you were miserable without her."

"Oh, I don't think I could be miserable if I tried," said Reggie.

"Most people find it so easy to be miserable. But I don't think you're like most people."

"I certainly don't find it easy to be miserable; not natural, at least. You see, Gerty's only away for a month, and it wouldn't do the slightest good if I was miserable."

"You have great common sense. Really, common sense is one of the rarest things in the world. Ah, Hayes, that is you, is it? Do you know Mr. Reggie Davenport?"

Lord Hayes made a neat little bow, and took some tea.

"There is a footman waiting to know if you were in," he said. "Somebody has called."

"Please tell the man that I'm not in, or that I'm engaged."

Reggie started up.

"Why didn't you tell me to go?" he said. "I'm afraid I've been here an awful time."

"Sit down again," said Eva. "You are my engagement. I don't want you to go at all."

Reggie sat down again.

"Thank you so much," he said.

"There has been," said Lord Hayes, stirring his tea, "there has been a most destructive earthquake in Zante. The town, apparently, has been completely demolished."

Reggie tried to look interested, and said "Indeed."

"Do you know where Zante is?" asked Eva. "I don't."

"I think it's in the Levant," said Reggie.

"That makes it worse."

"Zante is off the west coast of Greece," said Lord Hayes. "I was thinking at one time of building a villa there."

"Ah," said Eva, "that would be charming. Have you finished your tea, Hayes? Perhaps you would order the carriage for to-night. I have to go out at half-past ten. You must find it draughty here with your bad cold. You would be prudent to sit indoors."

Reggie looked at him with sympathy as he went inside.

"I'm sorry he's got a cold," he said.

"It is an intermittent catarrh," said Eva, with amusement. "There is nothing to be anxious about—thanks."

Lord Hayes had gone indoors without protest or remonstrance, but he was far from not feeling both. The polite indifference which Eva had practised earlier in their married life—the neutral attitude—had begun to wear very thin. When they were alone, he did not care much whether she was polite or not, but he distinctly objected to be made a fool of in public. Why he had not made a stand on this occasion, and insisted that he had no cold at all, which was indeed the case, he found himself wondering, even as he was making his retreat, but that wonder brought him no nearer to doing it. Investigation into mesmerism and other occult phenomena are bringing us nearer a rational perception of such forces, and we are beginning to believe that each man has a set of moral muscles, which exercise moral force, just as he has a similar physical system which is superior or inferior to that of another man. And to judge by any analogy which is known to us, it appears inevitable that when one moral organisation strips as it were to another moral organisation, that a fight, a victory and a defeat will be the result. Eva's prize fight with her husband had lasted more than a year, and though it was practically over, yet the defeated party still delivered itself of small protests from time to time, which resembled those anonymous challenges, or challenges in which it is not distinctly stated that "business is meant," and which are common in the columns of such periodicals as register the more palpable sort of encounters.

Lord Hayes, in fact, still preserved his malignant potentialities. It was a source of satisfaction to him that he still retained a slight power of annoying Eva in small ways. This he did not venture to use in public, because, if Eva suspected anything like a whisper of a challenge not strictly in private, she would take steps to investigate it, and these public investigations were not to his taste. But in private he could vent a little malignity without being publicly pommelled for it.

Thus it came about that, when they were seated at dinner alone that night, Lord Hayes said,—

"May I ask who that young man was with you? He was here yesterday, I believe."

"Didn't I introduce you?" said Eva. "I thought I did. It was Reggie Davenport."

"What do you intend to do with him?"

"I beg your pardon?"

"Is he to be a sort of Jim Armine the second?"

Eva finished eating her soufflé without replying, and Lord Hayes rather prematurely thought the shot had told.

"Oh! dear no," she said at length, "nothing of the sort. I am very fond of Reggie Davenport. Quite devoted to him, in fact. He is quite the nicest young man I ever saw."

"I thought you were very fond of Jim."

"How dull men are," said Eva. "Any woman would have seen at once that it was he who was fond of me. But with Reggie—he asked me to call him Reggie—it is reciprocal, I think. I should advise you to be jealous."

"I should not think of such a thing," said he. "Nothing makes a man so ridiculous as to be jealous."

"Except, perhaps, to be complaisant," said Eva, not sparing herself in the desire not to spare him. "I think that is absurder still."

"I have no intention of being complaisant."

"That is such a comfort," said Eva; "it is a great thing to know that one's honour is safe in one's husband's hands. You are my guardian angel. Are you coming to the ball to-night? Yes? I shall be upstairs in my room. Please send a man to tell me when the carriage is round. And don't keep me waiting as you did on Thursday."

Eva went upstairs into her room, and found, among her letters, Reggie's photograph, which he had already sent. She took it up and looked at it for a few moments, and placed it by the side of Gertrude's. Something, perhaps the scene at dinner, had made her restless, and she walked up and down the room, with her long, white dress sweeping the ground behind her.

"What is the matter with me?" she thought to herself impatiently. "Surely I, of all people—"

She sat down again and opened some of her letters. There was one from her mother, who was coming to stay with them for a week or two.

"I hear such a lot about you," she wrote; "everyone seems to be talking about nothing else except Lady

Hayes and her beauty and success. And when I think that it is my own darling little Eva, I can only feel full of gratitude and thankfulness that a mother's prayers for her own daughter's welfare have been answered so fully and bountifully. But I hope that, in the riches of love and position and success, which have been so fully granted her, she will not forget—"

Eva tore the letter in half with a sudden, dramatic gesture, and threw it into the paper-basket. She was annoyed, ashamed of herself for her want of self-control, but a new spring of feeling had been rising in her this last day or two, that gave her a sense of loss, of something missed which might never come again, a feeling which she had experienced in some degree after her marriage, when she found out what it was to be linked to a man who did not love her, and whom she was beginning to detest. But now the feeling was deeper, keener, more painful, and from the mantlepiece Reggie's photograph looked at her, smiling, well-bred, well-dressed, and astonishingly young. Surely it couldn't be that!

An hour later a message came that the carriage was round, and she went downstairs again, impassive, cold, perfectly beautiful. As she swept down into the hall, Lord Hayes, who was standing there, with a pair of white kid gloves in his hand, was suddenly struck and astonished at her beauty. He felt freshly proud at having become the owner of this dazzling, perfect piece of life. He moved forward to meet her, and in a burst of pleased proprietorship, laying his hand on her bare arm,—

"My dear Eva," he said, "you are more beautiful than ever."

Eva looked at him for a moment fixedly; then she suddenly shook his hand off.

"Ah! don't touch me," she said shuddering, and moved past him and got into the carriage.

Lord Hayes, however, had one consolation which Eva could never deprive him of, and that was the knowledge that she was his, and the knowledge that she knew it. She might writhe and shrink, or treat him with indifference, or scorn, or anger, but she could never alter that, except by disgracing herself, and she was too proud and sensitive, as he knew, to do anything of the sort. Consequently, her assaults on him at dinner on the subject of complaisance did not trouble him for a moment. It was morally impossible, he felt, for her to put him into such a position, for her own position was as dear to her as he was odious. His lordship had a certain cynical sense of humour, which whispered that though this state of things was not pleasant, it was distinctly amusing.

Meantime, as the days went on, if Eva was beginning to be a little anxious about herself, Mrs. Davenport was not at her ease about Reggie. Gertrude's letters came regularly, and he liked to let his mother read them, and they, at any rate, betrayed no dissatisfaction. But in one of these which arrived soon after the last interview recorded between Lady Hayes and Reggie, Mrs. Davenport suddenly felt frightened. It was a very short sentence which gave rise to this feeling, and apparently a very innocent one:—

"What on earth does Lady Hayes want my photograph for?"

Reggie was sitting by the open window after a particularly late breakfast, smoking into the window box. His back was turned to the room, and he was apparently absorbed in his occupation. He had read Gertrude's letter as he was having breakfast, and when he had finished, he had given it to his mother, saying—

"Such a jolly note from Gerty; you will like to see it, mummy."

Mrs. Davenport read it and looked up with some impatience at the lounging figure in the window seat.

"What's this about Gerty's photograph and Lady Hayes?" she asked. "I don't understand."

Reggie did not appear to hear, and continued persecuting a small, green fly that was airing itself on a red geranium, and was consequently conspicuous.

"You may smoke in here, Reggie," said Mrs. Davenport, raising her voice a little; "come in and sit down."

Reggie turned round somewhat unwillingly. He had heard his mother's first question, and it had suddenly struck him that it was rather an awkward one. A very frank nature will, on occasions, use extreme frankness to cover the deficiency of it, and he decided that the whole truth, very openly stated, was less liable to involve him in difficulties than the subtlest prevarication.

"Oh, Lady Hayes said she wanted Gerty's photograph and mine," he said, walking towards his mother. "Of course, I gave them her, and she gave me hers in exchange. I told Gerty all about it in a letter."

Mrs. Davenport looked up at him, and observed that his face was flushed.

"What an odd request," she said.

"I don't see why. I know her quite well, somehow, though I have only known her such a short time."

There was a short silence. Mrs. Davenport was casting about in her mind as to how she might learn what she wanted, without betraying her desire to know it.

"Did you write to Gerty yesterday?" she asked at length.

"No, I didn't," said Reggie, frankly. "I was out all day and then I went to the Hayes in the evening."

"Are you going out to Lucerne at the end of the month?"

"No, I think not; somebody told me—Lady Hayes, I think—that it was awfully slow. I told Gerty the Arbuthnots were going out, and suggested she should leave Mrs. Carston with them and come back to London. I like London, somehow, this year."

Mrs. Davenport was beginning to understand. She could have found it in her heart at that moment to label Eva with some names that would have astonished her.

"Does Lady Hayes talk about Gerty much?"

"Oh, yes, a good deal; at least, she lets me talk about her whenever I want to."

"Is that a good deal?"

Reggie frowned. He had been acting for this last week or so with such spontaneity, obeying so instantaneously his inclinations, that he found it hard to answer questions about these things. It is always harder to recall what we have done unthinkingly, than what has been the result of thought or conscious effort.

"I don't know," he said. "We talk about her now and then, but we talk about a thousand things. I don't know what you mean. Lady Hayes said the other day that she was sure Gerty would detest her."

"I think Lady Hayes is probably quite right."

"Then it would be very unreasonable of Gerty," said Reggie, frowning again, "and I don't know why you think so. Why should Gerty detest her?"

"Does she strike you as the sort of woman Gerty would like?"

"I don't think I ever thought about it till Lady Hayes mentioned it, and I disagreed with her."

"You told me the other day that you and Gerty agreed that you only liked good people. I don't think Gerty would think her good."

Reggie flushed angrily.

"I don't really see what you are driving at," he said rather vehemently, because he did see. "I think I won't talk about her any more if you don't mind, mummy. You see she's very kind and delightful to me, and that's all that I have any right to judge by, and I'm sure she'd be just as nice to Gerty."

He sauntered out of the room with rather exaggerated slowness, feeling a little uneasy. He was just conscious that this new element which had come into his life was a very absorbing one, and he wondered a little how absorbing it was in proportion to other things. Eva showed to him a different side to that she showed to the world; she was careful when he was there not to say quite what she was in the habit of saying, when she was with others. She regarded him as a child—a very charming, delightful child—and she knew that the greatest respect, as one of the most finished artists of human life has said, was due to children. In fact, according to his data, Reggie's glowing, adoring picture of her was faithful enough. Why Eva behaved like that to him is a question which concerned her alone, and of which the answer was even now working out in her mind. She had tried the world for two years, and had found it distinctly wanting. It amused her at times, but it bored her more frequently. The frantic interest which she had taken in men and women was beginning to pall a little; even the interest she had taken in herself was not so deep as it had been. It must be remembered that the world, as she knew it, was a certain section of society which, however much its units differ in individuality, is, to a certain extent, all dulled and choked in the limitations of its class, the inexorable need to be well dressed, to be successful, to be smart. Diversity of interest is the only thing that will make interest long lived; and diversity was exactly what was wanting. The gossip, the whispered scandals, the scheming, the jostling, were new to her at first, and she had drunk them down eagerly, but in her heart of hearts she knew that she was just a little tired of it all, and she was beginning to behave as others behaved, not because it was the most amusing thing that could be done, but because others behaved so. On this stale, gas-lit atmosphere Reggie had come like a whiff of fresh air. He had not the smallest interest in scandal or gossip, or any of those things in which her world found its entire interest settled. He was new, he was fresh, and he was young.

Just now that meant a good deal to Eva, for it was the type to her of all she had missed. He was, again, distinctly of her own class—he could not offend the most fastidious taste—Eva would never have cultivated a grocer's assistant, however fresh—and he was extremely handsome and attractive in appearance. Her feeling for him was made out of one large factor, and several small ones; for his pleasant manner, his frank good breeding, his beauty, she liked him; for his serene, stainless youth she had a sort of liking that was quite new to her.

That the conception he had formed of her was very far from representing her, she knew well. She had deliberately held the reckless, cynical, unprincipled part of her nature rigorously in check when she was with him. She was sympathetic, simple, divinely kind to him because she liked him so much and knew that he would detest the other half of her. But now a mixture of motives led her to determine to let him know all. It had come to this, that she felt that inevitable longing to throw her nature open to him, to drop this elaborate suppression, to let him see her as she was, and judge her. Our deeper emotions are thickly entwined with the fibres of honesty, which makes even those who are least honest, in ordinary life, scrupulously truthful and open when those deeper emotions are touched. To say that Eva was in love with Reggie would be both overstating it and understating it. He was the symbol to her of her lost ideals, which she found she had loved now she had lost them; and, humanly speaking, she found him very attractive as a substantial embodiment of these.

Eva was sitting in her room one morning, a few days after the talk Reggie had had with his mother, wondering how she had better carry her resolve out, when an idea struck her. She got up and wrote a short note to him:—

"I wonder if you would care to come to the opera to-night with me," she said. "Tannhäuser is being played, and I think I remember your saying you thought the overture very pretty. Do come. Dine here first."

"Jim Armine shall come too," thought Eva. "He shall chaperone us. Besides, I can't be worldly all alone with Reggie. I must have some one to be worldly with. Decidedly that is the best plan."

CHAPTER VI.

The opera began at half-past eight, and Eva, in her note to Reggie, had mentioned "seven sharp" as the hour for dinner, because she wanted to hear the overture. Reggie had routed up an "arrangement" of the music that afternoon, and had got his mother to play it to him, but whether it was that Mrs. Davenport's musical education had been conducted in her youth on the same principles of æsthetics that used to instil into the young idea the system of "touches" to indicate foliage, or that Reggie did not attend much—in any case, he pronounced it totally unintelligible, and, in his mind, reconsidered his previous verdict of it.

Reggie's "seven sharp" partook of the nature of "seven," but in a less degree of the nature of "sharp," and Jim Armine had already arrived and was talking to Eva. As he opened the door—he was already sufficiently at home to dispense with the formula of being shown up— Eva felt her resolve waver, but determined, if she could, to do what she had intended. She wheeled her chair a few inches further round, so as to be with her back to the door, and began talking in a hard, cold voice.

"Of course, there will be a tremendous scandal about it," she said to Jim, "but you know what the woman is like. Didn't you see her here a fortnight ago? Hayes thought her divine. Of course, men are always blind in such matters. If a woman is beautiful enough, they think she must be good. Now, women do just the opposite. If a woman is beautiful enough, they think she must be a villain. They are, probably, much more likely to be right than men. Ah! Reggie, you've come, have you? I know what your seven sharp is."

Reggie shook hands with her, and looked inquiring.

"Whom were you talking about?" he demanded.

"Oh! it would have been applicable to most women," said Eva. "There has been, or will be, a tremendous scandal about most of us, and it seems to me that most women have been here during this last fortnight. We have been having a week of parties, and Hayes will have to sell one of his villas, I expect. The parties have all been very stupid, but so are the villas, for that matter. Come, let's go in to dinner. Which of you gentlemen will take me in? You're the nephew of a marquis, are you not, Jim? Then you shall go in first, and Reggie and I will follow."

"I've been making my mother play the overture to me," remarked Reggie, as they sat down, "and I can't understand a note of it."

"Oh! the overture is the epitome to the play," said Eva; "you have to know the plot, and then the overture is easy enough. Let's see, I'll give you a little sketch of it. Tannhäuser is a good young man, Reggie—something like you—and he goes to Venusberg. Well, Venusberg is not at all the place for a good young man. There is no propriety of any sort observed there, and they are very lax about etiquette and other things. Never go to Venusberg, Reggie, or, if you do, take Mrs. Reggie with you. If she won't come—and I don't expect she will—you had better not go at all. It is said to be very unsettling."

Jim Armine laughed. Lady Hayes was inclined to be talkative, and he always thought it worth while listening to her when she was talkative, because she always had something to say whenever she said anything. He wondered a little why she had taken it into her head to say this just now, but she always talked with a purpose, and he was content to assume the purpose. But Reggie was wofully puzzled. He had not known her like this, and he very much wanted explanations.

"I don't understand," he said. "You know I'm very stupid. Do tell me what you mean."

Eva cast one look at his anxious, frowning face, and trifled with her fish.

"I must do it," she said to herself; "I cannot let things continue as they have been."

"Oh! it gets easier further on," she continued, "as Humpty Dumpty said; and you'll understand it all when you hear the overture again, according to your new lights. Of course, the Venusberg is only an interlude in Tannhäuser's life, and everyone has interludes in their lives, or else they would not be human. Tannhäuser is a pilgrim, and the pilgrims march about to slow music all the time. Venus, of course, does not go about to slow music—quite the contrary, in fact; and, when you hear the two together, the contrast is very striking. Tannhäuser goes away from Venusberg, you know, before the end, and dies in the odour of sanctity."

Eva stopped for a moment, and Jim Armine laughed again.

"You are admirably lucid," he said. "You seldom explain yourself so well."

"Thanks for the compliment," said Eva. "And you, Reggie, do you find me lucid?"

Reggie was listening to her with a puzzled air.

"I expect I shall understand better when I've seen it," he said.

"Yes; you can't fail to understand it then," said Eva, "or, if you don't, you will be even more charming than I thought you. I wonder if you are capable of it. I am talking nonsense to-night; you must forget it to-morrow."

"As long as you remember it just during the opera," said Jim maliciously.

Eva's mind was thoroughly made up, and she choked the rising misgivings.

"He must know some time," she thought, "and it is best I should tell him."

"You are going to be Adam in the garden of Eden, possibly for the last time," she said with mock solemnity, which covered her own earnestness; "to-night the fruit of the tree of the knowledge of good and evil will be offered you—"

"By the woman?" asked Jim, indicating Eva.

"On the contrary," said she, "by Augustus Harris. Every man since Adam has had it offered him sooner or later, Reggie, and the majority of them eat it. The apple, in this case, is Tannhäuser, accompanied by my comments on it. It's a funny sort of apple. I'm giving you the core first, which is rather dry, probably, and the fruit comes afterwards, like dessert after savouries."

"The core is rather hard," remarked Reggie unceremoniously.

"Oh, it will taste quite different when you chew it up with the fruit."

"Give us some more of the core," asked Jim.

"Well, there's Venus, of course," said Eva, "about whom I haven't told you anything yet. She is just the opposite to the pilgrim's march; she regards things from an entirely different standpoint, you know. I'm always a little sorry for Venus. Tannhäuser goes away just when she has got very fond of him."

Eva stopped a moment and looked at Reggie.

"But, of course, you mustn't consider her at all. Tannhäuser is usually done on Saturdays, you know, and Venus would not go at all well with Sunday morning service. Poor dear, how the Litany would bore her! She stops in the porch, when you go into church, and when you come out she is gone. She hasn't gone, really, you know; she is only having a stroll, and she always comes back, very often before Monday. If she doesn't come back, most men go to look for her, and they usually find her again."

Reggie stifled a sudden sense of misgiving with staunch loyalty, and smiled at Eva.

"I told you I was stupid," he said, "the first time I saw you, and I confess to being absolutely stupid now. I don't understand you a bit."

Jim regarded Reggie as a successful interloper, and could not resist the temptation to be slightly malicious.

"After all, it is the most delightful thing in the world to be able to keep up our mysteries," he said. "Nothing intelligible is so charming as what is mysterious. When you understand anything, the charm is gone."

"Nonsense, Jim," said Eva; "don't pay any attention to what he says, Reggie. It is very easy to be unintelligible."

"Yes, it seems to be," said Reggie, rather absently, but resenting Jim's remark, which savoured of patronising.

Eva laughed.

"You won't get any change out of him, Jim," she said. "He has often assured me he is very stupid, which no stupid person is capable of doing. I must go and put on a cloak. There is just time for you to smoke a cigarette before the carriage comes."

Eva got up and left the room, and Reggie lit a cigarette, and strolled to the window. He had no particular liking for Jim Armine, and Eva's words had disturbed him. He was growing more conscious of the fact that his life was beginning to find a new centre, and a mystery which was quite new to it. His strong, genuine liking and admiration for Gertrude had not diminished a whit, but he did not conceal from himself that he thought with more excitement about Eva. But he felt himself able to retain both these interests without any sense of compromise. He was engaged to marry

Gertrude, and he would have been genuinely puzzled if it had been suggested to him that such an engagement, to some minds, limited his liberty in becoming indefinitely interested in another woman. In fact, the extreme simplicity of his character appeared to be going to land him among some perilously complicated and unknown shoals. He was young, ardent and unreflective, and these divine gifts are capable of dealing back-handed blows in the most inopportune and unexpected ways.

But Eva's words this evening had startled and perplexed him, and his bewilderment was touched with distrust. He expected, as Eva had told him, to find the key to his perplexity in the opera to-night, and he half realised that the explanation might be appallingly significant. Years afterwards he remembered those few minutes, which he spent looking out of the window, with much greater clearness than he remembered what followed. A mental, like a physical shock, often produces a dimness in the memory. Men who have been in great peril of death will remember with great vividness the most insignificant circumstances just before that peril; how they were walking round the slippery corner of rocks coated with ice, how a little purple gentian grew just above the crevice where they found a handhold, how at their feet was a trickle of water, where the sun had melted the snow. Then came the slip, and the activity of the mind seems suddenly quiescent. As they slid powerlessly down the icy stair, they noticed nothing, even the bitterness of death was passed—they were inanimate arrows from the bow of natural laws.

In the same way the little details of those few minutes when he waited for Eva to put on her opera cloak were engraved indelibly on Reggie's mind. Years afterwards the faint, acrid smell of red geraniums brought back the whole evening with a throb of sudden awakening. The window was open, and the flower-box outside was in full scent and colour. A canary creeper climbed the trellis-work at the sides of the windows, and twined its green, muscular stalks round the painted wooden squares. Between, a row of gaudy geraniums grew up from a groundwork of low mignonette, not yet in full flower, and in the front of the box a fringe of dark blue lobelias shivered on their hair-like stalks in the evening air. Beyond lay the grimy, dusty, square garden, and over the road, between the house and it, bowled silent, smooth-running carriages, within which he caught sight of the shimmering of silk and jewels, and over all brooded the hot, weary sky, exhausted with the long, sultry hours, but beginning to grow a little more serene, a little less stifled in the cool of the evening.

Reggie looked at these things not knowing he was noticing them, and forbearing to guess what Eva meant. He was surprised to hear the door in the room behind open, and to find that Eva was ready, and his cigarette was nearly smoked out. He had not thought that she had been gone more than a few seconds.

"Well, Reggie," she said, "have you been thinking it all over? Are you prepared for the great change. I think it is coming to-night, but, of course, there is nothing so easy as prophesying, and nothing so inconclusive. Well! we shall see. At present the carriage is waiting, and we must be off."

It was still early when they arrived at the opera house, and the orchestra were just beginning to tune up. The house was still comparatively empty, but it was beginning to fill rapidly, for all London had suddenly discovered that Wagner was worth listening to, and that an overture was not necessarily as dispensable as a preface.

But at last the tuning was over, the violins had caught their A's correctly, and had hit the "four perfect fifths," the drums had been screwed up to the necessary tension, and the wind instruments were in their places, pregnant with the miraculous birth of sound. For these five strings, these tubes of brass were going not to interpret, but to present the actual mysteries which passed through the artist's brain. Music is, as it were, the speaker in the first person, whereas painting only deals with the vision secondhand. The painter represents a blaze of light by certain pigments—yellow, red, white—but these are only the symbols of what he wishes to tell us. He may not take liquid sunlight and place it on the canvas. His art is but a symbol, an algebra of tints to express certain other things. No colour he can use is in itself luminous, the resemblance it bears to light is only imagined by the spectator, in proportion as the artist presents us with contrasts, with sombre shadows or brooding clouds, and it is only by the aid of what he tries to represent that we can see his vision at all. But with the musician it is different—he deals with his materials direct; he takes sound pure, not a symbol of sound; his vision is woven of the waves of air which are eternal and original, not of chemical combinations of white lead, or the blood of cuttlefish. He mixes pure sound in his thought, and out of it "frames not a sound but a star." And Wagner, above all other musicians of all time, has taught an incredulous world what can be done with sound, his beautiful slave and master, just as Stevenson taught his faithless generation what could be done with steam. The emotions and passions of humanity are his harp, and this harp, touched by a master's finger, tells us what it knows. Thus in Tannhäuser he has presented us with the great problem of all time—the war between the lower, the bestial side of man, and something which mankind itself has declared to be higher—the pure, steadfast soul. He tears the hearts out of the breasts of Galahad and Messalina, bleeding and palpitating; he threads them together on his golden string, and then, the artist's work being over, he tosses them to us, and says "Choose." The materials for choice are all there, the whole of the data are before us, and as Tannhäuser chose once, so "chance" has ordained that each of us should choose, and the same thing called "chance" ordained that Reggie should choose that night.

There was a pause, a silence after the conductor had entered, and then the wooden instruments gave out half the problem. The slow, deep notes of the "Pilgrim's March" rose and fell, walking steadfastly on in perilous place, weary yet undismayed. Then followed the strange chromatic passage of transition, without which even Wagner did not dare to show us the other side of the picture, and then the great animal, which had lain as if asleep, began to stir; its heart beat with the life of its waking moments, and it started up. The violins shivered and smiled and laughed as Venusberg came in sight; they rose and fell, as the march before had done, but rising higher and laughing more triumphantly with each fall—careless, heedless, infinitely beautiful. But below them, not less steadfast than before, moved the pilgrims. The riot was at its highest, the triumph of Venus and her train seemed complete, when suddenly Reggie started up. He stood at his full height a moment, watching the curtain rise on Venusberg.

"I see, I see," he cried.

Then he turned to Eva.

"You are a wicked woman," he said, and next moment the door of the box closed behind him.

Eva had been seated opposite him, and she had watched his face during the overture. Before he spoke, she knew what would happen, but she did not repent of her resolve. As he left the box, she made two hurried steps as if to follow him, and then stopped, turning round again towards the stage. The electric light fell full on her diamonds, on the gleam of her white dress, on her incomparable beauty. The fan that she had held had slipped down and lay at her feet, and her hands were clenched together.

"He is right," she said aloud. "Ah, my God! he is quite right."

Jim Armine looked up as Reggie left the box, but as his chair was towards the stage he saw nothing except that he had gone. But when Eva rose, he turned half round, and caught her words. It would not have required much penetration to see that something had happened, and it was not unnatural that he hesitated to ask Eva what was the matter. But the next moment she had picked up her fan, and had seated herself in her old place. She opened her mouth to speak once, and Jim waited, but she said nothing.

"Where's Reggie gone?" asked he at length.

Eva summoned her wonderful power of self-control, and spoke in her natural voice.

"I think he has gone home," she said with a certain finality. "Isn't the scene charming? Really, they mount these things very well in England."

The evening passed on; men from other boxes came and paid their respects to Lady Hayes, and, as usual, she snubbed some, was a little amused by others, and appeared indifferent to all.

Towards the end of the third act, Lord Hayes made his appearance and made some true remarks on the state of the weather and the prevalent influenza. Eva listened to his remarks with somewhat unusual attention, and went so far as to inquire how his mother was, who, in spite of her fortified condition, was "down" with the epidemic. But when the curtain fell for the last time, and Tannhäuser had died in "the odour of sanctity," she turned to Jim.

"I wonder if that ending is really natural," she said. "Do you think any man leaves Venusberg so utterly behind after he has been a *habitué* there? I wish Reggie had stopped. He would have given us some very spontaneous criticisms on the subject."

"Do you think spontaneous criticisms are the most valuable?" he asked.

"Perhaps not; but they are very interesting. After all, experience may vitiate one's judgment as much as it matures it."

"What a very odd doctrine," laughed Jim. "But I don't suppose you really believe it yourself."

"Oh no, probably I don't," she replied, "but I don't know what I do believe, and what I don't. Will you give me my cloak? Do you want a lift? No? Good-night!"

When Eva got home she went straight up to her room, and her husband followed her and sat down on a chair opposite to her, as if waiting for her to speak. But Eva had quite as successful a power of silence as he, and sat saying nothing, till he found it unbearable and, in a fatal fit of fidgeting, went across to the mantelpiece, where Reggie's photograph was standing. Eva's eyes followed him slowly, with a still impatience.

He took up the photograph and looked at it for a moment.

"Ah! this is your young friend Reggie Davenport, is it not?"

Eva yawned slightly and nodded assent.

"I thought he was at the opera with you to-night?"

"He was."

"But surely he was not there when I came."

"No, he had gone away."

"Ah! I suppose he got tired of it. It is possible to get tired of Wagner."

Eva stood up suddenly. Her self-control was beginning to break down, and the knowledge of what had happened, the entire success of her own scheme of letting Reggie know the truth about her, was being supplanted in her own mind by a great sense of loss. She felt reckless, at revolt with the world, intolerably intolerant of her position. As she stood there, watching her husband leaning on the back of a chair with the photograph of Reggie in his hands, the desire to fling the truth of it at him became too strong to resist.

She made a quick, silent step to his side, and plucked the photograph out of his hands.

"I should not touch that again if I were you," she said, speaking in a low, rapid voice. "You had better leave it alone for the future. Oh! my meaning is clear enough. I am in love with Reggie Davenport. Yes—in love with him. He is not at all like a second Jim Armine, as you suggested the other day. No, this is quite a different thing. And he is in love with me, while he is engaged to that girl whose photograph stood next his there. It is a sweet position, is it not? Here am I married to you—in love with a young man who is engaged to someone else who is in love with him, while he is in love with me. Ah! Hayes, I lost a great deal when I married you, while you got what you wanted. You wanted to be my owner, did you not? You wished to be master of my beauty. I know how beautiful I am; there is not another woman in London who can touch me. You wanted someone who would give that stamp to your dinner parties and country house parties that I give it. You have had the best of it. And I married you because I wanted position, because I wanted to know the world. That I have got—I know it by heart. It is as dull as a week-old newspaper. Ah, God! how I know it. I did not know what it was to fall in love; I was inexperienced, ignorant. No, I don't blame you. I pity myself."

Eva stopped for a moment, and put Reggie's photograph down on the mantelpiece again, next Gertrude's. She looked at them for a single second, and then took the girl's photograph, and, with a sudden, ungovernable frenzy, tore it to bits, and threw the pieces in the grate. That wild-animal burst of jealousy would not be smothered. Then she went on, still speaking rapidly,—

"You need not be afraid of scandal, Hayes, or anything else of that sort. I have broken with Reggie for good. He thought me kind and good, and all that is womanly, and so I wished him to know the truth about me. Have you ever been in love? If so, you will understand it. I shocked him horribly by explaining to him about Tannhäuser, and at the end of the overture, he suddenly understood what I meant, and he got up and left the box, having told me that I was a wicked woman. It was very fine. I admired him immensely for it. But that sort of thing is rather trying. I managed to behave decently while the play lasted, but I have broken down. That is all there is to tell you. I don't really know why I told you at all."

Lord Hayes listened to his wife with much composure.

"Dear me, how very sensational!" he said, "and how very Quixotic of you. I should not have thought you were capable of Quixotism. You are a most remarkable woman. I think I shall go to bed. The new story by Paul Bourget which I am reading will seem quite flat after your little romance. Good-night!"

Eva felt a sudden sense that he was justified in his quiet scorn of her. How was it to be expected, she reasoned to herself, that he should behave to her, as far as in him lay, otherwise than she behaved to him? Her regret at all she had lost was not entirely resentment towards him. For the first time since she had known him, she was generous to him, showed a willingness to meet him half-way.

"Wait a moment," she said, "I have not quite done."

He paused in an uncompromising attitude with his hand on the handle of the door, ready for some fine return shot. But Eva's impulse was strong within her, and she spoke.

"I do not blame you," she said; "I assure you of that. I only blame myself. You were willing to be very kind to me, and I believe you are willing still. In fact, I am very sorry for you, just as I am very sorry for myself. I do not wish to make it worse for either of us. I want to make a bad job as good as it can be made. I did not tell you what I have told you, in order to disgust you or pain you. We are travellers in the same compartment in this very tiresome journey called life. We are inevitably shut in here until it is time for one of us to get out. Do not let us quarrel; it will only make the journey worse."

Lord Hayes came a step closer.

"Do you find this journey called life so tiresome?" he asked. "I should have thought you would have enjoyed it."

"I wish I was dead," said she, simply.

Then, quite suddenly, all her self-control gave way. She dropped her face in the sofa cushions and sobbed as if her heart would break. Lord Hayes was by no means a fool, and he saw very plainly what the reason for this sudden outburst was, and obviously it was not very complimentary to him, however complimentary it might be to another.

He closed the door quietly, and sat down in a chair a little way from her. He had no notion of being tender, and he lit a cigarette till she was herself again. The sobs grew quieter after a while, and in a few minutes Eva sat up again. Lord Hayes chucked the end of his cigarette into the fireplace.

"My dear Eva," he said very calmly and quietly, "I know quite well, of course, what this all means. You are in love with that young fellow, and that quite accounts for your very—your very extraordinary behaviour. But I don't mind that at all, I assure you. You may be in love with him as much as ever you like. The only thing I should mind would be any scandal on the subject, and I feel quite sure that nothing of the sort will happen. You have been very candid to me—very candid indeed, and I will follow your lead. I know perfectly well that your position and title and wealth are much too dear to you to let you risk any possibility of losing them. You would lose everything by a scandal, and I do not believe you would gain anything. This young man is engaged to another girl, as you say, and he is obviously a very good young man, and will do nothing he should not. In any case, you would have to live at Boulogne or Dieppe, or some of those hideous little French towns, among a set of second-rate people. That is absurd on the face of it. No, I am sure this 'tedious journey called life,' to quote your own words again, would be much more tedious there. For the rest, I fail to see how I am to prevent our quarrelling. It never has been a wish of mine that we should. So once more, good-night!"

Eva was sitting up looking at her husband, with an intensity that was not pleasant to contemplate. He felt it perhaps, for once, when he met her eyes, he looked away again immediately and he faltered in his speech. The utter, entire absence of generosity, of anything like manly feeling in what he said, seemed to Eva to be a new revelation of meanness, the like of which she had never encountered. He turned and left the room at these last words, and Eva was left sitting there.

CHAPTER VII.

Mrs. Davenport had spent the evening alone. Her husband was away for the night, and Reggie, as we have seen, had gone to the opera.

Whatever Reggie was he was not secretive, and his obvious pleasure that afternoon at Lady Hayes's invitation did not savour of the sweetness of consciously forbidden fruit. But his very frankness, which, as has been mentioned before, was capable of dealing unpleasant back-hand blows, had also a dazzling power about it, which, like the rays from a noon-day sun, renders it impossible to tell what lies behind, though it would be very false to describe it as partaking of the nature of dissimulation. It seemed to say, "I am not responsible for the weakness of your eyesight; I show my mystery or my want of mystery to you with all my heart, and you are at fault if you cannot form any conclusion which it is." To continue the metaphor, Mrs. Davenport would have felt not ungrateful to some abatement in its brilliance partaking of the nature of an eclipsed frankness, a shadow cast on the disc by some external object, or, at any rate, she would have been glad to take the opinion of someone who was possessed of smoked glasses, or a natural tendency to observe correctly. Had she known it, Lord Hayes would have been exactly the individual required, but it was no discredit to her acuteness that the idea never entered her head, quite apart from the impracticability of putting it into execution.

She had just dined and was glancing through the pages of a novel from Mudie's, when the drawing-room door opened, and Reggie appeared. He paused a moment when he saw his mother, and then advanced into the room. His attempt to look unconcerned and contented was singularly unsuccessful.

Mrs. Davenport laid down her book, frightened.

"Ah! Reggie, what's the matter? What has happened?"

Reggie turned away from her, and fingered a small ornament on the mantelpiece.

"Nothing," he said hoarsely. "I came away from the opera. I—"

He turned round again, and knelt by his mother's chair.

"Don't ask me just now," he said. "There has been a scene, and I came away. Lady Hayes said things that disgusted me. I didn't think she was like that."

Mrs. Davenport offered a short mental thanksgiving. Until the relief had come, she had not known how much Reggie's intimacy with Lady Hayes had weighed on her. She waited for a moment to see if Reggie would say more. Then—

"Won't you tell me more, dear, or would you rather not?"

"Yes, I want to tell you," said he. "At dinner she told me all about Tannhäuser and Venusberg, and I didn't understand her. Then, when the overture was played, I suddenly understood it all. It was horrible; it was wicked. If anybody else had said that, I should simply have thought it was very bad form, but that she should!"

Mrs. Davenport had not quite realised before how serious it was, and Reggie's tone, even in his renunciation of Eva, was a shock to her.

"That she should say those things!" repeated Reggie. "But when I understood it, I couldn't stop there. I don't remember very clearly what happened. I told her she was a wicked woman, and then I came away."

The excessive baldness of his narrative struck Mrs. Davenport as convincing, and she felt a little reassured. But Reggie had not meant to reassure her, and he soon undeceived her.

"Why should she have said those things to me?" he went on, getting up, and walking about the room. "Why, if she was like that, couldn't she have kept it from me? I should have been content to know only half of her, and to have adored that."

"Ah!"

Mrs. Davenport winced as with a sudden spasm of pain; then pity for Gertrude bred in her anger for Reggie. "What do you mean?" she said sharply. "I do not understand you in the least. You adored her, then; why not say love?"

"I didn't know it before," said he, "until this thing came, or, of course, I should have gone away. I am not a villain. But I know it now; I adored her, and I loved her—and—"

"And you do still?"

"Yes."

There was a long silence, and the hum of the London streets came in at the open window. Mrs. Davenport found herself noticing tiny things, among others that Reggie had placed the ornament he had been fingering perilously near the edge of the mantelpiece. In a great crisis our large reflective and thinking powers get choked for a moment, and the ordinary surface perceptions, which are as instinctive and unnoticed as breathing, are left in command of our mind. The sight of that ornament there assumed an overwhelming importance to her, and she got up from her seat and put it back in a safer place. Then she turned to Reggie, who was standing still in the middle of the room, with his back towards her.

"Sit down here, Reggie," she said quietly. "I think we had better talk a little. Do you quite realise what that means?"

"Ah, don't talk to me like that," he burst out. "As if I was not in hell already, without being reminded of it. Mummy, I don't mean that. You are all that is good and loving. You know that I know it. You are very gentle with me. I won't be angry again."

Mrs. Davenport's anxiety for Gertrude made her very tender.

"Ah, my dear," she said, "I do not care for myself. It is very immaterial that you speak like that to me. I should be a very selfish woman if I thought of myself just now. There are others to think of, you and—and Gertrude."

"Yes, I know, I know. But what am I to do? Tell me that, and I will do it."

"Go to Aix," said his mother promptly, "and go at once."

"Go to Aix!" said he. "Why, that's just what I couldn't possibly do. God knows, I have done Gertrude injury enough, without insulting her!"

"Your waiting here in London is the worst insult you could do her. You must see that."

"I can't do it!" he cried. "You know I can't. How can I leave Eva—Lady Hayes—like this?"

Mrs. Davenport got up, and waited a moment till her voice was more under her control. But when she spoke, her anger vibrated through it so strongly, that even Reggie, in his almost impenetrable self-centred wretchedness, was startled.

"Has it ever occurred to you that there is another concerned in this besides yourself?" she said. "Are you aware that Gertrude loves you in a way that it honours any man to be loved? Do you mean to make no effort to repair the injury you have done her? Be a man, Reggie; you have been a boy too long. Dare you say you ever loved Gerty, if you treat her like this—now? You wish to behave like a fool, and, what is worse, like a coward. I never thought I should be ashamed of you, as I shall be now, if you stop in London after what has happened."

Once more there was a dead silence. Mrs. Davenport, as she knew, had played her ace of trumps; she had brought to bear the strongest motive that she could think of to influence Reggie. If he would not listen to her because she was his mother, if he cared nothing about the effect his action would have on her opinion of him, she knew that there was no more to be done by her.

Reggie flushed suddenly, as if he had been struck.

"But what good will it do if I go?" he cried; "and where am I to go to? I can't go to Gertrude now."

"Your place is with her," said Mrs. Davenport. "If it is all over between you, it is your business to tell her. I don't wish you to tell her at once, but go there and wait a week. Don't be a coward, and don't think that it will be any the better for putting it off. What do you propose to do in the interval—to wait here? She will write to you, and you will not answer, or will you pretend that you are hers, as she is yours? That would not be a very honourable position, would it? Don't disgrace yourself and bring dishonour on us all. Have you no pride, even?"

Reggie looked up in amazement.

"Disgrace myself—bring dishonour on you—"

"Has it never struck you that you are on the verge of doing that?" said Mrs. Davenport.

It evidently had not, and Reggie received the possibility of it with deep perplexity. But the outcome was that he said wearily,—

"Do as you like with me. Yes; I will go."

"Ah! but what is the use of going like that?" said his mother. "You must go, not because I wish you to, but because you realise it, and mean to act up to it. The fact of your going is only a symbol that you are not quite disloyal yet. You are to go as if your heart was still whole; you are going to meet Gerty, to meet her to whom you promised so much. You told me Eva said things which disgusted you. Think of them; sting yourself into hating her. Oh! it will not be easy. I do not expect you will enjoy yourself."

Reggie sat still a moment; then he exclaimed inconsequently,—

"I am very tired. I shall go to bed. Yes, I want to see Gerty again very much."

Reggie, as he had said, had only that night realised how much Eva had entered into his life. It had not occurred to him before to put the case candidly to himself; not because he wished to shirk a conclusion, but because he regarded his feeling for Gertrude as sufficiently safe to warrant the assumption that things were all right. But when this sudden crash came—serious enough, at least, from his point of view, for he could not help regarding his words to Eva as a formal and complete rupture—he saw exactly where he stood. He was separated from Eva; but he was separated from Gertrude, not by any violent wrench, but by the gradual drift of the current, which he had not perceived till now. It had not occurred to him to be honest with himself before. Eva had been divinely kind to him, sympathetic, eager to share his confidence; it was no wonder that, in the blank which Gertrude's absence made, he had found pleasure in giving it her, and that the aforesaid blank became gradually filled with new interests. If the thought ever had occurred to him that the image of Eva was becoming a sort of palimpsest to that of Gertrude, he would have denied the imputation stoutly, perhaps the more stoutly because he was aware that he had not been at pains to find out.

Mrs. Davenport felt, when he had left her, that in a vague way she had expected all this. She had been quite aware that it is not possible for men to continue being boys indefinitely—that there is a time for everyone when they must ask themselves why they do a thing, or why they do not do it; and she knew that, for Reggie, that time had come. He was a boy no longer; that unconscious youth, which had moved Eva's interest, then her love, had gone; he had awoke from his long, happy dream to the grey, convincing morning of reason and of claims. That he would be the better man for it, she did not doubt; that he could not have been a man without, she knew; and yet she was full of regret, full of those aching thoughts "for days that are no more," which are even more poignant when we feel them for others than when we mourn over them for ourselves. Reggie had consented to go away—that was good; but was there not something left to be done? She knew from him that he had called Eva "a wicked woman," and had left the box. What, then, was Eva's feeling on the subject? If she was offended, so much the better; she might be induced to say so. If—worst chance of all—she cared for him, more than she cared for the hundred men who were dangling round her, was there still no possibility of making her say she was offended? All the mother's pride and protectiveness revolted against the notion, but it was worth trying. Mrs. Davenport had so clearly in her mind the best solution of the problem—namely, the disenchantment of Reggie, by any means, or, failing that, the prolonged absence from Eva—that she put her pride in her pocket. She remembered perfectly well her talk with Percy; how he had felt uneasy at this engagement, because it resembled too much Reggie's previous escapades: and surely, if he was right, Reggie's very curtailed entanglement with Eva came under the same head. Let him only get away, with obvious discouragement from Eva, and let Gertrude reassert her previous relation, unconscious of any interruption.

Lady Hayes had not passed a very good night. She was on the verge of doing a very difficult thing; that is to say, doing something directly opposed to her inclinations. In fact, she was, as she had told her husband, in love with Reggie Davenport, and such an experience was new to her. But this very simple and every-day phenomenon was curiously complicated in her case. She happened to be another man's wife, and the man with whom she was in love was about to be another girl's husband. She thought with some impatience of the hundred-and-one stories which are called realistic because they are improbable, in which the woman and man cast everything to the winds and say they obey the dictates of the divine mother of things, because that solution was very far from satisfying her. There is a book that says that love seeketh not its own, and, curiously enough, Eva found her thoughts straying to that short text, which has been abandoned as untrue by the apostles of evolution and modern life, who say that that particular gospel has served its time, that we now know a more excellent way. She had probably never devoted much thought as to whether she was modern or not, but she was surprised to find that so ancient a text seemed to represent her mood more clearly than less antique and hall-marked utterances.

She had had breakfast and was still sitting in the dining-room with her husband, when a footman came in bearing a card. Eva looked at it and pondered. Then,—

"Tell Mrs. Davenport I will see her; show her in here."

Eva got up from her place, and walked up and down the room. She was very pale, and she looked anxious and worn. But she stopped opposite the flower-stand in the corner, and put two orchids in the front of her dress.

Mrs. Davenport was announced, and remarked that it was a beautiful morning, and Lord Hayes assented. She had seldom seen him before, and he was dressed with extreme care, but appeared wholly insignificant. She remembered his enormous wealth, and it seemed to her to be a sort of label to prevent his getting quite lost in this large world. He reminded her of an undelivered parcel, waiting for its owner to turn up.

Lady Hayes sat silent for a few minutes, and then turned to her husband.

"Perhaps you would be so good as to go away," she said in a low, musical voice, "as I have things to talk over with my friend, or, if you like, we will go upstairs. Perhaps that would be better."

Lord Hayes got up with alacrity.

"The fact is," he said, "I was on the point of going. I have some business to do. I was wanting to talk to you some time later on, if it would be convenient."

"Certainly," said Eva. "I will see you about it later."

She dropped her eyes as he addressed her, and sat looking at the ground till he had left the room. Then she said to Mrs. Davenport,—

"What do you want with me?"

Her tone belied the curtness of her words, and she waited eagerly for the answer. These few moments after she had said she would see Mrs. Davenport, were spent in an agony to control herself. She was hungering for more news from Reggie, but in her hand she held a note, which had come from him by the early post, which made her decision doubly difficult. It was a wild, absurd production, imploring pardon, entreating her to let him know that she had forgiven him—only half coherent—

241

and Eva knew that he had really made his choice, or was willing to make his choice between her and Gertrude, if she would only say "Come." "I am going to Aix to-day," the note finished, "to see Gertrude. Cannot you send me one word, to say you forgive me? I behaved quite unpardonably."

Mrs. Davenport raised her eyes to Eva's face, and answered her bravely.

"I have come to talk to you about Reggie," she said.

Eva flushed, and unconsciously closed her hand on the note she held.

"What about him?"

"He is not very happy," said Mrs. Davenport, gently, "and I think perhaps you can help me."

"Ah! I think I probably can," said Eva. "I am glad you have come to see me. I am afraid I have made mischief, and I am sorry. It is odd for me to be sorry; I suppose it's a sign that I am growing old. You know for some time he has been seeing a good deal of me. That was my fault; I ought to have stopped it. And last night I gave him a sudden shock. He only knew one little bit of me, and I thought it was better—"

Eva stopped, for her voice was trembling, and Mrs. Davenport waited.

"It was better," she continued, after a moment, "that he should know the rest of me. Then, when he knew, he called me a wicked woman, and went away straight from the opera. It was splendid. I admired him immensely. But it appears he is sorry he did so. I have just got a note from him imploring forgiveness."

"Ah! the foolish boy," said Mrs. Davenport, half involuntarily.

"Yes, I quite agree with you. You see it puts me in a difficulty. I like him very much—so much that I should be sorry to do him an injury. I should do him an injury if I allowed him to fall in love with me again. On the other hand, I like him well enough to be very sorry not to see him again, and I have to choose."

Eva stopped again, and Mrs. Davenport laid a hand on hers.

"Yes, yes," she said eagerly.

Eva was gradually regaining her control over herself.

"I want him to be very happy," she said, "and his best chance of happiness, I am sure, is with that girl; I forget her name. I have never seen her, but Reggie has spoken of her to me. He ought to go to Herefordshire, or wherever it is, and live among the daisies with his beloved. He is not made for this sort of thing; he is too good. I don't at all wish to spoil his life or the girl's life."

Mrs. Davenport bent forward again in her chair.

"Ah! Eva, you will do it, won't you? I am sure you are right. He will be very happy with her. Do write to him, and say you are offended; make him angry, touch his pride, be as brutal as possible."

"But I don't feel brutal," said Eva. "It is rather hard on me. Oh! I can't, I can't," she exclaimed suddenly.

Mrs. Davenport saw how matters stood at once, and she paused. She had not expected this complication.

Eva started up as she made this self-betrayal, and stood with the colour rising in her cheeks, furiously angry with herself, and wondering how Mrs. Davenport would interpret it. She blamed herself for ever having seen her; she had passed a sleepless night and her nerves were disordered. But the other lady spoke again, almost at once. She saw that it made it harder for Eva, but she saw that the only thing to be done was to pretend to have noticed nothing. So, before the silence grew portentous, she went on, but with more tenderness in her voice,—

"Yes, of course it is hard for you," she said. "It is very hard to be unselfish in this weary world. But it is worth an effort, is it not? And that you are fond of Reggie ought to make it easier. You don't wish to spoil his life, as you say."

"How did he behave last night when he came home?" asked Eva, suddenly.

"He is changed," said Mrs. Davenport. "I think you would see it. Somehow, he is a boy no longer; he has become a man, and he finds it not pleasant."

"Ah! that is so, is it?" said Eva. "It was horribly stupid of me. But it makes it easier for me. He was so young, somehow—which I have never been. Are you sure you are right?"

"Yes, quite sure."

"That makes it easier for me, and perhaps for him. Does he take things hard?"

"I don't think Reggie has known anything before which he could take hard. He has been very happy."

"You mean he will be less happy now."

"For the time, yes," said Mrs. Davenport; "but I feel sure it will be for the best. He is one of those people who are made to be happy, and I am sure he will have less unhappiness this way than if you took any other course."

"I must think about it," said Eva, turning and walking up and down the room. But even as she spoke she tore Reggie's letter in half, and threw the pieces into the grate. "It is hard for me, is it not?" said she, stopping in front of Mrs. Davenport, "but it appears I am to be the victim."

"Reggie looked very like another victim last night," said the other.

Eva looked away.

"Did he—was he very unhappy about it?" she asked.

"Not too unhappy."

"What do you mean?"

"From what I know of him," said Mrs. Davenport, "especially since this sudden change has come, if you speak now, you may make the whole difference to him. Make him angry and sore, and then let him go off to Aix, and I think Gertrude will do the rest. I wonder if she will guess what has happened. I hope not."

"How she will hate me!" murmured Eva, "and so will Reggie. It is really hard to see what I am to gain by the arrangement."

"Ah! don't go back now," entreated Mrs. Davenport. "See, I have no pride left. I implore you to do what I ask. You are very powerful; I know your power too well, and so does Reggie, God help him!"

"I wonder if it is really better to be unselfish than selfish," mused Eva, more to herself than to Mrs. Davenport, "or to try to do good at all. We are so very short sighted that we may be doing the worst thing possible. Who were those very ingenious people who did harm when they wanted to, in order that good might follow? Anyhow, if I do this, I shall not have chosen the selfish course. I suppose there will be an imperishable reward for me somewhere. Even so, perhaps I am really doing the selfish thing by doing as you ask me; it all depends, doesn't it, on how much I like him? whether I like him enough to be unselfish; whether the burden of being selfish wouldn't be harder to bear than the burden of being unselfish."

"I know how little I matter to you personally," said Mrs. Davenport, "but you will know at least that I think you have done a very noble thing, something of which not many are capable; something it was very hard for you to do."

"Ah! you don't understand me a bit," broke out Eva. "I assure you that no one's opinion has an atom of weight with me. I fear evil report as little as I covet good. Let me think for a few moments."

Mrs. Davenport was silent; she hardly heard Eva's last speech, for all her thoughts were on her possible decision. That she had not dismissed her at once, had not refused to see her, she felt was a favourable sign. Eva, she knew, was quite capable, in spite of a certain intimacy between them, of having sent a message that she saw no one in the morning. Mrs. Davenport feared her and her cold, hard power, as she feared nothing else in the world. She sat there pale, almost trembling, while Eva passed slowly up and down the room, for a few minutes. But at the end of one of these turns, when she was by the door, she passed out, and Mrs. Davenport heard her step ascending the stairs. She waited there while the minute hand crept round the dial of the great bronze clock on the mantelpiece, and it was half-an-hour before Eva appeared again, with a large, unsealed envelope in her hand. She looked very weary, but as faultlessly beautiful as ever.

"I have not sealed it," she said, "because I thought you might like to read it, and while I am about it I might as well do it handsomely. At the same time, I would sooner you did not read it, but I shall neither blame you nor try to dissuade you if you wish to. With it is Reggie's photo—the one he gave me. You need not take them. Will you read it? No? Then I will send a man with it at once, as you don't care to look at the letter. There is no reason why you should be turned into a penny post because your son has called me a wicked woman. He was quite right, by the way—perfectly right. I—"

Eva stopped suddenly, for there was that tremor in her voice which had been there once before at this interview.

"I will not betray myself," she determined, biting her lip, in a splendid effort to keep command over herself.

"There is just one thing that I should like to ask you," she went on almost at once; "send me a line now and then, to tell me about Reggie, and whether it is all right between him and the girl. I liked him very much, you know, and I shall never see him again, I suppose."

Mrs. Davenport was much moved. She had guessed, and guessed correctly, that Reggie would not be the only sufferer, and that Eva had behaved heroically, and tears partly of relief, but partly of gratitude and admiration, started to her eyes.

"God bless you for what you have done!" she whispered. "I can say no more than that."

The tension broke.

"Leave me quickly," cried Eva, as the large, painful sobs began to break from her throat. "Go at once!"

"Eva, Eva," cried Mrs. Davenport, stretching out her hands to her.

"Go—go at once!" cried the other.

She turned rapidly from her, and Mrs. Davenport, without another word, left the room. She just saw Eva sink in the arm-chair she had been occupying before, and bury her face in her hands. Mrs. Davenport closed the door quietly and went out.

She had left behind her, and she knew it, a sorrow greater and more desolate than Reggie's weaker nature would ever know. She remembered Percy's prediction, that some day Eva "would do something sublimely unselfish, and that would be when she fell in love."

It was still only about mid-day when she left the house, and she had purposely said "Good-bye" to Reggie before she went, for, presupposing the success of her expedition, of which Reggie knew nothing, her presence was unnecessary and undesirable. If, on the other hand, she was unsuccessful, she had determined to go to the station and meet her husband, and acquaint him with the state of things. She drove about for an hour or so, and then changed her mind, and determined to make an effort to see Reggie before he set off.

She arrived home just as he was starting, and they met in the hall, and when she saw his face she drew a deep breath of satisfaction and relief. He was unmistakably angry.

"You are just off, are you, dear?" she said quietly. "Give Gertrude my love, and—and be very brave and make an effort, dear boy. It will not be easy. God bless you, my darling?"

"She wrote to me this morning," whispered Reggie hoarsely, as he kissed his mother. "I will never speak to her or think of her again. Ah! Mummy, good-bye! you have saved me."

CHAPTER VIII.

After Mrs. Davenport had left her, Eva remained in the dining-room for an hour or more. She had chosen, and the choice was not easy. But it seemed to her as if the struggle came afterwards rather than before. The letter she had written to Reggie rose before her, and her heart cried to her for mercy. But the clear knowledge which she had arrived at, that his chance of happiness grew in direct relation to remoteness from herself, remained unclouded, and at no moment of that hour's agony would she have reconsidered her decision. That she had so decided was a matter of wonder to her, for it is always a surprise to find that we are better, not worse, than we think; but her investment in unselfishness gave her no quick returns, for at present, as she well knew, Reggie was as miserable as she was. The sacrifice of two victims called down no immediate answer from the blessed gods in the way of a sudden cessation of pain.

But when that hour was passed, she went upstairs to her husband, to see him about the business he had mentioned. She felt strongly the necessity of being active, of doing something, no matter what, which might possibly take her a little out of herself. Our moral nature has to go to bed when it is hurt, and it is well to leave it there, and not fidget at the bandages to see how it is getting on.

The business resolved itself into affairs connected with the ironworks at Trelso, and Lord Hayes told her that he was going down that afternoon, and would stop the night there, returning the following day. And Eva, longing for distraction, found none there. Her mother and Percy were in town, and she drove off, and fetched them back to lunch.

The sight of so well-appointed a house, and the thought that, in a measure, it was part of her environment, as being the mother of its mistress, always put Mrs. Grampound in an excellent humour, at times bordering on a sort of mature playfulness.

"And how is my little daughter behaving?" she asked Lord Hayes, as soon as they were seated at lunch. "I hope she is doing me credit, and you, too, of course. I don't like the way girls behave now. I'm sure they do things we should have got dreadfully abused for when we were young, and now no one takes any notice whatever. Dear Eva, what a lovely piece in the middle of the table. That is new, is it not?"

"The beauty of it is that it's very old," remarked Eva.

"Really, it looks so bright and fresh. And talking of brightness and freshness, I met Mr. Davenport the other day. He spoke of you a great deal, as if he knew you quite well."

"He is a great friend of Eva's," said her husband, watching her. "Why hasn't he come to see you to-day, Eva?"

"Chiefly because he left by the mail for Aix this morning," said Eva. "He asked me to say good-bye to you for him."

Lord Hayes had the satisfaction of believing this to be untrue, but that was small compared with the complete failure on his part to ruffle Eva's bosom with an uneven breath, or raise the slightest tinge of colour to her face.

"I'm quite in love with him," she went on slowly, without looking at her husband. "I feel quite desolate without him. Hayes, you must be particularly kind to me all day. Though, of course, you mustn't hope to compete with Reggie in my affections."

Lord Hayes smiled, and took some jelly. Most people know that particular moment experienced at varying distances from Dover pier, when they are not quite sure whether they enjoy the motion or not. Lord Hayes was, metaphorically speaking, being a little tossed about, and if he did not yet think with longing of *terra firma*, he was not sorry to remember that he would be alone at Trelso that evening.

"What a beautiful thing it is, is it not," he said, addressing Mrs. Grampound, "when a wife reposes such confidence in her husband, that she tells him she is in love with someone else. Truly there can be no secrets between such."

Mrs. Grampound tittered shrilly. To state the truth, as Eva had done, is often the surest, sometimes the only, way of producing a complete misconception. She failed to notice the acidity in Lord Hayes's face and voice, and thought the scene quite too charming. But Percy noticed and wondered.

"What shocking things to say to each other," cried she. "Eva, you naughty child, how can you? And you deserve I should scold you too," she said, turning to her son-in-law.

"Reggie has scorned me and my homage altogether," continued Eva gravely, speaking chiefly in order to produce a sort of counter-irritant to her own pain, on the same principle as that on which children, suffering from toothache, may be observed to bite their lips. "He has gone off to Aix to see his *fiancée*. He gave me her photograph—wasn't that a cruel thing to do?—and his own. Really, it was most shameless. I was never so humiliated before. I think, when Hayes goes away to Trelso, I shall take the train to Aix and sit watching the hotel windows, and serenade him in the hotel garden. It's quite a new idea for a woman to serenade her lover. Why did you never serenade me, Hayes? I should like to see you serenade on a cold night under a silk umbrella. Can you sing, by the way? You'd have to leave a good deal to the lute, like the man in Browning who serenaded at a villa during a thunderstorm. Your mother wouldn't approve of serenading, would she? The evening fever sets in about that time, I think, from eleven till two—of course, the damp wouldn't matter if you had Jaeger boots with eight holes in them."

"Eva, you naughty girl," said her mother again.

Yes; there was just a little too much motion. Metaphorically speaking, Lord Hayes went below.

"I've got to go to Trelso this afternoon," he said. "I hear that the men are getting more and more discontented. There is an organised body of Socialists down there, who incite them and refer to me as a brutal tyrant. What a very odd way to spend your life, you know—going about the country calling us names. I can't think what they imagine they will get by it."

"It is rather hard to call you a brutal tyrant," said Eva with some amusement. "Now, if they had said so of Reggie, or of me, for example— Yes, Percy, you may smoke here, or let's go up to the top of the porch. There is a tent there, and it is deliciously cool."

The two gentlemen stayed behind a moment, and Eva and her mother went on. Lunch made Mrs. Grampound even more effusive than usual.

"I do so love to think of you here in your beautiful house, darling," she said to Eva, as they passed up the great marble stairs; "with your husband devoted to you, and all that. A charming little scene at lunch, so playful and delicately touched. But you always were clever, dear. It is such a happiness to me to think of you like this. That yellow collar you have on your liveries is very becoming. How much do you pay your *chef?* Ah, what a charming little room this tent makes! I suppose you and your husband often sit here."

She subsided into a low chair, and looked at Eva affectionately, or, at any rate, with an air of proud proprietorship.

"I am very rich," murmured Eva. "I have every thing that money can buy—I have a title—yes, what more can I want?"

Mentally she was far away. The boat got into Calais about two-thirty. She had looked it out in a Bradshaw that morning. He had just left Calais, going south to join Gertrude. He would be at Aix next morning early. She felt if she could only know exactly what effect her letter had had on him, she would be more content. Her heart ached for the sight of him, ached with the pang of that self-inflicted wound which had sent him away irrevocably, she hoped, or feared—which was it? There was half-an-hour at Calais, she remembered, on her journeys to Algiers; enough to lunch in, to buy a book in, to be rather bored in. There was—ah! the curtain that separated the little tent from the drawing-room was drawn aside, as she had often seen it drawn aside lately, when she said she was not at home to visitors—and Lord Hayes entered.

"I have come to say good-bye," he said, "I must be leaving at once for the station. I shall be back to-morrow, Eva, soon after lunch, I expect; we are dining with the Davenports."

"Ah, yes, I had forgotten," said she. "Good-bye! I shall see you to-morrow."

"What are you going to do this afternoon?" inquired her mother, after she had kissed her hand to Lord Hayes as he drove off.

"I am going to Wimbleton House. There is a garden-party. It is a bore, but I promised to go." Eva paused to see the sudden alacrity with which she knew her mother would receive the news, before she added—"Perhaps you would like to come with me."

"I should enjoy it very much," said her mother. "I am so fond of garden-parties, and they do them so well there."

"I didn't know that you knew the Duchess," remarked Eva, and let the subject drop.

She returned home and dined alone, and spent a long evening upstairs in her room. She reviewed again minutely from the beginning, not because she wanted to think of it, but because she could not avoid it, the events of the last weeks. It was as if a sudden light had burst in upon her soul, showing her what was meant by love, and then, just as she comprehended it, the exigencies of its very nature, the compulsion she was under to reveal herself, and that second compulsion which would not allow her to do for Reggie anything but what her sober reason told her was best for him, had left her face to face with this horrible blankness. A spring had broken out which could never, she felt, cease to flow, but she stood there, with mouth gagged, unable to drink of its coolness. In her heart she believed that, even now, if she wrote one word to him—"Come"—in two days he would be with her. But her longing and her firm renunciation seemed indivisible. She could no more have apostatised on her renunciation than she could have compelled herself to be quit of her love. Her nature was of too large and serene a type for her to feel again that one outburst of jealousy when she had torn Gertrude's photograph in half. At that moment all the worst side of her heart had leapt out—the tigress element; the animal within her had raised that one howl of anguish, but after that it had lain still, cowed to the deeper pain of that in her which was human and divine. At the moment of her renunciation a light had shone on her darkness, and though the darkness comprehended it not, it wondered and was still; and when in that light she saw and decided what course she must, for all reasons, take, the animal did not venture even to lift its head and growl.

Reader, are you burning to tell me that all this suffering on the part of Eva and Reggie—even if you allow that such a very proper chastening for the lax self-indulgence with which they slid into the mutual positions they now occupy is a subject fit to be treated of at all in a moral and Christian country, or whether you hold that I might as well describe the infliction of the cat o' nine tails on a righteously-condemned convict for some well-defined and properly-chastened offence—that this suffering was perfectly well merited; that, had Eva been a woman of even decent moral principles, or had Reggie not been subject to the calviest of calf loves, it would never have happened; that, above all, it was their, particularly her, fault? I plead guilty to all these indictments, or rather I put in no defence for my prisoners, which is the same thing. I admit that Eva was not—according to the best lights, which you, no doubt, are judging her by—a woman of decent moral principles; that it is a tenable view that this infatuation of Reggie's was only a calf love; but his last, remember, for I have told you that he was a boy no longer; and, above all, I admit that it was their, particularly her, fault.

Now, with regard to Eva's morals, you are judging her, I imagine, by your own standards, which, after all, are the only standards by which one man can judge another. No one can judge by other men's standards, whether they be lower than their own or higher—the

result is a loss of moral perspective. You cannot take
observations, except by applying your eye straight to the
telescope; if you stand above it and squint, you will
obtain an incorrect idea of what you wish to see. And in
addition to venturing to assume that you judge her by
your own standards, I will go further and assume,
broadly, what those standards are. I have noticed that
when people—as I, for the sake of argument, have made
you do—refer to moral principles, they refer to a code
which may vary in magnitude and comprehensiveness,
but which is based on one principle—the avoidance,
even in thought, of certain things which they regard
instinctively, almost hysterically, as being impossible,
because they are wrong. But the moral principles very
seldom go so far as to say they are wrong; they stop short
at impossible—they are contrary to its nature—and that
is enough. Eva, I am afraid, had no morals at all of this
kind. To take an exaggerated instance, I am afraid, if the
truth were known, vitally and essentially, she kept her
hands from picking or stealing not because it was wrong,
but because she did not want the things she might have
stolen. It is a very shocking confession, and it is driving a
principle home to admit it, but it serves to illustrate
under a distorting, or, at any rate, a very high-power lens,
the difference between her and you. But—and this, I
again assume, is the purport of the whole matter in your
mind—it was her own fault. Ah, if I could only tell you
how freely I grant you that. And what is there, in
Heaven's name, of all the sufferings we ordinary people
undergo, that is not our fault? From the slippers which
the labourer's wife has omitted to put down to warm for

her lord, and which give rise to recriminations and perhaps a few silent tears, to the pangs of remorse for some wrong done which we can never undo, what is there of which we are wholly guiltless? The supremely-suffering-babe-unborn-innocent-utterly-milk-and-water heroine of the severely classic romance is not common in this dingy, work-a-day world. It would be presumptuous in me to say she does not exist, but I have never seen her yet. She is a very beautiful and ennobling conception, and she always gets a full reward in the last chapter, where she is joined to her only love and lives happily ever afterwards, and sometimes is seen again in the epilogue, surrounded by a group of golden-haired, clean-limbed children, with their father's pensive eyes, who utter sentiments which must fill her maternal heart with pride and joy ineffable. But have you never, even in those beautiful epilogues, been faced by a grey, shadowy doubt that life is not quite like this, that even villains have good points, and heroines bad ones; that virtue does not always bring so full a reward, and that vice is not discomfited with that sublime completeness; in a word, that human nature is much more complex, more subtlely compounded than the epilogue would indicate, that a nature capable of a sublime action is also capable of one or of many that do not fall in with your moral principles, and that something is to be said even for the villain? But Eva, I maintain, though not a heroine, and though the bank of ineffable joy had not given her a blank cheque to be filled up at her pleasure, was not a villain. She had done something which no right-minded person would approve in allowing herself to fall in love with Reggie, and in allowing him to fall in love with her; and what is more, she had done something short-sighted. Not knowing the nature of love, she had tried to play with that perplexing emotion, and was finding now that it was not merely playing with her, but ordering her about in a most autocratic manner. She had committed a folly, and in this world we pay more heavily for a folly than a sin. She was bewildered, unstrung, unhappy, by her own fault, no doubt; but if we never pity those on whom justice makes its pitiless claims, whom shall we pity? Are we to class her with the villain, since we cannot class her with the heroine? After all, do not most of us belong to a class which it would be unjust or impossible to class with either the one or the other? There are more gradations between the noon-day sun and the starless night than the epilogues allow for. At any rate, all you Rhadamanthine judges, she was paying for it, and surely that is all you demand. Come a little further with me; your desire for justice, justice to the uttermost farthing, will not be disappointed.

Eva woke next morning from that dreamless sleep which only quickens our capabilities for suffering, woke with a start of pain into the full consciousness of her unimaginable future. But the absence of her husband was at least a mitigation; she felt she could not stand any extra burden just then. But would this horrible emptiness never cease—would there come no assuaging of her agony? It is hard, directly after some severe shock has been sustained, to believe in the possibly healing powers of time—all we feel is that the impossible to-morrows and to-morrows will stretch away until death, and none will be less impossible than the last. And when one is young, strong, serenely healthy, that is a serious thought. Surely Eva was paying for her folly. And still she never reconsidered her decision; she still saw with undoubted clearness that Reggie, leaving herself out of the question, would eventually be happier with Gertrude; that, for him, there were pleasant places open on this weary earth, into which he would, in all probability, soon pass and leave her for ever. His best chance of happiness lay there, and herself she did leave out of the question utterly and fearlessly. There is something to pity, and perhaps, after all, there is something to praise.

There is nothing so unbearable as this consciousness of force that cannot be converted into effort, or reach fruition. It strikes with an unavailing hand at the gateways of our soul, but it cannot pass out and fulfil itself. And to Eva the sensation was wholly new. The coldest, least human of our species are just those who throw themselves with the most irresistible singleness into the force which has thawed them, when that unthawing comes. When their long winter is passed, the sap streams more fully into its channels, than in those who live, as it were, in most temperate climates, where the sap never wholly quits the trees. And Eva had none on whom to spend the force of her late waking love. The one who woke it was gone—gone by her own will—and the stream had no other outlet.

The hours passed wearily on till noon. After lunch she had calls to make, and about five o'clock she returned home to dress for a ride. Lord Hayes had not yet come back, and she left word that she would be in before seven. But the exercise, the sun, the meeting of half a hundred people she knew had its due effect, and made the horror of that empty house the greater. To her it was a house full of ghosts, of dead possibilities and living horrors, and it was not till much before eight that she dismounted again at her door. The gloaming was rapidly deepening into night, the lamps had already been lit, and the white star on her horse's forehead glimmered strangely through the dusk. She asked the man whether Lord Hayes had returned, and learned that he had come back soon after she had gone out. They were to dine at the Davenport's at a quarter to nine, and Eva went straight to her room to dress. Lord Hayes, the man said, had already dressed and was sitting in his room, writing. He had given orders that he was not to be disturbed. Eva had two minds as to whether she should go to the Davenports that night or not, but the desire to see Mrs. Davenport, to learn whether Reggie had really gone, and how he had received her note, were too strong. She would be wiser, she knew, to say nothing about him, but the craving of her nature took no account of wisdom.

Half an hour later, she came out from her room, dressed for the party, faultlessly beautiful. She had put on the diamonds she had worn two nights ago at the opera, and they lay on her breast like a living embodiment of light. Just as she came out on to the landing, a man came upstairs to say the carriage was round, and she turned aside to go to her husband's room to tell him.

She opened the door, and to her surprise found the room was dark. Then she called him, but got no answer. The man who had announced the carriage was still standing on the landing, and she turned to him.

"Where is Lord Hayes?"

"His Lordship went into the room an hour ago, my lady," he said. "I have not seen him come out. He is not in his dressing-room."

Eva stood for a moment with her hand still grasping the door, for the space in which a new thought may strike the mind. Her eyebrows contracted, and the diamonds on her breast were suddenly stirred by a quick-drawn breath.

"There is no light in there," she said. "Bring me a lamp quickly."

She waited in the same position while the man fetched a lamp.

"Take it in there," she said; "no, give it me."

The man followed her in.

By the writing-table, with his face fallen forward on the paper, sat her husband. His arms sprawled on each side, and every joint was relaxed. Eva looked at him for a moment, and then touched him.

"Hayes!"

There was no answer.

"Hayes, Hayes!" she said, raising her voice.

She set the lamp down on the table, close to the thing that sprawled there, and, taking him round the shoulders, dragged him up off the table. But the head fell back over one shoulder, and the two hands rattled against the wood-work of the chair, as his arms slipped off his knees.

"Quick, quick!" she cried to the man. "What are you standing there for? Don't you see he is ill? Let the carriage go off to the doctor's and bring him back. You fool, run! Send a man here at once!"

Eva ran to the bell and rang it furiously. There was a sound of hurried footsteps on the stairs, and two men came running up.

"Lord Hayes is ill," said Eva. "Take him to his room, and lay him on the bed."

She could not bear to stop in the room to see that nerveless thing being moved, and went out to the passage, where her maid met her. The atmosphere of terror had spread through the whole house, and servants were running up.

"Oh! my lady, what is the matter—is he dead?" asked that somewhat hysterical young woman, clasping her hands.

Eva turned fiercely on her.

"Nothing is the matter. What do you mean by saying that? Run downstairs and get some brandy. Quick! do you hear?"

The two men passed out close to Eva with their grim burden. She shuddered as they moved slowly along to the bedroom door. Then, after a moment she followed them. They had laid him on the bed, but, even in that attitude, the limpness was not that of a living man.

"Leave me, wait till the doctor comes, and bring him up," said she.

When she was alone, she lit the candles and brought them near his face. She took up one of the open hands, and felt for the pulse, but found it not. Then, looking up suddenly, she saw her own face in the glass, set in a half circle of light from the diamonds on her neck. For a long moment she gazed, and then, setting the candles down, she unclasped the necklace, and dashed it on to the ground.

BOOK III.

CHAPTER I.

Mrs. Carston was a widow, with only one daughter. She was a woman to whom querulousness had, by habit, become a second nature, but she had, as she often remarked, cause enough for complaint. Her husband, of whom she had been very fond, died suddenly, leaving her with one girl, a younger son, and less income than she could comfortably manage on. Then, two months later, her son died, leaving her alone with Gertrude. Her health, never very good, was much weakened by the double shock, and of late years she had become a *habituée* at Aix for four or five weeks every May, when there were plenty of English people there, with whom she used to talk gossip, and bemoan her unfortunate health.

Gertrude managed to be very happy during the earlier part of that month. The enchanted valley, in which there falls not hail nor rain nor any snow, had a great charm for her, and she used to avail herself of the early morning hours, when her mother was undergoing her baths and douches and treatment, to wander far among the thick, dewy meadows, over which the mountains keep watch. She would pick great bunches of the early gentians and meadow sweet, and tall, tasselled grasses, and make their sitting-room bright with their wild, free beauty. The flowers sold in the market place had less attraction for her; they reminded her of towns, and she found it sweeter in the country. She had, too, at first, a very happy background to this pure joy of living, in the thought of Reggie. Ever since the winter, her love for him had been undergoing a slow, steady change; it had deepened and widened imperceptibly from day to day, and, looking back on the early days of their courting, the hours now seemed to her to have been unmomentous and shallow, save that they held the germ which had ripened into this. And he was going to join them, as he had said, in a few weeks, and she felt she particularly wished to be with him again, in the way that she would be at Lucerne—away from his world and her world. Those quiet hours had for her in anticipation a glorious possibility. She would make Reggie feel all that he was to her, make him understand the new depths which she knew had been opened by her love in her nature.

She did not usually see her mother till the twelve o'clock *déjeuner*, and one morning, about five days after their arrival, she had got up earlier than usual and walked down to the lake. The day before, Reggie's letter, announcing Lady Hayes's sudden desire to have her photograph, had arrived, and for an hour or two she had been filled with perplexing doubts, of which she felt ashamed. But her true and deep loyalty had soon reasserted itself, and she had chased them from her mind. She told herself that she was absolutely unjustified in ever letting the vaguest uneasiness rise into her thoughts. Whatever her feeling was, it had sprung from that irrational pique with which she had received Reggie's remarks concerning Eva six months ago. She had then conceived in her mind a dislike and distrust for a woman she had never seen, and that weed she had allowed to grow until, just before she left London, she had refused to go to lunch with her for no reason at all. Decidedly it was time to pull the weed up.

So she went out next morning feeling a wider happiness than ever. That act of loyalty was finding a full reward, and the meadows had never looked so green, nor the water so lovely, nor the background of her thoughts so satisfying. The post had not come in when she left the hotel, and the certainty of a letter from Reggie awaiting her return added its solid contribution to her happiness.

The tall, graceful figure, walking swiftly along the poplar avenue out of the town, was very characteristically English. Several French women, as she passed through the streets, turned to look at her, wondering who was that English demoiselle, who walked so fast; why she was at Aix at all, and, above all, for what conceivable reason she should want to walk. But none of them failed to smile pleasantly when Gertrude gave them a "*bon jour*"; her face was so irresistibly happy and handsome, and they went back to their work smiling, and forgetting for the moment to scold Jean or Pierre for putting their dirty little fingers in the washtub.

Gertrude got down to the lake while the sun was still behind the big range of hills to the east, though, looking back, she could see the tops of the mountains behind, and even the lower pastures beneath them touched by the new gold. She sat down on the landing-stage and watched the glory spreading downwards, till it reached the clear, white town she had left, and finally the sun itself swung into sight over the serrated outline of the eastern hills. The small, blue ripples tapped an invitation on the sides of the pleasure boats lying at anchor, and Gertrude determined to have a short row before going back. The boat-keeper expressed astonishment and dismay when he heard that mademoiselle proposed to row herself, but Gertrude stripped off the light jacket she was wearing and told him to get two light sculls, and, with a laugh, disdaining his outstretched hand, she jumped into the boat and pushed off.

Life was very sweet that morning. She was going to write to Reggie and tell him to come very soon, before they left Aix, for it was a nice place, and he could row as much as he liked, and go for long walks, and there were horses to be had. As she paddled quietly along, she pictured herself here again with him in a week or two. He would be sure to come. Had he not said he did not care for London, and he did happen to care for her? She wanted her mother to know him too, for she had only seen him at present on fugitive visits, and her "ideas" about him were vaguer than Gertrude wished.

The sun was already high when she landed again, but the dusty mile of road up to Aix was short in her anticipations. There would be a letter for her from someone she cared about, infinitely dear to her, but, as the advertisements often say, "of no value but to the owner." So she walked up not feeling the sun, only conscious of an inward glow of happiness which nothing could touch.

Yes—the post had come in, and the polite porter looked through the letters. Miss Carston? No; none had come this morning. "Was he quite sure?" Yes; but perhaps mademoiselle would like to look through them for herself. Mademoiselle did like to do so, and she went upstairs to see her mother, feeling that the doubts, which she had buried the day before, had celebrated a private resurrection on their own account.

"Summer had stopped." There are no words for it but those. Was the sky still as blue? Possibly, but not for her. And when the sky is not blue for us, it is noticeable that we do not care very much, even the most unselfish of us, whether it is blue for others or not.

Gertrude, in fact, passed on the stairs a colonial bishop and his wife, whom she had been accustomed to make the sharers of her intense joy in its blue spring; but when the lady recorded her opinion that it was a lovely day, Gertrude felt that the remark was singularly ill-chosen.

She found her mother upstairs, preparing to come down. It was one of her bad days, and Gertrude knew that even greater attention than usual would be required of her.

"I have been wanting you ever so long—these two hours at least," said her mother, as she entered. "I wish you could manage to think about me sometimes. But that is always the way. Invalids never matter. They can look after themselves."

Gertrude kissed her mother and took off her hat.

"I am so sorry," she said, "I went a longer walk than usual, right down to the lake, and had a short row. Did you have your massage earlier this morning? You are not usually ready till twelve, and it is not twelve yet."

"No, I had it at ten, as usual. Why should I have it earlier?"

"I thought you said you had been waiting for me so long. However, here I am now. I won't be out so late another morning. What did you want me to do?"

"Mrs. Rivière met me at the bath," said her mother, "and wanted me to go for a picnic this afternoon, and you. I think I shall go. I want a breath of fresh air; they are going up to the Monastery, on the far side of the lake. We shall have to dress up, I suppose. Princess Villari is going, and the Prince too, I think."

Gertrude frowned slightly. She detested Mrs. Rivière with all the power with which a healthy, honest mind can detest *mondaines* of a certain description.

"Did you say we would come?" she asked.

"Why, of course I did. I suppose you don't want to go now. Really, considering what I have to go through, it might be expected that my only daughter would not object to coming with me for a picnic, where perhaps I may get a little distraction. And the doctor particularly told me to get up in the hills now and then."

"Mother, why do you judge me so hastily?" said Gertrude. "Of course I will come; I only asked you whether you had accepted. What time shall we start? It will be delicious up there. Must I put on my very best frock?"

"Gracious me, yes," said Mrs. Carston. "I wish you had a better. And you're getting dreadfully brown. Gertrude, I wish you would take a little more care of your complexion. You won't be fit to be seen in a low dress when we get back to England. Ah, there's the bell. Give me your arm, dear, I am a mass of aches to-day. Have you heard from Reggie this morning?"

"No, there were no letters for me to-day," said Gertrude, cheerfully. "I shall have to blow Reggie up when I write again. Or shall I not write until he writes to me?"

"I forget whether you know Princess Villari," asked her mother. "You've seen the Prince, haven't you?"

"I never spoke to her," said Gertrude. "But I saw her last night at the Cercle; she was going into the baccarat room, talking at the top of her voice, and smoking."

"It's becoming quite the thing to smoke," remarked Mrs. Carston. "I should smoke, if I were you, this afternoon, if everybody else does. It is no use making an obvious exception of oneself. It looks so odd."

"Oh! I think it's horrid for women to smoke," said Gertrude. "It's unfeminine. Don't you think it is?"

"Nonsense; I wish you would, if others do," said her mother; "but you are always so determined. If you don't wish to do a thing, you won't do it. Take me to that seat at the small table. I can't talk to Mrs. Mumford any more."

The rest of the party were all coming from the "Splendide," the great hotel at the top of the hill overlooking Aix, and as the road from there went by the Beau Site, where Gertrude and her mother were staying, it had been arranged that the party from the upper hotel should call for them as they passed, and pick them up. Mrs. Carston told Gertrude that they were going to drive down to the lake in the Prince's four-in-hand, take boats there, and walk up to the Monastery, where they would have tea.

Gertrude and her mother were sitting in the verandah, facing the road, after lunch, when the brake drew up at the entrance to the hotel. A woman, brilliantly beautiful and marvellously dressed, was driving, whom Gertrude recognised as the Princess. She was smoking a cigarette, and held her whip and reins in the most professional manner. By her side sat Mrs. Rivière, and, in the centre of the seat just behind, a handsome, foreign-looking man, who, when they stopped, and he saw Gertrude and her mother coming down the steps, leaned forward to the Princess, and said,—

"Who is that very handsome girl there, Mimi? Is she coming with us?"

The Princess turned to look, and gave a shrill, voluble greeting to Mrs. Carston.

"Charmed to see you! Get up and sit next my husband. Villari, you know Mrs. Carston, don't you? And is that your daughter with you? I am so glad you were able to come, too. Steady, you brutes! Bring the steps, quick! These animals won't stand quiet. Villari, get down and help them up."

"It's Miss Carston," she said to him, as he passed her; "isn't she handsome? Very *ingénue*, I imagine. Do you know her, Mrs. Rivière?"

"I met her the other day," she replied. "I don't think they've been here very long. How beautifully you drive!"

"That's one of my English accomplishments," said the Princess; "and I haven't forgotten it, you see. Dear me! it's more than a year since I've been to England. We're going in November. Villari's bought a country place there, you know. Are you right behind there? Go on, you brutes, then! Ah! you would, would you?"

The Princess gave a savage cut with her whip at one of the leaders, who appeared to want to go home, and they started off at a hand-gallop.

"For God's sake, take care, Mimi!" said the Prince, leaning forward, as they swung round a corner with about three-quarters of an inch to spare; "the streets will be full to-day—it's Saturday."

"Blow the horn, old boy!" remarked the Princess. "Tell them we're coming. I must go fast through here, you know, because I've got the reputation of driving like the son of Nimshi. Do you know who the son of Nimshi was, Mrs. Rivière? He comes in the Bible."

By about an equal mixture of the favour of Providence and the dexterity of the Princess, they got through the town in safety, without impairing the reputation of the latter as being a furious driver, and the horses settled down to a steady pace on the road to the lake.

The Prince had managed to seat himself next Gertrude, leaving Mrs. Carston to the attentions of Mr. Rivière. The rest of the party were composed of English visitors staying at the "Splendide," and the whole party numbered ten or twelve. A second glance assured him that she was even handsomer than he supposed, and, as it was one of the Princess's maxims that husband and wife were, both of them, perfectly free to receive or administer any attentions they pleased, without injuring their mutual relations, it followed, naturally, that he made himself agreeable.

"I hope you and your mother are not given to nervousness," he asked, when it was plain that the Princess intended to keep her reputation up, "for my wife is a perfectly reckless driver. However, she is also the best driver I ever saw, and she has never had an accident yet."

Gertrude shrank from his somewhat familiar scrutiny of her face, and she answered him coldly—

"Oh no, thanks. I am never nervous, and my mother is not either. Are you, mother?" she asked, leaning back, and addressing her directly.

"Not when the Princess is driving," said Mrs. Carston, graciously, smiling at the Prince.

"I was just telling Miss Carston there was no need to be when my wife is driving. I acknowledge it doesn't look the safest form of amusement. Mimi, you'll have a wheel off presently."

"Then we'll go like a fox terrier when it wants to show off," remarked Mimi. "It would look rather nice, I think."

"I saw you two nights ago at the Cercle," continued the Prince to Gertrude. "I wanted my wife to introduce me, but she didn't know you, she said. I suppose you haven't been here very long."

"No; only a week," she said, again feeling a little uneasy.

"Then, of course, we may hope that you will still remain here a considerable time."

"I shall be here about a fortnight or three weeks more."

"Ah! you stop here about as long as we shall," he said; "personally, I would stop longer, but we have to go back to Vienna for a time, and we go to England in November."

"You hunt, I suppose," said Gertrude, carelessly.

"My wife is very fond of it, and that is reason enough for our going. She is half English, you know," said the Prince, making concessions to ingenuousness.

"Here we are at the lake; let me help you down; the boats are waiting, I see. Let me give you my hand."

"Thanks, I can manage for myself," said Gertrude, preparing to dismount.

She turned round to catch hold of the rail, and in doing so, somehow, her foot slipped off the step. The Prince had already dismounted, and was standing below. He made a sudden, quick movement towards her, and just saved her a rather nasty fall, by catching her strongly round the waist and lowering her to the ground. Poor Gertrude was furious with herself, and flushed deeply.

"I hope you are not hurt," he said, bending towards her. "I was very fortunate in being able to save you."

Mrs. Carston saw what had happened from the top of the drag.

"Dear Gertrude," she cried, "you are always so precipitous—why don't you thank the Prince?"

"As long as Miss Carston was not precipitated, her precipitousness is harmless," said the Prince. "I am afraid you are shaken," he said to Gertrude.

"Villari, you must not try to make puns in English," screamed Mimi; "go and hold the horses a minute till they've taken out the baskets. There's no such word as precipitousness."

Meanwhile Gertrude had recovered her equanimity, and confessed to herself that the Prince had merely chosen between letting herself be hurt or not hurt, and that it was hard to say why she was angry with him. She walked to where he was standing at the horses' heads.

"I am so grateful to you," she said; "you saved me a very bad fall."

"Please don't thank me for the privilege I have had. It is for me to thank you."

Gertrude made a great effort to conquer her increasing aversion to him, which was quite inexplicable, even to herself, and smiled.

"You are very unselfish. Do you always find it a privilege to help other people?"

"Decidedly not," said he, looking straight at her.

Gertrude turned away, and he followed her to join the others, who were standing at a little distance.

"There are the boats," explained the Princess, "and as there are ten of us and three of them, we'll divide ourselves between them. We'd better take a man each to do the rowing, and if any of us like we can take an oar. I love rowing, and I know you row, Miss Carston. Your mother was telling me you were out this morning. Shall you and I go in a little boat by ourselves, and row across? Let's do that."

The Prince remonstrated.

"Mimi, you mustn't take Miss Carston off all by yourself like that. It isn't fair on the rest of us."

Mimi looked at him with malicious amusement in her eyes.

"Miss Carston shall decide for herself," she said. "Will you offend me or offend the Prince?"

Poor Gertrude was not used to a world where chaff and seriousness seemed so muddled up together, and where nobody cared whether you were serious or not. She was accustomed to mean what she said, and not to say a good many things she meant, whereas these people seemed to say all they meant, and only half to mean a good many things they said.

"I'm very fond of rowing," she said simply. "I should like to go with you."

Princess Mimi looked mischievously at her husband, and Gertrude, not knowing exactly what to do with her eyes, glanced at him too. He was waiting for that, and as their eyes met he said,—

"You are very cruel; your thanks to me do not go beyond words."

The Princess came to her rescue.

"Come, Miss Carston, you and I will set off. There's a sweet little boat there, which will suit us beautifully."

The Princess's method of rowing was to dip her oar into the water like a spoon very rapidly, for spasms which lasted about half a minute. In the intervals she talked to Gertrude.

"I am so glad to be coming to England again," she said. "Villari has had a lot of tiresome business which has kept him at Vienna during this last year, and we haven't set foot in it for sixteen months. I am tremendously patriotic; nothing in the world gives me so much pleasure as the sight of those hop-fields of Kent, with the little sheds up for hop-pickers, and the red petticoats hanging out to dry. I think I shall go and live in one. Do you suppose it would be very full of fleas? I shall build it of Keating's powder, solidified by the Mimi process, and then it will be all right. Do come and live with me, Miss Carston. Do you know, we've taken a tremendous fancy to you. May I call you Gertrude? Thanks, how sweet of you. Of course you must call me Mimi."

It was quite true that she had taken a great fancy to Gertrude, and Gertrude, in turn, felt attracted by her. She, like others, began to discount the fact that she smoked and screamed and drove four-in-hand, in the presence of the vitality to which such things were natural and unpremeditated. There was certainly no affectation in them; she did not do them because she wished to be fast, or wished to be thought fast, but because she was fast. Between her and Mrs. Rivière, Gertrude could already see, there was a great gulf fixed.

Later on in the afternoon the two strolled up higher than the others on the green slopes that rise above the Monastery, and sat down by a spring that gushed out of a rock, making a shallow, sparkling channel for itself down to the lake. The Princess had what she called a "fit of rusticity," which expressed itself at tea in a rapid, depreciatory sketch of all town life, in removing flies from the cream with consideration for their wings, and watching them clean themselves with sympathetic attention, and, more than all, in her taking a walk with Gertrude up the mountain side, instead of smoking cigarettes. Prince Villari had asked if he might come too, but Mimi gave him an emphatic "No." Nobody had ever accused Prince Villari of having the least touch, much less a fit, of rusticity.

The Princess had the gift of prompting people so delicately, that it could hardly be called forcing, to confide in her, and so it came about that before very long she knew of the existence of our Reginald Davenport, and his relation to her companion.

Then Gertrude said suddenly,—

"Do you know Lady Hayes?"

Mimi was startled. The question had been very irrelevant. But she answered with a laugh,—

"No; but I am told I should not like her. They say she is too like me. But why do you ask?"

"Reggie wrote to me about her this morning. He says she is delightful."

"Oh! I don't say she isn't," said the other, "but you see there isn't room or time for two people like me in one place. I never have time to say all I want, and if there was somebody else like that, we shouldn't get on at all."

"Oh! but Lady Hayes is usually very silent, I believe," said Gertrude.

"Yes; but you have to listen to the silence of some people, just as you have to listen to the talk of others. It takes just as much time. I expect she is one of those."

The Princess looked at the figure beside her.

"How happy you must be," she said with something like envy; "and I think you will continue to be happy. And Mr. Davenport is coming here, is he? You must introduce me at once, and I will give you both my blessing. That's something to look forward to. Come, we must go down, the others will be waiting."

Mimi was rather less noisy on the way home than usual. Prince Villari remarked it, and supposed that the fit of rusticity was not yet over. She bid a very affectionate good-night to Gertrude at the door of her hotel, and asked her to come and see her in the morning, and then altered the terms of the visit, and said she would come down to their hotel herself, and hoped to find Gertrude ready for a stroll before lunch.

She remained silent at dinner, and afterwards, when she and her husband were sitting in their room by the window, to let in the cool evening breeze, he felt enough curiosity to ask,—

"What is the matter with my charming wife that she is so silent?"

"I was thinking about Gertrude Carston," said Mimi. "She is engaged to be married."

Prince Villari puffed his cigar in silence for a few moments.

"Ah! that is interesting," he said at length. "I shall come with you to-morrow to offer my felicitations. How very handsome she is."

"I wish you would do nothing of the sort, Villari," said his wife. "Flirt with somebody else, if you must flirt with somebody. Flirt with me, if you like."

"That is a most original idea," he said. "I never heard of a husband flirting with his wife before."

"It's no manner of use trying to flirt with Gertrude Carston, my dear boy; so I warn you solemnly. She is awfully in love with her intended, and, in any case, she wouldn't flirt. She will only get angry with you."

"She would look splendid when she was angry," said the Prince meditatively.

Mimi got up from her seat.

"Look here, Villari," she said, "I don't often ask a favour of you, and I am not particular in general as to how you conduct yourself. I am never jealous, you know, and we have ceased to be lovers—we are excellent friends, which I think is better. As a friend, I ask you to leave her alone."

"I never suspected you of jealousy," he said; "but you ought to explain to me exactly why you wish this, if you want me to do as you ask."

"Benevolent motives, pure and simple," said Mimi at once. "You won't get any amusement out of it."

"Never mind me," murmured he.

"Very good," continued Mimi. "I cancel that—and she will hate it. Just leave her alone. Flirt with Mrs.

Rivière. She would enjoy it. You were rude to her to-day; you never spoke a word to her—good, bad or indifferent."

"Mimi, you are inimitable," said the Prince, looking at her with satisfaction. "Really, you never disappoint one. I expected to find all sorts of surprises in you; but it seems I haven't got to the end of them yet. To discover such a spring of benevolence in you now is charming. Do you know I feel like your lover still."

"Then will you do what I ask?"

"Yes; I think I will," said he. "After all, I shall flirt with my wife a little longer."

He rose up from his chair, and took her hand in his, and raised it, lover-like, to his lips.

"You're a very good old boy, Villari," she said. "We've never yet come near the edge of a quarrel, and we've been married, oh! ever so long. How wise we are, aren't we? Let me go, please. I want to write some letters. You told Mrs. Rivière you'd go to the Casino with her. It's time you were off. Be awfully charming to her, will you?"

"I'll let her show me to all her acquaintances, and be introduced to them all, if that will do," said the Prince.

"That's a dear," remarked Mimi. "That'll do beautifully. Trot along!"

CHAPTER II.

Gertrude's pleasure at receiving the telegram announcing Reggie's immediate arrival was not untouched by surprise. The vague thoughts, which for very loyalty she would not allow to take shape in her mind, in connection with Lady Hayes, formed themselves into a dark cloud on the horizon, distant but potentially formidable. But when she came downstairs on the morning of his arrival, and saw him standing in the hall, with the early morning sunlight falling on his tall, well-made form and towering, sunny head, there was no room in her mind for more than one feeling, and she was content. He had not seen her coming downstairs, and on the bottom step she paused, held out her hands, and said,—

"Reggie!"

That moment was one of pure and simple happiness to them both. He turned and saw her, the girl to whom he had given his heart and his young love, and for him, as for her, at that moment none but the other existed. Gertrude felt that the thoughts of that golden future, which had so filled her mind one morning, as she walked down to the lake, were now beginning to be fulfilled. As for him, the chief feeling in his mind was one of passionate, unutterable relief; the long nightmare was over, for the moment he felt that childish, pure happiness of waking from a bad dream and finding morning come, and the sun shining into a dear, familiar room.

He had not had a very pleasant journey. The anger which Mrs. Davenport had seen in his face, and from which she had taken comfort, burned itself out and left him face to face with blankness. His passionate desire to see Eva rekindled itself, but that was impossible, and the sight of Gertrude he felt, in another sense, was impossible too. Several times he had been on the point of turning back, but the essential weakness of his character forbade so determined a step. But certainly, at that first moment of meeting her, he felt, with that unquestioning irresponsibility, that in natures not so sweet creates egoism, that the solution was here, and the relief was great.

"Ah, it is good to see you, Gerty," he said, when the first silent greeting was over. "I didn't know how much I wanted to get to you, until I saw you standing there."

"It was nice of you to come so soon," she said, drawing her arm through his, and leading him out on to the verandah; "but why did you come so suddenly? Nothing is wrong, I hope?"

Reggie had foreseen and dreaded this question, and he had devoted some thought to it. But Gertrude had given it a form more easy of reply than that he had anticipated.

He looked at her affectionately.

"Nothing is wrong," he said with emphasis, and, to do him justice, he believed at that moment with truth.

"Everything is as right as it can be now," he went on; "now I am here with you, and oh, Gerty, nothing else matters."

"No," she said softly; "nothing else matters."

They stood there looking at each other, silent, almost grave—for happiness is no laughing matter—until a waiter came out with a tray on which was Gertrude's breakfast. Reggie went upstairs to his room to get rid of his travel stains, and Gertrude ordered breakfast for him to be served at the table on the verandah where she had her own. But it was not to be expected that the change in Reggie which Mrs. Davenport had noticed would escape her, and though, in the grave, silent joy of that first meeting, she had not consciously noticed it, she remembered it now, and it struck her exactly as it had struck Mrs. Davenport.

"He has become a man," she said to herself, and the thought flooded her mind with a new joy. He had said that nothing was wrong; their meeting had been all and more than she had expected, for she felt he fulfilled his part of that union of soul which she had thought of as the germ which lurked in their first months of courtship, and which she felt she had become capable of by degrees only. But, lo! he had changed too. Truly, the golden future was dawning.

Such moments are rare. We cannot live always at the full compass of our possibilities, any more than a horse can gallop at full speed for ever. That great characteristic of the human race, limitation, forbid us to walk for ever on the circumference of our circle. That most disappointing of phenomena called reaction will not be denied, and the hearts which are capable of the highest emotions in the highest degree, are not only capable, but necessarily liable to their corresponding depths. But at present, disconsolate reflections of this kind had no footing in Gertrude's mind. She knew her emotions were expanded for the present sweet moment, even to the limits of her imagination, and room for further thought there was none.

All that day and all the next day the joy grew no less deep. On the afternoon of the third day an invitation came from Princess Villari for Mrs. and Miss Carston to come to tea, also to bring Mr. Davenport if he was there. Gertrude wanted to go, and so *sans dire* did her mother, and she soon convinced Reggie—who was of opinion that tea-parties were bores—that he wanted to go too. It is always flattering to the male mind to know that a lady particularly wants to see you, especially when that lady is described in so promising a way as that in which Gertrude alluded to the Princess.

The Princess had a genius for doing things in the best possible way. If she had given a soap-bubble party, the pipes would have been amber tipped, the soap, "Pears' scented," and even in an informal affair of this sort, her arrangements were indubitably perfect. Her sitting-room opened on to the verandah of the hotel, which in turn communicated with the garden. Tea and light refreshments were provided in all these three charming places, on a quantity of small tables, giving unlimited opportunities for any number of *tête-à-têtes*. The steps and the verandah were bright with sweet-smelling flowers, and in the room, where their fragrance would have been overpowering, were large, cool branches of laburnum and acacia. Needless to say, she had advertised the hotel-keeper that she would be using the verandah and hotel gardens that afternoon, and that, with her compliments, those places would be "*interdite*" to any one but her guests.

The Princess was extremely glad to see Reggie, and she couldn't help congratulating him, if he wouldn't think it very interfering of her, but she had made great friends with dear Gertrude, and Gertrude had told her all about it. And here was Mrs. Rivière coming, and did Reggie know her; she was a great friend of Lady Hayes, whom she was sure he must have met in London.

Gertrude was standing some little way off, but she heard the name mentioned, and she could not help turning half round and looking at Reggie. Reggie's back, however, was towards her, and he was making his bow to Mrs. Rivière.

Mrs. Rivière was very busy about this time on modelling herself after the Princess, but having nothing in her composition that could be construed into tact or ability, the result was that the imitation was limited to talking in a loud voice, and saying anything that came into her head.

"Charmed to meet you," she was telling Reggie in shrill tones, "and all the men here are going to be dreadfully jealous of you at once. Your reputation has preceded you; it came to me by the last mail; how nobody could get in a word edgeways with Lady Hayes, because she was always talking to you, and how your photograph stood on the mantelpiece in her room, and she would never allow the housemaids to dust it, but she dusted it herself every morning with a pink silk handkerchief, also belonging, or belonging once, to you. Oh, don't deny it, Mr. Davenport—and how she sat out four, or was it forty—I think forty—forty dances with you at some ball one night."

Mrs. Rivière paused for breath, well satisfied with herself. Her monologue had been quite as rapid as the Princess's and, she flattered herself, quite as fascinating. Mimi had moved away when Mrs. Rivière came up, and was talking to Gertrude, a few yards off. But Gertrude did not hear what she was saying, for the shrill tones of Mrs. Rivière's voice rose high above the surrounding babble of conversation, and seemed as if they were spoken to her alone. Reggie's back was still turned towards her; his face she could not see.

Reggie was conscious that Gertrude was within hearing, conscious also that Mrs. Rivière did not know his relations to her. Eva's name had caused the blood to rush up into his face, and Mrs. Rivière had been delighted with the success of her speech. The Princess had caught a few of her last words, and, looking up at Gertrude, she saw that she had heard too. She wheeled suddenly about, and approached Mrs. Rivière.

"There are simply twenty thousand people whom I don't know here," she said; "you really must come and introduce me to them. Who is that there in a green hat with little purple, bubbly things on it? I want to know anyone who wears purple and green. They must be so very brave; I respect brave people enormously. Come and introduce me. Villari has asked a lot of people I never saw before. I shall talk to him about the woman with purple bobbles!"

She drew Mrs. Rivière away, and Reggie turned round and found himself with Gertrude.

"I heard what that woman said to you," said Gertrude, simply. "It is only fair to tell you that."

She waited, looking at him expectantly, but he remained silent.

"Reggie," she said, touching his arm.

He raised his eyes and looked at her.

"Come and walk round the garden, Gerty," he said, "I have something to say to you."

Gerty's loyalty struggled again and again conquered.

"What you have to say to me can be said here, surely," she said gently and trustfully. "I do not even want you to deny the truth or any of the truth of what that woman said. I am ashamed of having told you that I heard. Forgive me instantly, please, Reggie, and then we'll have a stroll."

Reggie paused, and it was a cruel moment for Gertrude.

"Yes, I will say it here," he went on at length. "Do you remember my telling you, three days ago, on the morning I came, that everything was right now I was with you? That was true."

"And it is true, and you have forgiven me?" asked Gertrude.

Was the ghost of Venusberg not laid yet? Else what was that murmur which Reggie had heard again, when Mrs. Rivière spoke of Eva, like the burden of a remembered song?—"She is not gone really, she has only gone elsewhere?" Was that the smell of red geraniums borne along from the flower-beds by the warm wind, faint, acrid, as you smell them in the dusty window-boxes of the great squares and streets in London? There should be no geraniums here, only wild flowers— meadow-sweet, dog-rose, violet—

The sound of Gertrude's voice had long died away, but Reggie stood silent. An overpowering feeling of anxiety swept over her; the trust that she had felt in his assurance that all was right was suddenly covered by a rolling breaker of doubt. And that silence cost her more than any speech.

At last it became unbearable.

"Speak, Reggie," she cried, "whatever you have to tell me."

"Come, let us go round the garden, where we can be quiet," he said, and together, in silence, they followed a path leading down between dark evergreen bushes to the garden gate.

They sat down on a garden seat where they were hidden from the crowd gathering on the lawn.

"Let us sit here, Reggie," she said. "Just tell me, and when you have said 'yes,' forgive me for asking that it is true that everything is right."

"Ah! God knows whether it is true or false," he cried.

For him again, the army of Venus laughed and rioted as it had rioted once before in the crowded opera house. Again a woman, pale, wonderful, with dark eyes, sat beside him, beating time listlessly to the music with her feathered fan. She had worn that night her great diamond necklace, and the jewels had flashed and glittered in the bright light, till he could scarcely believe they were not living things. And he had thought it was all over, past and dead. Oh no! "she is not gone really; she has only gone elsewhere ... she often turns up again."

Gertrude felt her heart give one great leap of strained suspense, and then stand still for fear.

"I don't understand," she cried. "Tell me all about it, and tell me quickly. Yet, yet, you said it was all right, didn't you, Reggie, and you wouldn't tell me a lie? Ah! say it is all right again, say it now. I cannot bear it. I should like to kill that woman for what she said. It was not true, was it? Tell me it was not true."

The ghost of Venusberg loomed large before Reggie's eyes, blotting out the green bank of trees in front, the pure sky overhead, the mountains sleeping in the still afternoon, blotting out even the tall, English figure by him, leaning forward towards him in an agony of fear, hope, despair; he saw the gleam of electric light, the gleam of jewels, the gleam of another woman's eyes.

"I will tell you all," he said. "I saw Lady Hayes for the first time after you had left London, and from that time till four days ago I have seen her constantly. Then one night she showed me she was like all those women she moved among, and from whom I thought her so different. She was like Mrs. Rivière, Princess Villari—all is one after that. It was at the opera, at Tannhäuser—"

The intensity of Gertrude's suspense relaxed a little. It was all over, then—

"Ah! we heard the overture together. Do you remember? You said you did not like wicked people."

"Yes, I know. When I saw that, at that moment I loathed her. She had said to me things no woman should say, and when I heard the overture I understood, and told her she was a wicked woman. And not till then— you *must* believe me when I tell you this—not till I had vowed never to see her again, did I know—my God! that I should say these things to you—did I know I loved her. I have been through heaven and hell, and they are both hell."

Reggie paused.

"That is not all," said Gertrude.

The suspense was over, and despair is as calm or calmer than joy.

"I couldn't leave her like that," he went on. "I could not hate her utterly at the first moment that I knew I loved her, and I wrote to her asking her forgiveness, and she told me—she wrote to me, that she never would see me again, that I had behaved unpardonably. She made me angry. And I came straight off here the same day."

"And now?" asked Gertrude.

"God only knows what now," said he, leaning his head on his hands.

There was a long silence, and the babble of laughter and talk came to them from the lawn, which was filling fast. Then Reggie heard Gertrude's voice, very low and very tender, speaking to him,—

"Poor Reggie, poor dear boy. I am very sorry for you."

She laid her hand on his knee, and then, drawing closer to him, as he sat with down-bent head, leaned forward to kiss him. But in a moment she recollected herself, and by an effort of supremest delicacy, before he was conscious what she had intended, drew back with one long look at him, in which her soul said "Farewell."

She had something more to say, but it was not easy for her to say it. The uprootal of all one loves best makes it difficult to talk just then. But easy or not, it had to be said, and it was better to say it now.

"I am sure you told me the truth," she began, "when I met you three days ago, and you said everything was right. We know nothing for certain, do we; we can only say what we think, and I am sure you thought that. Anyhow, these last three days have been very sweet. And now, Reggie, there is only one thing more to say ... you are free, absolutely free.... I am not so selfish as to wish to bind you to me.... I love you ... surely I may tell you once more what I have told you so often ... I love you with all my heart and soul, and I do not think I shall change. But we must wait. If that day comes when you say to me, 'Will you have me?' I shall say 'Yes.' But, you must say it in the same spirit in which I shall say 'Yes.' You know what that means, don't you? Ah, Reggie, I don't blame you. How could I do that?"

"Gerty, Gerty," cried he, "I would give all the world to be able to say that to you. I know what you mean. But I am helpless, dumb, blind, deaf. I can do nothing. I am tossed about. I don't know what is happening to me. And that you should suffer too."

Gertrude smiled, ever so faintly.

"It's a difficult world, isn't it," she said, "but it has its ups and downs. I have been very happy almost all my life."

"Forgive me, forgive me," he cried. "Gerty, say you don't hate me."

A deep tremor ran through her. When she met his imploring gaze, the desire of her young, strong love to gather him into her arms, to comfort him, to *make* him feel the depths of her yearning for him, to lose all for one moment in one last, clasping embrace was very hard to resist. "What harm is done?" whispered one voice within her, but another said, "He is not yours; he belongs to the woman he loves." For one moment she hesitated: tenderness, love, memory, wrestled with that other voice, but prevailed not. There was that within her stronger than them all.

"I love you more than all the world," she said, "and there is nothing to forgive."

For one moment she stood looking at him, treasuring the seconds that passed too quickly, knowing that before a short minute had passed that last look would be over. Such a pause is purely instinctive, and when instinct tells us that it is time to take up one's life again, it is impossible to stay longer.

That moment came all too soon, and Gertrude spoke again.

"Come, we must be going back. They will wonder where we are. Ah! there is the Princess. Reggie, pick me that tea-rose."

The Princess felt vaguely reassured. The look in Gertrude's face when she heard what Mrs. Rivière was saying was not pleasant, and it remained in her mind with some vividness. But the last remark which she had overheard was distinctly encouraging.

"Really, you two people are too bad," she said. "You are here to amuse me and my guests, and show these little French people how magnificent, clean, nice, English boys and girls are. I've been entertaining a lot of stupid people, whom I didn't want to see, and who wouldn't have wanted to see me if I hadn't been a Highness. But I've got a great notion of my duty as a hostess. Didn't somebody write an "Ode to Duty"? You might as well write an "Ode to Dentistry." They are both very unpleasant, but they both keep you straight."

She led the way back to the lawn, and Gertrude and Reggie followed.

Society may be a farce, but it is a very grim farce. The devout but rejected lover, who has proposed to the lady of his love beneath an idyllic moon, goes to bed that night as usual, and if, in the agony of his mind, he has forgotten, to take the links out of his shirt in the evening, he will have to do it in the morning. The bows of his evening shoes will want untying just as much that night as on any other, and next morning he will find himself at the breakfast-table just as usual, having washed and brushed his teeth and combed his hair. The unkempt, haggard lovers of fiction have no existence in real life. Edwin does not refuse to shave because Angelina will have none of him, nor does he use his razor, in nine hundred and ninety-nine cases out of a thousand, for any more anatomical process than that of removing his superfluous hair. And Gertrude did not go home in floods of tears and refuse to be comforted, but she talked to several old acquaintances, and made several new ones, and quite a number of people said, "What a delightful girl Miss Carston is." But her grief was none the less deep for that.

Among the old acquaintances, Prince Villari chose to number himself.

"I hear Mr. Davenport, whom my wife says you were expecting, has arrived," said he. "Would you do me the pleasure to introduce him to me?"

Reggie was standing near Gertrude at the time, and she said,—

"Reggie, Prince Villari desires me to do you the honour to introduce you to him."

"Mrs. Carston has been so good as to accept a most informal invitation to dinner from my wife for to-night," continued the Prince. "She said we might hope that you and Mr. Davenport would join us too."

Gertrude did not flinch.

"I should be charmed," she said. "Reggie, you are not engaged, are you?"

The Prince smiled in anticipation of a "sweet, secret speech," but he was disappointed. Reggie considered it an honour, and ventured to inquire at what time they should come.

"My wife has refused to allow Mrs. Carston to go home. She says it would be too cruel to entail that double journey over the most dusty mile of road in Europe twice in one day. May I add," he said, turning to Gertrude, "that it would also be too cruel if you went. It is already half-past six, and we dine in an hour. I see the people are all going. Let me show you the garden. Ah! I see Mr. Davenport has found an acquaintance. Won't you come with me down as far as the gate? There is a seat there commanding a lovely view."

Ah! but how Gertrude's heart knew that seat and that lovely view! Had she not looked on it once already this afternoon?

The Prince was disposed to be particularly amiable.

"I am sure you must love this view," he said. "I know it's a great bore having views shown you, and that sort of thing, but I must say I think this view really is enchanting! Those mountains there look so fine in this evening light! They always remind me of the English lake scenery. My wife raves about English scenery; she says it is part of the only satisfactory system of life in the world, and belongs to the same order of things as roast beef and five o'clock tea, and daisies and large cart-horses. Ah!

here is Mrs. Rivière; I suppose she has been looking at the scenery, too."

As a matter of fact, Mrs. Rivière had been doing nothing of the sort. She had come to a secluded corner, in order to smoke a cigarette and carry on a promising flirtation with a somewhat mature French count. But the mature French count had gone his way, and she was finishing her cigarette alone.

"I have been looking for that fascinating and wicked Englishman," she said. "Yes; isn't the view charming? You really don't know, Miss Carston, how dreadfully you are compromising yourself by going about with him. Take my word for it, as a married woman, that it endangers your reputation. Really, I don't know what young people are coming to. It's perfectly frightful. I heard all about him from a very dear friend of mine in London."

Gertrude felt an overwhelming desire to stop this sort of thing. Mrs. Rivière had run herself out by this time, and stood taking little puffs from her cigarette, and thinking how very Mimi-ish she was becoming. Gertrude stood by her a moment in silence, and Prince Villari thought the contrast between them very striking indeed. There was an expression in Gertrude's face which puzzled him somewhat and he waited in patience for an explanation which he felt sure was forthcoming.

"You mean Reggie Davenport?" she said at length.

"Reggie!" screamed Mrs. Rivière, "really you are getting on at a tremendous pace. I honestly tremble for you."

"Your fears are misplaced," said Gertrude, looking down at her. "I have been engaged to him for eighteen months."

She turned round after saying these words, and walked slowly back, the Prince by her side, without troubling herself to see the effect produced on Mrs. Rivière. They walked in silence for some yards, and then the Prince said,—

"May I offer you my congratulations on the double event—on your engagement, and your defeat of Mrs. Rivière? It was really very fine."

"Thanks," said she, without tremor or raised colour. "I don't like Mrs. Rivière. I think she is insupportable. Ah! there is Reggie. May I go and speak to him?"

The Prince walked gracefully off in another direction. He never made himself *de trop*.

"Reggie," said she, "it was necessary, I found just now, to let Mrs. Rivière believe we were engaged, and I think, perhaps, we had better not let it be known what has happened just yet. I have good reason for it. But tell your mother. I am tired. I think I shall go indoors. Stop and talk to the Prince."

By a merciful arrangement of Nature's, a great shock is never entirely comprehended by the victim all at once. A numbness always succeeds it first, and the torn and bleeding tissues recover not altogether, but one by one. At present Gertrude was conscious that she did not wholly take in all that had happened. Volition and action in small things went on still with mechanical regularity, and it is doubtful whether any of those about her saw any difference. She wandered into the Princess's room which opened on to the verandah, and was pleased to find it untenanted. She threw herself down in a chair, and took up the paper, which had just come in by the mail. There was a famine somewhere, and a war somewhere else, Mr. Gladstone had gone to Biarritz, the Prince of Wales had opened a Working-Man's Institute and Lord Hayes was dead. His death, it appeared, was sudden.

The paper slipped from Gertrude's knees and fell crackling to the ground. So he was dead, and his wife a widow, like herself, she felt. She sat there for some time without stirring. So Lady Hayes, then, was free, and Reggie, as she had told him herself that afternoon, was free too. How very simple, after all, are the big problems of life, and how very cruel. Surely Eva could not help loving him. Anyone who knew him must love him; who could tell that half so well as herself, who loved him best? Was he not lovable? Surely, for she loved him. And what would Mrs. Rivière say? Her thoughts wandered blindly on, touching a hundred different points with accuracy, but without feeling, till they all centred round the main event.

Ah! the cruelty of it, the diabolical chance which placed these things on the devil's chessboard, for the devil to move and manœuvre with. She was to be the victim, it seemed; she was to give up the object of her long tender love to another woman, more beautiful, less scrupulous than herself, and her jealousy sprang to birth, full armed, terrible. Did the irony of fate go so far as this, that that woman, for whom she had herself declared Reggie free, should be free also? Her rejection of him— that was nothing, a wile to bring him back more humbly to her feet. Ah, yes, they would be married in St. Peter's, Eaton Square, probably, and Gertrude would go there, and sing "The Voice that breathed o'er Eden," and eat their—his—wedding cake, and be introduced to the bride, and throw a slipper after them for luck. Yes that was all extremely likely, one might almost say imminent. At this point Gertrude began to perceive that she was getting hysterical, and with a violent effort of self-control, she got up and walked to the window. The sun was just setting, and over the lawn strolled a tall figure, preceded by a still taller shadow. Reggie's eyes were bent to the ground, and he walked up close to the verandah without seeing her. The sight of that familiar, best-loved figure produced another mood in Gertrude; she watched it silently for a time, and then said to herself under her breath,—

"Pray, God, let her love him very much;" and then aloud, "Reggie."

At the sound of his name he looked up and saw her.

"Come in here a minute," she said. "I have something to tell you."

Reggie nodded assent, and came along the verandah, until he reached the low, French window opening on to it.

"Come in," said Gertrude, "it's the Princess's room, but she isn't here. Sit down there."

Gertrude paused.

"The paper has just come," she said at length. "There is something I have read which I wish to tell you, Reggie. It affects you very deeply—I have just read it. Lord Hayes is dead."

"Ah, God!—"

The exclamation burst from him involuntarily. He could have checked it no more than a man can help wincing at a sudden, unexpected blow, or starting at a sudden noise. But into those two words he had cast all the cargo of his soul—hope, longing, love. Gertrude had heard them, had comprehended them, had swallowed the bitter draught.

A moment afterwards he saw that he had told her all, more convincingly than he had done even this afternoon, for he saw she realized it to the full.

"Ah, Gerty, what can I do?" he said, when the silence had become unbearable. "You know how it is with me. How can I help it? I wish I were dead, though the gates of hell were yawning to receive me."

"You did not wish you were dead two months ago," she said with a flash of scorn, "not even though the gates of heaven were open to receive you. You are not so easily contented now."

Reggie looked piteously at her.

"I know. I deserve all you could say of me. Much more than you ever would. I am a brute, a villain—I deserve to be shot. Yet you did not speak like that this afternoon; I am glad you have said it, though; I don't feel less guilty, God knows! but I am not so bad as not to feel thankful for any punishment."

"Let us say good-bye now," said Gertrude. "We shall not meet again like this."

She held out her hand to him, but volunteered no more intimate embrace. He grasped it, held it for a moment, and let it drop. Even the touch of hand had been something sacred before to him and her, he felt, but there was something dead between them; her hand was as another's. But to Gertrude that rush of memories was too great. Her strength had been too severely taxed already.

"Ah, Reggie," she cried, "do you leave me like this?"

"God help you!" he said, "and me too."

"Reggie, my darling," she cried suddenly, "shall that woman stand between you and me? Did you not promise me your love? Where are those promises? This is all a dream. Come to me again as you were once. You did not love anyone but me, you said—and once you told me you disliked wicked people. What has happened to those words of yours? Were they not true? It is a pity if they were not, for I have written them on my heart. Ah, my darling, my darling—" She threw her arms round him in a last embrace. "Reggie, dear," she whispered, "this is good-bye. I did not mean what I said just now. I did not know what I was saying. That was the best of me that spoke this afternoon when I said you were free. You are quite free. I hope she will love you as much ... as much as I have done—as I do. That will be enough. And now go. Leave me by myself. Good-bye, dear; good-bye."

She went with him on to the verandah, where the dusk was already falling, and as soon as he was outside the room, she turned quickly from him and went back, closing the glass door after her.

CHAPTER III.

Lord Hayes was buried with his fathers and forefathers in the little churchyard at Hayes, and after the funeral Eva came back again to her London house. Mrs. Grampound came to see her occasionally, was tearful and voluble, and could hardly conceal her satisfaction at the handsome settlements Lord Hayes had made on his widow.

"So thoughtful of him," she would say, wiping her eyes, "to leave you the London house for life. He knew that you could not do without a few months in London every year; and the villa at Algiers, too, for the winter, in memory of the honeymoon. So unselfish!"

Mrs. Grampound seemed to think that his lordship's disembodied spirit might have preferred to keep the villa at Algiers to itself, and that the fact that he had left it to his widow seemed to imply that he renounced all rights of visiting these particular glimpses of the moon. But Eva assented, with the ghost of a smile, as the impossible interpretation occurred to her.

Reggie's letter to Mrs. Davenport, telling her that his engagement with Gertrude had been broken off, had arrived, and it was not very pleasant reading. He mentioned that this was prior to the news of Lord Hayes's death, and that he was coming back to England;

and with all his old frankness, he said that he had written to Eva a letter of sympathy on her husband's death.

But if Reggie's letter gave pain to Mrs. Davenport, not to mention that Gertrude was not altogether happy just now, surely there was the corresponding balance somewhere. Eva, for instance—things were taking a fresh turn, were they not, for her? Her husband was just dead—that was true; but though the loss of a husband is not, in the general way, a matter for congratulation, her case was a little exceptional. And this morning a letter had come for her from someone she was very fond of, saying a few words for the sake of decency, and a few other words which, for the sake of decency, had better have been left unsaid. Reggie had told Eva that all was over between himself and Gertrude, and that he was coming back to London. The letter ended almost imperiously, "I shall come to see you—you *shall* see me."

Yet Eva was not the owner of the balance of happiness to make all square. How was that? But Eva was very conscious herself, as she sat with Reggie's letter in her hand, why she was not happy. Reggie was coming to offer himself, body and soul, to her, and there was nothing in the world that she desired but to give herself, body and soul, to him. It seemed very simple. Unfortunately it was only more impossible.

She had decided only a week ago that he was happier, or would be happier with another than with her. She knew it, she knew it; she was convinced of it by instinct and reasoning alike. It seemed to her that there was nothing she knew except that—that, and a certain dull remorse when she thought of that moment, when she had found the thing, which had been her husband, lying like a broken doll in the dark room. She wished she had made more of that bad job; he was so weak, so inadequate, surely it had not been worth while to spar with one so immeasurably her inferior. And he had been very kind to her, as kind as she would let him. He had been like a little dog, which had been purely amiable at first, but had got to snap instinctively when it was approached, from the certainty that it was going to be teased. She recalled that shrinking, hunted look that she had seen so often on his face when he had snapped at her and she had turned on him with a whip. To do her justice, the provocations, or, at any rate, the challenge had usually been on his side, but after all, would it not have been better so many times to have let it pass—not to have slashed so savagely? Ah, well, he was dead; Eva envied him now.

For the road to her happiness was as impassable as ever; her husband's death had made no difference to that. She knew that Reggie's best chance of happiness was not with her, but with another, and, unfortunately for Eva, she found that this fact could not be overlooked. And that necessity of securing his happiness came first; it was the most essential part of her love for him; the impossibility she had felt on that morning after they had seen Tannhäuser, or rather heard the overture together, of doing anything that was not for the best of his happiness, as far as in her and in her sober judgment lay, remained as impossible as ever. The existence of her husband, she felt then, was altogether a smaller matter. If she had felt it good that she and Reggie should love one another, she would have been content to go on living as they had lived before, seeing each other in ball-rooms, in crowded dining-rooms, in any publicity, just touching his hand, just reading that secret knowledge in his eyes, and she knew that he would have waited indefinitely as blissfully as herself. But her knowledge of herself and him rendered that impossible, and it was impossible still. Surely it was very hard; she did not ask for much, and that little was infinitely impossible.

Meanwhile, the hours were bringing Reggie closer to London, and closer to her. "I shall come and see you—you *shall* see me!" The words rang in her head, till it seemed the whole air held nothing but them. That imperious note, the first she had heard from him, was terribly dear to her, as it is to all men and women, when the one they love commands that which they long to do. He was changed, Mrs. Davenport had said; he had become a man. Eva felt in his words that the change had come—he spoke to her as a man to a woman. He pleaded no longer, he demanded, he announced his claims. She pictured him coming to her, bold in the assurance of his love. "You are mine," he would say, "you are mine, and I am yours. Let us come away together. Ah! but you shall come; you dare not say 'no.'"

Against the sight of him, the sound of his voice, the touch of his hand, Eva knew she would be powerless. The impossibilities on which she dwelt would sink, she well knew, into nothing by the side of that one great impossibility—that of resisting his claims when he came to seek and have her. Surely nothing on earth, not duty, nor unselfishness, nor wisdom, was so strong as Love, the soft, delicate-winged Love, which neither strove nor wept, but only smiled and smiled, until its claims, its claims in full, were willingly poured into its outstretched hand.

Eva rose from where she had been sitting, and walked upland down the room. Dressed in black from head to foot, she looked like an image of despair. She looked round the room, not hers, she felt, but his. That was the chair where he used to sit; the last day he had been there, he had pushed it back into the window and had sat in the sun, because he said he had a cold. He had been smoking a cigarette and had put it down on the window sill, where it had made the paint blister and burn. She had brought him a little Benares ware ash-tray, to put it in after that. Ah! there was the ash-tray, with the stump of a cigarette still in it. The servants ought to have cleared it away—and yet—well, perhaps it was too small to notice. In any case, she would not speak about it. No, on the whole she would speak about it, and she rang the bell. They should dust the room more carefully, she said to the man; that cigarette end had been there a week. After all, it did not matter, she added, as she took the ash-tray up. "No, leave it where it is; but let the room be dusted more carefully another time." Poor, momentous little cigarette-end!

He will see her, will he? Ah! but he shall not. Eva, who had always felt herself so strong, was suddenly weak. If she knew that he was there, was waiting to know if he could see her, how could she say she would not see him, and if she saw him, how could she not yield? It was impossible, impossible. Meanwhile, she had a day and a night in which to decide what to do. He would not be in London till to-morrow morning. Many things may happen in a day or a night. She might go away, away somewhere where he would never know and could never follow her. And where in the world was that? Where would not she follow him? Perhaps nowhere in the world, out of the world somewhere—perhaps—perhaps....

There was a piece of green, unturned grass next the grave where her husband lay, in that peaceful churchyard where the trees sang low together in the wind. How would it do to go there, to be quite quiet at last? "Perchance to dream?" Yes; but surely if she dreamed at all, she would dream of Reggie. One might do worse, she thought, than dream of him.

How odd that she had not thought of this before! It was so very simple, so very satisfactory. She only cared for one thing in this world, and that she could not have. So why wait here?

But he must never know—that would spoil it all. He must never even suspect. Eva had an intense horror of anything like melodrama, and she wished everything to be as natural as possible. If only she could hire a madman from a lunatic asylum to shoot her—no, shooting would not do—it was noisy, messy, a hundred things it should not be. Surely doctors knew plenty of ways by which one could glide quietly out of the world without suspicion— they knew so many ingenious devices by which they can keep us in the world, that they must know some to let us out. Some clean, soothing drug which presented no traces at a *post-mortem* diagnosis—that was the word, was it not? Eva smiled when she pictured herself going to a doctor and asking for a drug of this description. A suspicious mind might perhaps attach undue importance to such a visit, if made a few hours before her death. What fools people were!

Eva pondered, till after a moment a sudden thought struck her. Was not suicide, of a kind, more misleading to those—to him to whom she wished it to be misleading, than death from apparently natural causes? Her husband had died four days before, and, nominally, she was a more or less broken-hearted widow; to Reggie, at least, broken-hearted enough, for it was part of the concealment which she had practised to him, to hide her relations with her husband, and when she decided to let him know the rest of her, that was a side issue which she had not shown him. Would not the self-sought death of a heart-broken widow be the most complete disguise to her action, far more complete than the clumsy death by pistols or overdoses? "It is always a good thing to add details," thought Eva to herself. The worst of it was that such a death was somewhat melodramatic; but when the actor quits the boards for ever, it may be excusable that he makes one concession, in spite of his own distaste, to set the audience in a roar. Yes, she would have it so.

Lord Hayes used to dabble in chemistry in an amateur way, and Eva remembered his showing her, in his laboratory at Aston, a little bottle full of a harmless-looking liquid, the smell of which reminded her at first of soft cool peaches, but afterwards of the almond icing on the top of wedding cakes. He had told her that it was prussic acid, and that one drop of it on the tongue would kill a man. She remembered the incident clearly, because when she smelled it she had shuddered, and had thought of her own wedding cake. The bottle was sure to be there still—it stood on the second shelf to the right as you opened the door of the laboratory, and it had a large, red label on it. It was curious how accurately the whole thing came back to her.

The bottle was at Aston, and he was buried in the churchyard there. She regretted the necessity of melodrama, but she would not be alive to regret it afterwards. Eva had no fear, only a longing to get it over—to be quite sure that nothing would stop her carrying out her intention of putting herself out of the reach of him she loved. She would go down to Aston that afternoon; meanwhile, there were three or four hours to be spent in London. Well, there were very few preparations to make. When we take that longest journey of all, there is no packing to be done, no arrangements to be made, as when we go away for a three days' visit. All arrangements are made for us; death provides us with an excellent courier who will forget nothing.

There were just two notes she wished to write—one to Mrs. Davenport, saying that she had heard from Reggie, to say he was coming back to London, and that he wished to see her; that she had given him his *congé* once for all and had no intention of seeing him, and that it would save her trouble if Mrs. Davenport would communicate this to him.

It was not a very easy note to write for many reasons, but the other was even harder; it was to Gertrude Carston, and ran as follows:—

"You will wonder what I, of all women in the world, can have to say to you. Do not resent my writing till you have read. I have done you a cruel wrong and I am sorry for it. I allowed Reggie Davenport to fall in love with me, when I might have stopped it. If I had cared for him it would have been different, for my husband is dead, and he would have married me. In that case I should not have been sorry as I am now. But I never cared for him at all; I did it thoughtlessly, and, as far as I had any motive at all, because it amused me. My husband was the only man I ever cared for; he is dead and I wish I were dead too. It is but poor amends that I can make, but this I promise you, that I will never see Reggie Davenport again. Be very patient with him; he will love you as well as you love him, and that I know is not a little. He will come back to you and you will not hate me then.

"I wish I could have seen you to tell you these things. I think you would have believed me; and I must ask you to believe me now. You will have heard of my husband's death. May you never know what that means. If you like, show Mr. Davenport what I have written to you; it will be good that he should know that I never cared for him.

"I am not so bad as you think; I did my best to stop him caring for me when we saw Tannhäuser together; he went away to you, I know, next morning, and I hoped that that would have been the end. Perhaps, if you saw me, you would be sorry for me now. Above all, remember he will come back to you; it will be with you as if I had never come between you. The fault was mine, do not cast it up to him."

This letter took some time in the writing. It was not easy to write, but when it was done, Eva closed it for fear of drawing back, and sent both off at once to the post. She longed to finish some one of those things that lay before her to do, so that she could not go back from finishing them all. She was afraid of being weak, but not from fear of death. It was far easier to die than to live with that impassable barrier between her and happiness.

She arrived at Aston about four o'clock. She had sent a telegram to the house saying that she was coming for a few nights, and a carriage was at the station to meet her.

She went first of all to the little laboratory opening off
what had been her husband's study, and found that she
had remembered the place where the bottle stood, with
its red label. She uncorked it to make sure it was right.
Yes, the almond on the top of wedding-cakes—her
wedding-cake—it was exactly that smell. Then she drew
her black veil over her face and went out again. There
were certain grimly comic details which she had
determined to go through, in order to lend probability to
her act, and, with this purpose, she went into the
hothouses, and the gardeners who were working saw her
pick an armful of delicate orchids and white lilies. She
tore the plants up like one possessed, and with her load
of sweet-smelling whiteness, they saw her go down the
path that led to the churchyard.

There were several loiterers there, among them the
old sexton, who remembered afterwards that a lady,
dressed in black, scattered a mass of flowers over Lord
Hayes's grave, and then threw herself down on the fresh-
turned earth, and lay there for half an hour or it might
have been more. He knew her to be Lady Hayes, and
when he went away, for the dusk was falling, he left her
still there.

But when the sexton had gone, Eva got up. "One
scene more of this weary farce," she said half aloud. "Ah,
Reggie, Reggie, may you never know!"

In the gloaming she went back to the tall house,
standing stately among its terraces and garden beds. The

sun had sunk; only in the west was a great splash of crimson, the nightingales were singing in the elm trees, and white-winged moths fluttered about over the flower-beds. As she entered, she turned once more to look over the peaceful, unconscious earth. The river lay like a chain of crimson pools among the trees below the meadow; on the far bank was a brown-faced country lad fishing, and nearer, in the hayfields, were a few belated labourers returning from their work. Across the river she could see the red walls of her old home and the flower-beds gleaming in the light of the sunken sun. Then, for the first moment, a sudden spasm of regret, of longing, and of horror for what she was going to do came over her. It would have been better to have finished that last act at the grave itself, but an unaccountable repugnance to being found by the first passer-by had prevented her.

Next moment she had swept it away. Surely she was not going to turn coward now. She turned, and passed through the study, with step as firm as ever, and with all her indolent, unrivalled grace of movement, into the laboratory beyond.

THE END.